The shadow leaned forward, hands moving in persuasive gestures. She backed away, shaking her head.

Suddenly, she cried out, turned, started to run. The assailant lunged at her, and I heard the ring of a knife.

I ran forward. The assailant—male—looked up, saw me coming. I was a large man, and I carried a walking stick, within which was concealed a stout sword. Perhaps he knew who I was, perhaps he'd seen me and my famous temper at work. In any event, he flung the woman from him and fled.

She landed hard on the stones and boards, too near the edge. I snatched at the assailant, but his knife flashed in the rain, catching me across my palm. I grunted. He scuttled away into the darkness, disappearing in a wash of rain.

I let him go. I balanced myself on the slippery boards and made my way to her . . .

Regency London Mysteries by Ashley Gardner

THE HANOVER SQUARE AFFAIR

A REGIMENTAL MURDER

A
Regimental
Murder

ASHLEY GARDNER

BERKLEY PRIME CRIME, NEW YORK

A REGIMENTAL MURDER

A Berkley Prime Crime Book / published by arrangement with
the author

PRINTING HISTORY
Berkley Prime Crime mass-market edition / May 2004

ISBN: 0-425-19612-7

Berkley Prime Crime Books are published by
The Berkley Publishing Group,
a division of Penguin Group (USA) Inc.,
375 Hudson Street, New York, New York 10014.
The name BERKLEY PRIME CRIME and the
BERKLEY PRIME CRIME design
are trademarks belonging to Penguin Group (USA) Inc.

PRINTED IN THE UNITED STATES OF AMERICA

10 9 8 7 6 5 4 3 2 1

Acknowledgments

I would like to thank my editor, Christine, and my agent, Bob, for their continued enthusiasm for these books. Thanks also go to author Glenda Garland for feedback on the first draft of the manuscript, and to Bill Haggart, who answered questions about cavalry regiments, pay of officers, and several other Peninsular War issues. Also, thanks go to the members of the Beau Monde e-group, ladies and gentlemen who love the Regency era and who generously share information. Thanks also to Chris Dickenson who helped brainstorm some of the book, and who is happy to sit with me in outdoor plazas discussing dead bodies. The most generous thanks goes to Forrest for reading all drafts of the manuscript, allowing me to bounce ideas off him, and generally putting up with the "creative process."

CHAPTER 1

London, 1816

A new bridge was rising to cross the Thames just south and east of Covent Garden, a silent hulk of stone and scaffolding slowly stretching its arches across the river. I walked down to this unfinished bridge one sweltering July night through darkness that belonged to pickpockets and game girls, from Grimpen Lane to Russel Street through Covent Garden, its stalls shut up and silent, along Southampton Street and the Strand to the pathways that led to the bridge.

I walked to escape my dreams. I had dreamed of a Spanish summer, one as hot as this, but with dry breezes from rocky hillsides under a baking sun. The long days came back to me and the steamy rains that muddied the roads and fell on my tent like needles in the night. The warmth took me back to the days I had been a cavalry captain, and to one particular night when it had stormed and things had changed for me.

Now I was in London, Iberia far away. The damp warmth of cobblestones caressed my feet, soft rain striking

my face and rolling in little rivulets down my nose. The
hulk of the bridge was silent, a dark presence not yet born.
That is not to say it was deserted. A street theatre distracted
passersby on the Strand and game girls stood at the edges
of the pavement. A threesome of burly men, arm in arm
and smelling of ale, pushed through singing a happy tune
off-key. They slithered and dodged among wheeled con-
veyances, never loosening their hold on one another. Their
merry song drifted into the night.

A woman brushed past me, making for the tunnel of
darkness that led to the bridge. Droplets of rain sparkled on
her dark cloak, and I glimpsed beneath her hood a fine,
sculpted face and the glitter of jewels. She passed so close
that I saw the shape of each slender gloved finger that had
held her cloak, and the fine chain of gold that adorned her
wrist.

She was a furtive shadow in the midst of the city night,
a lady where no lady should be. She was alone—no footman or maid pattered after her, holding slipper box or
lantern. She was dressed for the opera or the theatre or a
Mayfair ballroom, and yet she hastened here, to the dark of
the incomplete bridge.

She interested me, this lady, pricking the curiosity beneath my melancholia. She might, of course, be a high
flyer, an upper-class woman of dubious reputation, but I
did not think so. High flyers were even more prone than
ladies of quality to shutting themselves away in gaudy carriages and taking great care of their clothes and slippers.
Also, this woman did not carry herself like a lady of doubtful morals, but like a lady who knew she was out of place
and strove to be every inch a lady even so.

I turned, my curiosity and alarm aroused, and followed
her.

Darkness quickly closed on us, the soft rain our only
companion. She walked out onto an unfinished arch of the
bridge, slippers whispering on boards laid over stones.

I quickened my steps. The boards moved beneath my
feet, the hollow sound carrying to her. She looked back,

her face pale in the darkness. Her cloak swirled back to reveal a dove gray gown, and her slender legs in white stockings flashed against the night.

She reached the crest of the arch. The rain thickened, a gust of wind blowing it like mist across the bridge. When it cleared, a shadow detached itself from the dark arms of scaffolding and moved toward her. The woman started, but did not flee.

The person—man or woman, I could not tell which—bent to her, speaking rapidly. The lady appeared to listen, then she stepped back. "No," she said clearly. "I cannot."

The shadow leaned forward, hands moving in persuasive gestures. She backed away, shaking her head.

Suddenly, she cried out, turned, started to run. The assailant lunged at her, and I heard the ring of a knife.

I ran forward. The assailant—male—looked up, saw me coming. I was a large man, and I carried a walking stick, within which was concealed a stout sword. Perhaps he knew who I was, perhaps he'd seen me and my famous temper at work. In any event, he flung the woman from him and fled.

She landed hard on the stones and boards, too near the edge. I snatched at the assailant, but his knife flashed in the rain, catching me across my palm. I grunted. He scuttled away into the darkness, disappearing in a wash of rain.

I let him go. I balanced myself on the slippery boards and made my way to her. To my left, empty air rose from the roiling Thames, mist and hot rain and foul odors. One misstep and I would plunge down into the waiting, noisome river.

The woman lay face down, her body half over the edge. Her cloak tangled her so that she could not roll to safety, and her hands worked fruitlessly to pull herself to the firm stones.

I leaned down, seized her about her waist, and hauled her back to the middle of the bridge. She cringed from me, her hands strong as she pushed me away.

"Carefully," I said. "Do not worry, he is gone."

Her hood had fallen back. The jewels I'd glimpsed were diamonds, a fine tiara of them. They sparkled against her dark hair, which lay in snarls over her cloak.

"You are safe now," I said gently. "Who was he?"

She looked about wildly, as though she did not know who I meant. "I do not know. A—a beggar, I think."

One with a sharp knife. My hand stung and my glove was ruined.

I helped her to her feet. She clung to me a moment, her fright still too close.

Gradually, as the rain quieted into a soft summer shower, she returned to herself again. Her hands uncurled from my coat, and her panicked grip relaxed.

"Thank you," she said. "Thank you for helping me."

I said something polite, as though I had merely opened a door for her at a soiree.

I led her off the bridge and out of the darkness, back to the solid reality of the Strand. I kept a sharp eye out for her assailant, but I saw no one. He had fled.

Our adventure had not gone without attention. By the time we reached the Strand, a small crowd had gathered to peer curiously at us. A group of ladies in tawdry finery looked the woman over.

"Why'd she go out there, then?" one remarked to the crowd in general.

"Tried to throw herself over," another answered.

"Belly-full, I'd wager."

The second nodded. "Most like."

The woman appeared not to hear them, but she moved closer to me, her hand tightening on my sleeve.

A spindly man in faded black fell in beside us as we moved on. He grinned, showing crooked teeth and bathing me with coffee-scented breath. "Excellent work, Captain. How brave you are."

I knew him. The man's name was Billings, and he was a journalist, one of those damned insolent breed who dressed badly and followed the rich and prominent, hoping for a breath of scandal. Billings hung about the theatres at Drury Lane and Covent Garden, waiting for members of the haut ton to do something indiscreet.

I toyed with the idea of beating him off, but knew that such an action would only replay itself in the paragraphs of whatever scurrilous story he chose to write.

The curious thing was, the lady seemed to recognize him. She pressed her face into my sleeve, not in a gesture of fear, but betraying a wish to hide.

His grin grew broader. He saluted me and sauntered off, no doubt to pen an entirely false version of events for the *Morning Herald*.

I led the lady along the Strand toward Southampton Street. She was still shaking and shocked and needed to get indoors.

"I want to take you home," I said. "You must tell me where that is."

She shook her head vehemently. "No." Her voice was little more than a scratch. "Not home. Not there."

"Where, then?"

But she would not give me an alternate direction, no matter how much I plied her. I wondered where she had left her conveyance, where her retinue of servants waited for her. She offered nothing, only moved swiftly along beside me, head bent so I could not see her face.

"You must tell me where your carriage is," I tried again.

She shook her head, and continued to shake it no matter how I pleaded with her. "All right, then," I said, at my wit's end. "I will take you to a friend who will look after you. Mrs. Brandon is quite respectable. She is the wife of a colonel."

My lady stopped, pale lips parting in surprise. Her eyes, deep blue I saw now that we stood in the light, widened. "Mrs. Brandon?" Suddenly, she began to laugh. Her hands balled into tight fists, and she pressed them into her stomach, hysteria shaking her.

I tried to quiet her, but she laughed on, until at last the broken laughs turned to sobs. "Not Mrs. Brandon," she gasped. "Oh, please, no, never that. I will go with you, anywhere you want. Take me to hell if you like, but not home, and not to Mrs. Brandon, for God's sake. That would never do."

IN the end, I took her to my rooms in Grimpen Lane, a narrow cul-de-sac off Russel Street near Covent Garden market.

The lane was hot with the summer night. My hard-working neighbors were in their beds, though a few street girls lingered in the shadows, and a gin-soaked young man lay flat on his back not far from the bake shop. If the man did not manage to drag himself away, the game girls would no doubt rob him blind, if they hadn't already.

I stopped at a narrow door beside the bake shop, un-locked and opened it. Stuffy air poured down at us. The staircase inside had once been grand, and the remnants of an idyllic mural could be seen in the moonlight—shep-herds and shepherdesses pursuing each other across a flat green landscape, a curious mixture of innocence and lust.

"What is this place?" my lady asked in whisper.

"Number 5, Grimpen Lane," I answered as I led her up-stairs and unlocked the door on the first landing. "In my lighter moments, I call it home."

Behind the door lay my rooms, once the drawing rooms of whatever wealthy family had lived here a century ago. The flat above mine was quiet, which meant that Marianne Simmons, my upstairs neighbor, was either on stage in Drury Lane or tucked away somewhere with a gentleman. Mrs. Beltan, the landlady who ran the bake shop below, lived streets away with her sister. The house was empty and we were alone.

I ushered the woman inside. She remained standing in the middle of the carpet, chafing her hands as I stirred the embers that still glowed in my grate. The night was warm, but the old walls held a chill that no amount of sun could leach away. Once a tiny fire crackled in the coals, I opened the windows, which I'd left closed to keep birds from seeking shelter in my front room. The breeze that had sprung up at the river barely reached Grimpen Lane, but the open window at least moved the stagnant air.

By the fire's light, I saw that the woman was likely in her late thirties, or fortyish, as I was. She had a classic beauty that the bloody scratches on her cheek could not mar, a clean line of jaw, square cheekbones, arched brows over full-lashed eyes. Faint lines feathered from her eyes and corners of her mouth, not age, but weariness.

I took her wet cloak from her, then led her to the wing chair near the fire and bade her sit. I stripped her ruined slippers from her ice-cold feet then fetched a blanket from my bed and tucked it around her. She sat through the proceedings without interest.

I poured out a large measure of brandy from a fine bottle my acquaintance Lucius Grenville had sent me and brought it to her. The glass shook against her mouth, but I held it steady and made her drink every drop. Then I brought her another.

After the third glass, her shaking at last began to cease. She leaned against the worn wing chair, her eyes closing. I fetched a cloth, dampened it with water at my wash basin, and began to wipe the blood and grime from her hands.

Sitting this near to her let me study her closely. Her eyes were dark blue, wide, and handsome, and her hair, now tangled and loose, was darkest brown, bearing only a few strands of gray. Her mouth was regal and straight, the mouth of a woman not much given to laughter.

She was a lady, highborn and wealthy, who had been to a ball or soiree or opera. Who had managed to get herself away from her carriage and servants to walk alone to the unfinished bridge at the Strand for her secret errand.

I still did not know who she was.

Grenville would know. Lucius Grenville knew everyone who was anyone in London. Every would-be dandy from the Prince of Wales to lads just down from Eton copied his dress, his manners, and his tastes in everything from food to horses to women. This famous man had befriended me, he'd said, because he found me interesting, a relief from the ennui of London society. Most Londoners envied me my favored position, but I had not yet decided whether I should be flattered or insulted.

"Will you tell me who you are?" I asked as I worked.

"No." The voice was matter-of-fact, the timbre rich and warm.

"Or why you went to the bridge?"

Her closed eyes tightened. "No."

"Who was the man who accosted you? Did you have an appointment to meet him?"

She opened her eyes in sudden alarm. Then she focused her gaze on my left shoulder, holding it there as if it steadied her. "He was a beggar, I told you. I thought to give him a coin, because he was pitiable. Then I saw he had a knife and tried to flee him."

"Happy chance I was there to stop him." My palm still throbbed from the cut he'd given me, but it was shallow, my glove having taken the brunt of it. "That still does not answer the question of why you went to the bridge in the first place."

She lifted her head and bathed me in a haughty stare. "That is my own affair."

Of course she would not tell me the truth, and I had not thought she would. I wondered if the women at the bridge had been right, that she'd gone there to end her life. Suicide was a common enough means of ending one's troubles in these times—a gentleman ruined by debt, a soldier afraid to face battle, a woman raped and abandoned.

I was no stranger myself to melancholia. When I'd first returned to London from Spain, the black despair had settled on me more times than I cared to think about. My landlady had taken to removing my razor from my rooms any day that I failed to make an appearance for my breakfast coffee in her bake shop. The fits had lessened since the turn of the year, because my sense of purpose was slowly returning to me. I had made new friends and was beginning to find interest in even the most wretched corners of London.

She offered nothing more, and I carefully touched my cloth to the scrapes on her cheek. She flinched, but did not pull away.

"You may rest here until you feel better," I said. "My bed is uncomfortable, but better than nothing. The brandy will help you sleep."

She studied me a moment, her eyes unfocussed. Then, with a suddenness that took my breath away, she lifted her slim arms and twined them about my neck. The light silk of her sleeves caressed my skin, and her breath was warm on my lips.

I swallowed. "Madam."

She did not let me go. She pulled me into her embrace and pushed her soft mouth against mine.

Primal blood beat through my body, and I balled my fists. I tasted her lips for one heady moment before I reached up and gently pushed her from me. "Madam," I repeated.

She gazed at me with hungry intensity. "Why not? Does it matter so much?" Her eyes filled and she whispered again, "Why not?"

I could easily have accepted what she offered. She was beautiful, and her lips were warm, and she had quite entranced me. It was devilish difficult to tell her no.

But I did it.

She sat back and regarded me limply. I picked up the cloth I had dropped and resumed dabbing the blood from her face. My hands trembled.

Silence grew. The fire hissed in the grate, coal at last warming the air. My lips still tingled, still tasting her, and my body absolutely hated me. None would blame me, it said. She had come here, alone, deliberately forsaking protection, and had offered herself freely. The censure would go to her, not to me.

Except the censure from myself, I finished silently. I had already tallied too many regrets in my life to add another.

After a time, her eyes drifted closed. Her breathing grew steady, and I thought she slept. I returned the cloth to my washbasin, but when I came back to her, she was watching me.

"They killed my husband," she announced.

CHAPTER 2

I stared at her in pure astonishment. "I beg your pardon?"

Her voice trembled. "They made him bow his head and take the blame for their crime, and then they murdered him to make certain of it." Her eyes flashed. "May they rot in hell."

I could only gape. A spatter of rain struck the glass of the open window, and the casement creaked softly.

"Madam, who are you talking about?"

"The three of them. The triumvirate, I call them. They did everything."

"Who?" I went to her. "Who has killed your husband? You must tell me."

She blinked, as though just waking. "What?"

"You have just said your husband has been murdered."

Tears filled her eyes. "Has he?"

"You have said so."

She shook her head. "I am mistaken. I have made so many mistakes. Do not heed me."

My alarm grew. "You must tell me."

She blinked again, and then a sane light entered her eyes. She pulled away. "You gave me too much brandy. I do not know what I mean." Her gaze darted to me and away, color blooming on her cheeks.

I stared at her. Had she witnessed her husband's murder, that very night, perhaps? Was that what had driven her out to the bridge alone? Or did she fear for her own life because she knew the murderers' identities? And why the devil hadn't she simply run to Bow Street?

"Madam, you really must tell me what has happened."

She shook her head again. "No. I am tired. I must sleep." She closed her eyes.

I tried for a time to make her speak to me, to explain her fantastic declaration. She remained stubbornly silent. When I told her I would go out and fetch back a Bow Street Runner, her manner changed. Her haughty demeanor fell away and she regarded me with the alarm of a child. She begged me to say nothing, that she had dreamed it, that she had invented it in her stupor. I did not believe her, but I could see that something, at least, had frightened her badly.

I at last gave up. She was exhausted and incoherent and needed sleep. I would put her to bed and question her again in the morning.

She agreed to take my bed, but nearly collapsed when I helped her from the chair. I lifted her into my arms. She was light, her frame thin, as though she had been starving herself of late.

I took her to my room and laid her on the solid, square tester bed that had been here since I'd let the rooms from Mrs. Beltan. The thick mahogany bedposts and boards were worn and scarred from a century of use; births, deaths, and lovemaking had occurred in this bed time and again. Now my lady would use it for simple sleep, a healing sleep I hoped.

I had one more weapon in my arsenal and that was laudanum. A few drops of the opiate would let her sleep in sweet oblivion. I dropped the drug into a glass of water and stoppered the bottle again. She drank readily enough, as though relieved to have it, and lay down. I settled the blankets over her, then left her to let the laudanum do its work.

I took the bottle away with me. I did not trust her not to decide a large dose of it a pleasant way to keep from facing her troubles.

When I closed the door, her eyes had already slid closed, and her breathing was even.

I spent the rest of the night sitting in the wing chair she had vacated, my elbows on my knees, staring into the tiny flames of the fire.

I had laid her cloak and slippers before the fire to dry. The cloak was heavy velvet, the slippers mere wisps of cloth decorated with beads. They told me nothing about her except that she came from wealth and had fine taste in dress.

I still felt her kiss. She had flung herself at me scarcely knowing what she did. Her strange tale of murder could have been all invention, as she claimed, but her anguish had been real. Something had happened to her, something that had made her leave the safety of family and friends and venture to the unfinished bridge.

Her behavior reminded me of my own nearly fifteen years before when I had faced the worst night of my life. That night I had lost my wife and two-year-old daughter, not to battle or disease, but because of my own folly and blindness. I had not been able to see what I had done to the wisp of a young woman who had married me. She had hated life following the drum, and she had hated me. And so, one night, she had left me.

It amazed me even now that she had dredged up the courage to go. She had been like a little marsh grouse, tiny, weak, easily frightened. She must have truly loathed me to find the means to slip away from our rooms in Paris, where we had journeyed with the Brandons during the Peace of Amiens, alone and with a child. She had gone to her lover, a French officer of all people, and he had taken her away.

When I'd found her gone, truly gone, a madness had come upon me that I scarcely recalled. My wife had left a letter for Louisa Brandon, and Louisa had been forced to break the news to me. A young woman of twenty-five then, Louisa had already possessed a strength of will greater than that of any battalion commander. She'd taken the pistol from my hands herself, never mind that I must have tried to kill her with it. She'd ordered a subaltern to sit on me, and then had dosed me with coffee, brandy, and laudanum until I'd calmed enough to see reason.

I'd been hurt that day more than any in my young life, but Louisa had made me live through it and go on. The least I could do was help this woman live through whatever troubles drove her.

I looked in on her once or twice during the night, but she slept quietly, her breathing even and deep. She did not stir when I entered the room or adjusted the blankets. I left a candle burning so that she would not be in the dark if she awoke, but did not light the fire in the already warm room.

As I returned to my chair a third time, the double rectangles of windows lightened to gray. In the street below I heard the cries of the milkmaid who trudged through every morning offering her wares to the cooks and housewives of Grimpen Lane. "Milk," she cried. "Milk below!"

Her second cry trailed off, and at the same time, I heard someone clattering up the stairs. The tread was too heavy to be Marianne's, too heavy even to belong to Grenville's footman, Bartholomew, who was a spry lad with the strength of youth.

After a moment, I recognized, to my surprise and dismay, footsteps I'd not heard before in this house. I rose and opened the door.

Colonel Aloysius Brandon stood on my threshold, breathing hard from his climb. He was a large man in his forties with crisp black hair just graying at the temples, a hard, handsome face, and eyes as chill as winter skies. At one time he'd been my mentor, my commander, and my greatest friend. Since our return to London after Napoleon's first capture in 1814, Brandon had never visited my rooms. I had not thought he even knew where they were.

Now he stood on my doorstep, his eyes filled with cold fury. "Gabriel," he said. "Where is my wife?"

I regarded him in surprise and not a little annoyance. "Not here," I answered coolly.

Louisa readily visited my rooms whenever she needed to. Brandon knew that she did. He had never said a word, and I'd thought he'd learned since our falling out not to doubt her. But his ice blue glare now told me that for this past year and a half he had only been letting doubt fester in his soul, nurturing it in all its ugliness. After everything we'd been through, he hadn't learned a thing.

He followed me inside and slammed the door. A few shards of ceiling plaster settled like snow in his dark hair. "Where is she, then?"

"I have no idea. I have not spoken to Louisa in days."

He was not listening. He was staring at the woman's cloak that lay spread across the chair before my hearth, and at the slippers discarded there. His neck and face slowly turned purple and he raised his eyes to the closed bedchamber door.

The last thing the poor woman inside needed was Aloysius Brandon. I made for him, but he moved more quickly. He reached the door a second before I did and flung it open.

He stopped. The woman slept on under my blanket, undisturbed. A dark strand of hair had snaked across the white pillow, and one soft hand had curled under her cheek.

Brandon studied her for a long time, then he slowly turned and looked at me. I reached around him and pulled the door closed.

He continued to stare at me, his breathing deep and slow. "You have damned cheek, Gabriel."

"You draw a hasty conclusion, sir," I said. "She needed help, and I helped her. Any other assumption insults her."

"Her husband was disgraced. There is no help you can offer her."

Her husband. The one who she'd said, in her inebriation, had been murdered. But a husband in disgrace might explain her words, and despair. In the world of the haut ton, dishonor could be a living death. She may have meant murder in the sense that Iago might have expressed it, murder to his good name. Disgrace to her husband would be great disgrace to her as well.

But I wondered. Something seemed very out of place.

"Who is she?" I asked.

Brandon's look turned outraged. "You do not even know?"

My temper frayed. "For God's sake, what do you take me for?"

"I take you for a man who does as he pleases, with whomever's wife he pleases."

My heart beat hard. "One more insult, and we meet. Even if Louisa guts me for it."

At the mention of his wife's name, the fight suddenly went out of him. His eyes filled with contrite anguish, then he walked blindly past me to the middle of the room. He stopped and stared down at the cloak.

He must have been very certain of finding Louisa here. He had worked himself into a rage, ready to kill me and drag her home. He had wanted his fears proven, wanted to stand over Louisa and me, letting the role of the wronged man give him power. That opportunity had been snatched from him, and now he was at a loss.

"I do not know where she is, Gabriel," he said, his voice hushed. "I believe she has left me."

I stared at him. "Why do you think so?"

"You do not know. You . . ." He broke off suddenly and

swung around, his manner as stiff as ever. "This is none of your affair, Lacey."

All night, I had been told that things were none of my affair. "You charged in here looking for her, certain she was with me. You have made it my affair."

He looked down his nose. "It is a private matter."

"Then do not air it in public. If Louisa were to part from you, she would find some way to do so discreetly. She would not simply vanish."

A faint hope flickered in his eyes. "That is true."

"Doubtless she is somewhere sensible, with Lady Aline, perhaps."

"She is not. I have called on Lady Aline, and Louisa is not there."

Alarm touched me. "How long has she been gone?"

"A week Monday."

"Well, good God, did not it occur to you that she might have met with an accident? Or been taken ill?"

He shook his head again. "She sent a note."

I relaxed. A little. "Which said?"

"None of your damned business what it said."

I clenched my fists. "I am ready to tell you to go to the devil. I did not ask you to read it out to me, I asked for the gist of it. If I am to help you find her—"

Brandon reddened. "She said she wanted to go off and think. And I did not ask for your help."

"So you immediately thought she'd come to me."

His mouth tightened. "The last time my wife decided to go off and think, she ran straight to you, did she not?"

His voice was dangerously calm, with just a hint of tremor. We—Louisa, myself, and her husband—had given our word never to speak of the matter again.

"That was in another life," I said.

He looked at me as though he thought of the incident every night before he went to bed and first thing each morning. "It was not so very long ago."

I had wondered when he would reopen the wound. Louisa had made us promise not to. We had kept to our word so far, though that had not prevented Brandon from attempting, in a roundabout way, to kill me.

Where the discussion would have taken us, to words we could not withdraw or to a meeting with pistols on the green of Hyde Park the next morning, I do not know, because Marianne Simmons chose that moment to open my door and walk in unannounced.

"I am out of candles, Lacey. Borrow some?"

She was reaching toward the pile of candles on my shelf even as she spoke, never noticing Brandon or our expressions of suppressed fury.

She had obviously been out enticing gentlemen. Her cheeks were rouged, her lips artificially reddened, her golden hair pinned into childlike curls. Her gown was white muslin, very plain, a costume a bit out of date, but the thin fabric clung to her limbs, and her breasts, unfettered by stays, moved easily beneath it.

Colonel Brandon's color rose. "Who is that, Gabriel? What does she mean by bursting in here?"

Marianne turned, her hand still closing on a fistful of candles. She looked Brandon up and down. His suit betrayed that he certainly had a good income—with an inheritance of over ten thousand a year, the colonel could afford to frequent some of the best Bond Street tailors. But for all his wealth of dress, I saw Marianne sense that here was a gentleman who would not give an actress tuppence to buy her supper. This put him in a different category from Lucius Grenville, who had once handed Marianne twenty guineas in exchange for nothing.

I had wondered over the last months what had become of that twenty guineas. Marianne had purchased several new gowns and a bonnet, but the garments would never have cost her that much. She continued to gnaw bread from downstairs for her meals and to filch my candles and coal.

I cleared my throat. "This is Marianne Simmons. My upstairs neighbor."

Brandon's gaze flicked involuntarily to Marianne's

bosom, where her dusky tips pressed the gown's fabric. "Good God. What kind of a house is this?"

Marianne snatched up the candles. "Well, I like that. I don't think much of your friends, Lacey. Good night."

She swung away, bathing us in a waft of French perfume. She left the door open behind her as she, in high dudgeon, mounted the stairs to the next floor. Her door banged.

I was left alone with Brandon and fewer candles.

He regarded me in complete disgust. "When I allowed my wife to visit you, against my better judgment, I imagined you at least had taken respectable lodgings. Louisa shall not visit you here again."

He stopped, remembering that Louisa had removed herself, at least for now, from his sphere of influence. His eyes chilled. "I will leave you to it."

He marched out, back stiff, with the air of a man who has said all there is to say. I ground my teeth as I watched him descend the stairs, wishing I were more able-bodied so I could fling him out myself. Unscathed, he opened the outer door, strode out, and slammed it behind him.

I withdrew into my rooms and seethed for a moment, then I let out a frustrated growl. I had let Brandon get away without telling me the name of the woman in my bed.

SHE emerged from my chamber at ten the next morning. I sat at my writing table trying to answer letters, but my thoughts were too full and the pen had long since dropped from my fingers.

She had smoothed her hair with the brush I had placed on the washstand and had washed her face with the warmed water I had fetched from Mrs. Beltan. Her gown was stained and torn from her adventures, but her eyes were clear, the frenzy of the night before gone.

She hesitated in the doorway, regarding me in some embarrassment. The laudanum had done its work and she looked rested, though her face was still too colorless.

I nodded a greeting, keeping my expression neutral. "I have fetched breakfast for you." I gestured to the small table that held a plate of brown-crusted rolls and a fat pot of coffee. I paused. "Mrs. Westin."

At the name, her face went dead white. Her fingers tightened on the door handle, and she stared at me with darkened eyes. "How did you know?"

I lifted a small card from the writing table and held it up between my fingers. I had found, in a pocket sewn into her cloak, her reticule, which contained a card case. The small ivory colored rectangles within had proclaimed her as Mrs. Roehampton Westin.

She looked angry, but whether at me for taking such a liberty, or herself for not thinking to remove her card case, I could not tell.

When I'd read the name early that morning, I had understood better why she'd not wanted to tell me who she was. She was Lydia Westin, the widow of the unhappy Colonel Westin, late of the 43rd Light Dragoons. Rumor put it that he had committed a murder during the Peninsular campaign, a murder that had only recently come to light.

From what I had learned from gossip in the coffee-houses that summer, and from my former sergeant, Pomeroy, now a Bow Street Runner, a young man called John Spencer and his brother were seeking to discover who had murdered their father during the rioting after the battle of Badajoz in Spain in 1812.

At first it had been assumed that Captain Algernon Spencer had simply been killed in the frenzy. But now it seemed that his true killer had a name, and that name might well have been Colonel Roehampton Westin.

The happenings after the victory at Badajoz were, in my opinion, a blot on the reputation of the King's army. After the French had fled the town, the English soldiers had gone mad, beginning a drunken revelry that had lasted days. They had stormed houses, dragged families into the streets and shot them for sport, and looted all within. They had bayoneted those too feeble to get out of their way, and forced themselves onto women right on the muddy cobbles, ripping jewelry from their ears and breasts.

Not until a gallows had been set up in the middle of the square did the violence cease. I had been among those sent in to try to restore order. One of my own sergeants had threatened to shoot me if I did not help him plunder a house of a woman and her sister. I had lost my temper and let him know with my fists what I thought of his threats. The sergeant had been carried back to camp.

The death of Captain Spencer had been originally attributed to the rioting—Spencer had simply gotten in the way of soldiers too drunk to tolerate an officer trying to stop their entertainment. His son, John Spencer, wanting to determine "the actual man who pulled the trigger on my father," had searched letters and papers of those who had been at Badajoz, and had questioned many eyewitnesses in search of the answer.

What he had discovered was that a group of officers from the 43rd Light Dragoons, Westin included, had gone in, like me, to help restore order. They had apparently gotten caught up in the madness themselves and had turned on Captain Spencer, who had tried to stop them. During the fiasco, Spencer and another officer of their party, one Colonel David Spinnet, had died.

Colonel Brandon, I'd learned, had been asked to lend his testimony; he had supped with Westin the evening before Westin had gone out and committed the deed, and Brandon was prepared to swear that Westin was already drunk before he had even reached the town.

But now none of that would come to pass. I had recently read in the newspapers of Westin's death not a week before from a fall down a staircase.

Westin's wife stood now in my front room, head lifted, eyes glittering. Brandon had supposed her my lover.

"You have the advantage of me, sir," she said. "You

know who I am and doubtless all that my name means. I still do not know who you are."

I opened the writing table drawer and extracted one of my own cards from my careful hoard. I held it out to her, which forced her to leave the doorway and venture to me.

She took it from my outstretched fingers, turned it around, and read aloud: "Captain Gabriel Lacey." She lowered it, her eyes quiet. "I thought you might be he."

CHAPTER 3

I hired a hackney coach to take us through the hot and damp bustle of London to Mayfair. Haze shimmered in the air, rendering the classical lines of the Admiralty a distant white bulk as we passed through Charing Cross. We followed Cockspur Street, then commenced up Haymarket to Piccadilly, and thence into Mayfair through Berkeley Street and Berkeley Square. Even at the early hour, young ladies and gentlemen in their carriages, properly chaperoned, of course, were eating ices from Gunter's in the shade of trees in the oval park. These ladies were not the most fashionable—the grande dames would still be abed from their evenings out, not rising until perhaps three in the afternoon.

The hackney turned out of Berkeley Square into Davies Street, and so on to Grosvenor Street. We stopped before a plain brown brick house adorned with Doric columns that flanked a red painted front door, which was missing its door knocker, usually indicating that the family had left London. I knew the house's simple façade was deceiving—

the houses on this street held sons of lords, wealthy members of Commons, and gentlemen of high standing. My acquaintance Lucius Grenville lived but ten doors down in large and elegant splendor.

A footman in maroon livery hastened from his post and pulled open the door of the hackney as soon as it halted. He stared at me in surprise, then his footman's demeanor slammed back into place and he reached in to help his lady. I guided her out to him. Her perfume, diminished with the night, mingled with the scent of summer rain.

I descended after her and bade the driver to wait.

The footman looked a bit bewildered. He was young and tall and strong, as a good footman ought to be, and I was relieved to see devotion in his eyes when he looked at his mistress. He took his cue from me and led her to the door with as much tenderness as he might his own mother.

Before we reached it, a man halted on the pavement beside us. It was none other than the irritating journalist, Billings.

"Good morning, Captain." He tipped his hat. "Madam."

Mrs. Westin turned her face away. I gave her to the care of her footman and approached Billings, walking stick firmly in my hand. "Leave now," I advised.

"Good morning, Captain Lacey," the man said. "Returning home with Mrs. Colonel Westin at such an interesting hour of the morning. Good gracious heavens. What will everyone think?"

"Now," I repeated, "before I call a constable to clear you out."

He only gave me an insolent look and said to the air, "He is as rude as they say."

I advanced on him. His sneer turned to a look of alarm as I caught him by the elbows and tossed him into the street.

He landed on his feet, stumbled, then scrambled out of the way of a rapidly moving curricle. Before he could recover himself, I entered the Westin house and closed the door.

Lydia Westin's house was like she was, elegant and understated. In a world of ornate gilding and faux Egyptian furnishings, the Westin household had retained a more classical feel. Ivory paneling framed delicate moiré wallpaper hung with landscapes. Tapered-legged tables stood in niches along the black and white tile flooring, and fresh flowers filled vases hung on the walls flanking mirrors.

A straight staircase spilled down into the hall beyond the foyer, its dark polished rail ending in a graceful spiral. At the foot of these stairs, Lydia Westin waited, supported by a woman with iron gray hair. She was Lydia's lady's maid, I guessed, by her fine dress and mobcap. She eyed me severely.

The footman, closing the door behind me, hurried past and took Lydia's other arm. The worry in these servants' faces reassured me somewhat. They would take care of her.

Even so, I hated to leave. I lingered, hoping against hope that she would ask me to stay, to have breakfast, to speak with her. She would not, of course. She was tired and distressed and likely wished to see the last of me.

They were waiting for me to do something. I made a half-bow. "Good morning, then," I said. "I see that I leave you in good hands."

They turned her away, taking her upstairs. In a moment, she would be gone from my sight.

Between one stair and the next, Mrs. Westin stopped. She turned back, her hand on the railing. "William," she said. "Please take Captain Lacey to my sitting room. Bring him coffee. I should like to speak to him, at length, if he can spare the time."

Of course I could spare the time. I had no obligation, no one to go to. I could spend the entire morning and all afternoon with her if need be.

"Indeed," I said.

The maid looked unhappy, the footman, worried. They looked ready to hustle their lady upstairs and out of sight, protecting her from my gaze, like an Indian woman to her purdah.

"But, madam, we must not—" the footman whispered.

Mrs. Westin interrupted him. "I will speak to him, William. He can help us."

William snapped his mouth shut. The maid still looked reproving. Lydia gave her a cool nod and told her to take her upstairs.

As the two ladies ascended in a swish of silk, William returned to me. He had wide brown eyes and wisps of brown hair that stuck out from under his footman's wig. His gloved hands clenched and unclenched, as though he debated whether to obey his mistress or toss me out onto the pavement.

At last he sighed. "This way, sir," he said, and led me upstairs.

I waited in a drawing room whose windows faced a tiny patch of garden at the rear of the house. I sensed at once that this was *her* room, one she had created as her own sanctum. A small pianoforte stood in one corner, and the cream-colored walls were adorned with portraits of the family. The furniture had classical lines; its tapered-legged chairs matched the furniture downstairs. The divan, chairs, and cornices over the windows were decorated with gold studs laid out in simple scrolled patterns.

An hour had passed. William now led Lydia Westin in and seated her on a divan near the empty fireplace. He draped a rug over her legs and a paisley shawl about her shoulders. Her face was white, and the defiant sparkle that had shone in her eyes that morning had given way to quiet resignation.

She gestured me to sit and dismissed William.

"You were kind to stay, Captain," she said after William had closed the doors. Her voice was a weary slur.

I remained standing. "Not at all."

She toyed with the fringe of her shawl, as though gathering her strength to speak. Her portrait hung above her, painted, I guessed, when she'd been at least ten years younger. She had been extraordinarily beautiful then. Her painted face was a bit softer than the one that faced me now, and her eyes had lacked the pain I observed in them today.

Ten years ago, we had both been thirty. She had been an elegant Mayfair hostess, and I had been training cavalry in Sussex, preparing them, though I did not know it, to die on the battlefields of Spain. From what I knew of her, Lydia Westin, unlike my own wife, had not followed her husband to the Peninsula. She'd remained here in this fine house, attending the opera, hosting gatherings, keeping her skin soft and her slippers clean. She had lived the life my wife had longed for, the one I had not been able to afford to give her.

At last Lydia looked up at me. Her maid had combed out her dark hair, but had not dressed it, letting it lie loose about her shoulders. The girlish style did not soften the brittle woman who watched me.

"Captain," she began. "I have decided to confide in you a matter which . . ." She sighed. "I hope I am not wrong. But you have proved to be kind. You had no need to help me, and you continued to, even when I . . ." She flushed. "Even when I threw myself at you. Please forgive me. I can imagine what you must have thought of me."

"I thought you hurt and in need of rest."

"I was. Quite a lot. What I had decided to do last night . . ." She stopped again, lips trembling. "I cannot speak of it. I am only grateful you were there to stop it. You have proved yourself a gentleman, and so, I have decided to trust you."

"I hope I will prove worthy of it."

"My servants disagree with me. They believe me foolish, but will stand with me." She gestured. "Please sit, Captain. This will be long in telling."

I obeyed, settling myself on a damask chair next to the divan.

"My husband is dead," she said. "I remember babbling that to you in your rooms, after you gave me so much brandy. I told you other things as well. They were all true." She paused. "What I am about to tell you must go no farther than this room. You must swear this to me, upon your honor."

"Of course. You have my word," I said, my curiosity growing by the minute. "You told me that your husband had been murdered."

"I did. And he was."

Puzzled, I said, "But he fell down the stairs, at least the newspapers reported that he did."

"No." She stared into the middle distance, as though something there told her what to say. "My husband never fell down a staircase. Someone stabbed him, with a small, sharp knife through the base of his neck. Then they put him to bed. Or he was already there when they stabbed him, I do not know."

I stared at her, astounded. "Then why did the stories say—"

"Because we told them that." She switched her gaze to me. "Understand me, Captain. I and William, and my maid, and Millar—he is Roe's valet—told the journalists and Bow Street that my husband had fallen down the stairs. William and Millar lied themselves blue in the coroner's court, saying that they both saw him slip and fall. And so, the verdict was death by accident."

I frowned. "Why the devil should you try to hide the fact that your husband had been murdered?"

To my surprise, she smiled. "To save him the embarrassment of it, of course." The smile quickly faded. "I know you must think me mad, but I was afraid and so confused. This course seemed best."

"Afraid of whom?" Disquiet touched me. "Is it that you are protecting the murderer?"

"No, Captain, it is that I am protecting my daughter."

She leaned forward. "You must understand. We had been so raked through the newspapers until Chloe was ill with it. When I found my husband, I was of course ready to send for a constable. Then I stopped myself. I thought, why should he be murdered? Let the world think him dead by accident—a happy relief for his family. If the newspapers began crying murder, we would never know peace again. So you see, this is why I beg your silence. I want no newspapers, no constables, no Bow Street. I have sent my daughter away to her uncle in Surrey, but I want nothing of this to touch her—ever."

I traced the carved gold pattern on the arm of my chair. The lady of despair and fear I had saved last night had vanished, to be replaced by a cool-headed woman who had dispatched her daughter and sworn her servants to secrecy when her own husband had been killed. "I can imagine your feelings. But I still do not understand why you have taken this step. Why would you not want to find your husband's murderer?"

"I do want to find them. I do indeed. And make them pay."

"Them?" I repeated. "Last night, you said you knew *they* had murdered him. You called them the triumvirate."

"Yes, that is how I think of them, the three most devious and horrible men in existence. I am not afraid to name them. They are Lord Richard Eggleston, Viscount Breckenridge, and Major Sir Edward Connaught. The three of them murdered my husband, depend upon it."

"Why should they?" I asked. "Who are they?"

Her fine blue eyes glittered in anger and defiance. "They are officers of the Forty-Third Light Dragoons. They murdered an officer called Algernon Spencer at Badajoz and forced my wretched husband to take the blame for it."

Her words rang with conviction. The Spartan room echoed with it.

She smiled faintly. "Possibly you think me a madwoman, Captain. I cannot blame you after my behavior last night."

"Not mad," I said slowly. "You must have some reason for believing they killed him."

"No one else would have been wicked enough. And they feared him. He knew the truth, and who knows what he may have said in the dock or on the gallows? Safer to have him dead."

"Do you have proof of this? What I mean is, did they visit him the day of his death, did anyone see them commit this act?"

She sighed. "No. Millar and William say he had no visitors at all that morning, but that must be a mistake."

"If they were not here . . ." I began.

She glared at me, a fine lady gazing with scorn upon a disobedient servant. "I know they did this, Captain. I need no proof."

But a magistrate might, I forbore to point out. "Please tell me what happened that day—who discovered him, how you knew he'd been killed."

She was silent a long moment, then her gaze went remote again. "I found him. I wanted to speak to him. I wanted to tell him . . ." She paused, and I saw her rearrange her words. "I had a topic of importance to discuss with him. I wanted to tell him everything, the entire truth. It was ten; Roe was usually awake then, and waiting for Millar to bring his breakfast tray. I went to his bedchamber. He was still in bed; I thought him asleep. But when I reached his bed, I saw that he was dead."

"I am sorry," I said.

"He looked so peaceful. I thought he had died in his sleep. And do you know, I was glad." She looked up at me, her eyes glittering. "Glad for *him*. I thought, now no one can ever hurt him again. Not me, nor anyone else. And then I . . ." She paused, spots of color appearing in her cheeks. "I embraced him. I told him how sorry I was, how stupid I'd been."

I wondered very much about what. "Why did it occur to you that he'd been murdered?"

She pressed her palms together. "When I straightened from the bed, I noticed that I had a stain on the sleeve of my gown. It was not very large, and it looked black. I knew the gown had been cleaned before my maid dressed me, so I must have come by the mark recently. I could not get it out of my head that it must be blood, my husband's blood. So I leaned down and embraced him again, and then I knew where I'd obtained the stain.

"I sent for William, my footman. He is a trusty lad, and I wanted to spare Millar as long as I could. William was shocked when he saw my husband, of course, but he is remarkably well trained and resourceful." She smiled a little. "If ever I asked him to move a pet elephant into my upstairs chamber, I believe he would only say, 'Yes, my lady,' and fall to it."

I thought of the besotted look in William's eyes and agreed with her.

"He raised Roe's head," she said. "And I found it. A small mark on the back of his neck." She touched a spot just below her own ear. "Someone had stabbed him, Captain. Straight through the neck and up under the skull."

Such a wound could kill a man outright. I imagined he'd died quite quickly, and the absence of much blood bore out that theory.

"What did you do then?" I asked.

"My first instinct was to have William run for the constable. But something stopped me. I realized that if he ran out like the house was on fire, the journalists who hung about waiting for my husband to emerge every day would latch themselves on to him. They would know everything, and write every word. I just could not bear for Roe to die in the flame of notoriety. I wanted his death to be given some respect. So I called Millar and Montague, my lady's maid, and told them what I wanted to do. They were as angry as I at his death, and they also hate the newspapers.

They agreed to keep silent how he had died, even from my daughter and Mr. Allandale, her fiancé."

She subsided. Her lips trembled and she pulled the shawl closer about her.

"And now you have told me," I said. "Why?"

"Because I need help. Roe died in shame and disgrace, and he did not deserve that. I want that to change."

"What do you want me to do?" I asked. "Prove that these three men killed your husband?"

Her eyes held anger and determination. "No. Prove that they murdered Captain Spencer at Badajoz. Make the world know my husband had nothing to do with it. And when they die on the gallows for that murder, they will equally pay for my husband's."

I wondered briefly if she had loved her husband. Society marriages could be contracted with gain alone in mind—an heiress married an impoverished lord; a lady of a titled family married to lend connections to a wealthy nobody. My own marriage had been made for neither of these reasons, hence the complete rage of my father.

I shook my head slowly. "What you ask is—"

She flung back the blanket and got to her feet. Her maid had dressed her in a dark gray gown, against which her white skin seemed even paler. She began pacing unsteadily through the blocks of sunlight that poured through the windows.

"He did not kill that captain, I know it. Those three spoiled aristocrats did not want an ounce of shame to touch them, so they forced my husband to confess to something he did not do. He was willing to go to trial, ready to admit that he'd killed that officer in Spain rather than let others in his regiment be disgraced. That was the kind of gentleman he was. But he was wronged. Utterly wronged."

I thought again of the newspaper accounts, the stories, and Pomeroy's impartations on the affair. Westin, by all accounts, had been contrite and apologetic in the face of Spencer's sons' accusations. Lydia was now insisting that he had bowed his head so that the honor of others would not be tarnished, that his fellow officers would not be stained.

I found it all a bit odd. Would a man truly give up his life for the honor of others? And were those others so lacking in honor that they would allow him to do it?

"He was ready to admit to it," I said as gently as I could. "And he was the ranking officer."

She turned on me in fury. "Those three gentlemen cared nothing for rank," she snapped. "It was they who murdered Captain Spencer, you can be certain of it."

"Your husband told you this?"

"No. Nor would he. The honor of the regiment must be preserved at all costs, even when speaking of it to your own wife." Her mouth turned down. "But imagine it— three pampered, inebriated aristocrats let loose on the streets of a conquered town. They must have been delighted. Then when Captain Spencer tried to spoil their amusement, they killed him. I know it in my heart. My husband would have tried to prevent it, but they would not have listened." Her eyes sparkled, defiant, bitter.

"But Colonel Westin never confided in you."

She glared at me. I was a toad, waiting to be stepped on.

I did not tell her that I'd be honored to be trampled by her elegant foot.

"My husband was a moral man, Captain. Moral in the real sense of the word, not in the manner in which some preach morality while beating their servants black and blue with the other hand! He no more would have shot Captain Spencer than the Thames would flow backward. He abhorred violence and violent acts."

I was puzzled. "If he abhorred violence, why did he purchase a commission in the cavalry?"

One of the most violent professions I could think of. Cavalry charged, breakneck and reckless, down the throats of the enemy, chopping apart lines and boiling up dust and chaos while musket fire rained around them. Light Dragoons technically were not used to charge lines—that was the job of the heavy cavalry—but in practice, if any cavalry were at hand, they were thrown at everything. Some officers led their men so far through enemy lines that they were too winded to get back and were cut down one by one. At the beginning of the campaign, I had been just as reckless, but time had taught me the value of prudence.

Even so, after each battle, I had always been surprised to find myself still upright and walking.

Lydia Westin would not be cowed. "My husband was a colonel because his father was a colonel. The honor of the regiment again. Following in his father's footsteps. Roe was like that. He would sacrifice his happiness, his peace of mind—everything—for honor."

"Many do," I said dryly. "We live in honorable times."

"My husband's honor was true. It was the most important thing in the world to him."

Her eyes flashed. I could not tell if she had admired or despised her husband. Both, probably.

"He was prepared to admit to the murder," I pointed out.

"Oh, yes. How could he stand by and let those with great names be sullied? They asked it of him. When they heard that John Spencer was near to discovering the truth, they visited him. Here. Upstairs in his chamber for hours and hours. They played upon his sense of honor, knowing he'd agree. And he did it. He was willing to make the ultimate sacrifice. For them."

"But if he were willing to do so," I pointed out, "why do you believe they murdered him? Surely they would want him to go on to be arrested and tried."

"I thought of that." Her brow puckered. "It is one thing to agree to take the blame for a crime. But another when one actually stands in the dock. Who knows what he might have said? Would he have told the truth about what happened to Captain Spencer? Perhaps he would not have been believed, but then, some magistrates are quite canny.

They might have asked awkward questions." Her eyes dared me to tell her she was wrong.

I sat silently. Again I was struck by the incongruity of this woman traveling to the dark bridge in the rain. She believed her husband's innocence, would fight like a lion to preserve the honor he'd held so precious. This was a woman who would glare down her enemies and dare them to stop her.

So would she, in despair, decide to walk to an unfinished bridge and fling herself from it? Or had she gone for another purpose? Either action simply did not fit.

"Find these gentlemen," she said. "And make them admit that they murdered Captain Spencer."

I began to grow exasperated. While I'd listened, I'd allowed my senses to bathe in her beauty, but her vehemence was becoming unreasonable. "Not an easy thing to do. And you cannot tell me for certain that they did kill your husband." I held up my hand as she drew a breath for angry protest. "Think, Mrs. Westin. If they did not kill him, and you pursue them, the true murderer gets away with it."

She stared at me, startled, and I saw she had not thought of that. "But they must have done it."

I tried another tack. "What time did your husband go to bed that night? The usual?"

"Yes. Millar undressed him and left him in bed at half past eleven, his usual time to retire."

"And no one saw him until ten the next morning, when you entered his bedchamber, and no visitors came to the house and were shown up to see him."

"No." She said the word reluctantly.

"But that implies, does it not, that someone inside the house could have killed him. Such as one of your servants."

"No!" The cry rang sharply against the portraits. "They would not. They were devoted to him, and to me."

Perhaps. But once upon a time, my acquaintance Lucius Grenville had hired a well-trained, efficient butler

who had come with glowing recommendations from the
Duke of Merton, to whom said butler had been most devoted. The butler had, three months later, organized a
gang of thieves to rob Grenville blind. This had happened
during a huge gathering at New Year's at his house,
which I had happened to attend. Grenville and I had
caught the robbers together, and thus we'd begun our odd
friendship.

"What about this Mr. Allandale, your daughter's fiancé?"

She shook her head, but with less fervor than she had
when defending her servants. "He was not staying in the
house. He hired a house in Mount Street."

A house in Mount Street must be ruinously expensive, I
mused, even now that the Season was over. I wondered if
the good Mr. Allandale had asked to marry the Westin
daughter because of her parents' obvious wealth.

"Did it not occur to you," I said, "that the newspapers
would remark upon the convenient timing of his accident?
Sparing you the disgrace of an arrest, trial, and conviction?
Please do not be offended, but did none of them speculate
that it was your hand that pushed your husband to his
death?"

She smiled a fey, feral smile. "William and I thought of
that. We contrived it so that Millar and William claimed to
see him fall when I and Chloe were well out of the house.
Chloe was on her way to Surrey, to her uncle, and I had
dressed and gone out to attend a morning garden party
given by Lady Featherstone in Kensington. Everyone who
had not yet scattered to the countryside was there. They all
saw me. While I was gone, William and Millar arranged
my husband's body at the bottom of the stairs and ran for
a constable. They also brought back a doctor, an elderly
man. The wound was tiny and Millar cleaned it so it could
barely be seen. No one else found it."

Clever. No doubt she had chosen a garden party full of
gossips who would all clamor that Mrs. Westin had been
with them when news of her husband's accident was

brought to her. I imagined them describing her emotion, her paling face, her tear-filled eyes.

I said, "Does Mr. Allandale know the truth? Would he not ask why you had suddenly sent your daughter away?"

She shook her head. "I explained to him that Chloe was ill and needed to take the country air. He asked no questions, and said it was a mercy she had not been here to witness her father's death."

"This Mr. Allandale seems to be quite understanding," I remarked. "He stood by you and your family, even through the scandal of Captain Spencer?" A lesser man might have cried off, saved himself from being touched by the shame.

"Oh yes, he has stuck by us," Lydia said. "Like a cocklebur! He is most devoted." The derision in her tone was unmistakable.

I puzzled on this, but went back to the main problem. "But you believe that these three gentlemen, or at least someone hired by them to do the deed, entered your house sometime in the night and killed your husband."

"I do." She gave me a cold look, then relented. "I am sorry, Captain. I know it sounds ridiculous. But equally I know they must be responsible. I ask you—I am begging you—to help me."

I absently traced my forefinger. "I wonder that you would trust me. My own colonel was ready to swear that your husband was drunk enough to have committed the crime at Badajoz. Why do you believe I do not agree with him?"

She gave me a tight smile. "Because you would have already said so. And Mrs. Brandon told me that you had helped a young woman escape from her tormentor earlier this year. And that you brought a murderer to justice."

I wondered what edited version of the tale Louisa had imparted. True, I had helped a girl return to her aunt after she had been used by her purchaser for his amusement, but Louisa and I were the only two who knew the entire truth of the matter.

"Mrs. Brandon is too quick to sing my praises."

Again, the white smile. "She did not praise you. She claims you are highly exasperating. But that you are honest, and more interested in truth than in pleasing lies."

I was not certain whether to be flattered or annoyed.

"Make them tell the truth, Captain," Lydia Westin said. She caught and held my gaze. "Make them clear my husband's name and pay for all they have done."

I found myself agreeing. The story stirred my hazardous curiosity. She must have sensed that I could not have refused, and so ensnared me.

CHAPTER 4

I asked Lydia leave to speak to her servants. I hoped that the valet, who had been with Colonel Westin throughout the war, might be able to impart something about the incident in Badajoz. Also, I wanted to know what the servants could tell me about the night of Colonel Westin's death. Lydia might be convinced of who murdered her husband, but I was not so sanguine. The quicker I ferreted out the truth, the better.

She agreed to let me ask questions, though limited me to the three servants already in on the secret. I also mentioned Grenville. If I were to investigate the gentlemen she'd named, I would need an introduction to them. Grenville, beloved of society, whose acquaintance was much sought after, could smooth my way in that regard.

She was reluctant to let me enlist his help. I assured her that Grenville could hold his tongue, but I understood her hesitation. It was one thing to confide in a nobody like me, yet another to tell your secrets to the gentleman at the top of society.

At last she conceded, but made me promise to tell him nothing about the death of her husband beyond what was in the newspapers. I disliked to lie to him, but I agreed.

I spoke to William, Mrs. Montague, and Millar in the servants' hall. I explained that I had agreed to help Mrs. Westin as much as I could. They eyed me doubtfully, and I did not blame them their reluctance. She had literally plucked me off the street and asked for my assistance. I could sell them out to the journalists as easily as breathing for all they knew.

They answered my questions politely enough, but the stony light in their eyes told me that they had decided it their duty to answer me only because their mistress wished it.

I recalled asking similar questions of servants in a house in Hanover Square not long ago. My experience here was much different. Those servants had been inefficient, impudent, and lazy. They had stayed employed only by virtue of the fact that they would look the other way at their master's disgusting proclivities. The three facing me now had been hired by Lydia Westin. Their manners were impeccable, and they spoke correctly, deferentially, and coolly.

Only the valet, Millar, a Frenchman with a round face, betrayed emotion. He dabbed at his eyes with a handkerchief while he spoke, blinking back tears that would not completely cease. One person in this household, I thought, had looked upon Colonel Westin with true affection.

I did not, overall, learn much from them. They concurred that Colonel Westin had gone to bed at half past eleven on the night of the tenth of July and had been found dead in his bed the next morning at ten o'clock. No one had entered the house, as far as they knew, all night, though they admitted that between the hours of one A.M. and five, they would have all been asleep. No one had come in via the scullery early the next morning, save the coal man, but they all knew him and he had not lingered.

I thanked them for their time, a bit depressed at their lack of information, and left the servants' hall.

When I emerged onto the ground floor, I collided with a spare, blond gentleman just hurrying in through the front door.

He stopped short and stared at me. I waited for him to beg my pardon, to explain what the devil he was doing walking into the Westin house unannounced, but he merely raised his well-groomed brows and looked me over from head to foot. Annoyed at his impudence, I did the same.

The gentleman was younger than I, but not by much, possibly in his early thirties at the least. His blond hair was pomaded into place, but so artfully that it appeared to wave naturally. Women probably found him handsome. His face held the sculpted perfection of a Greek statue, and was just as alabaster. He could be described as beautiful; only a squarishness to his jaw saved him from a womanly appearance.

Lydia emerged on the landing above. She gripped the rail with a white hand.

"Captain," she said, "May I present Mr. Allandale. Mr. Allandale, Captain Lacey."

The understanding fiancé. He regarded me coolly. "Who is he, mother-in-law?"

"He was in the army with Colonel Westin," Lydia replied, stretching the truth a little. "I have asked him to look into the matter of Captain Spencer."

"I see," Mr. Allandale answered, still looking at me.

"He is also a friend of Mr. Grenville," Lydia continued.

Mr. Allandale's lip suddenly uncurled, and his expression changed to instant politeness. "Ah, yes. Captain Lacey. I have heard your name." He held out his hand. "You must take supper with us one day soon. A week Monday?"

Lydia remained silent. I spoke some polite, noncommittal words, and shook his offered hand.

Allandale nodded as though all were settled. "We will stay quiet, because of the colonel's death, you know. But I would be glad to make your acquaintance. Good morning, Captain."

It was a dismissal. I bowed to Lydia, who inclined her head and said nothing. Allandale saw me out the door, smiling and friendly all the way, but his eyes were watchful.

I returned to Grimpen Lane and wrote to Grenville, telling him I had come upon something interesting. I said nothing more than that, hoping to pique his curiosity. I had not spoken to Grenville in at least a month, and I did not know if he had even remained in town, nor if he would take offense at the presumption that he would help me the instant I asked. But I had to risk it.

I also boldly wrote to Lady Aline Carrington, asking if she knew of Louisa's whereabouts. Brandon had told me that Lady Aline had claimed to know nothing, but what Lady Aline would tell Brandon and what she would tell me was bound to be different. Lady Aline did not much like Colonel Brandon.

But it worried me that Louisa had not contacted me, even with a brief letter to assure me she was well. The most logical thing to assume was that Brandon had annoyed her in some way, and she had simply gone away to think things over, as he'd said, undisturbed. I could not discount, however, the possibility that she had been spirited away and the note sent as a blind. I knew the second speculation was not as far-fetched as it sounded. London abounded with opportunists waiting to seize a lady for a number of purposes. I'd heard of lone women robbed of all they had, and then held for ransom. Even a lady of good standing could be lured into a trap by someone pathetically requesting assistance. Once the generous lady entered the house, she could be seized, robbed, or worse.

I seriously doubted that Louisa would have gone out alone to some dire part of London. She was brave, but not

foolish. All of which pointed toward the first scenario—
she'd left to think something over.

But though I tried to make myself believe that the first
speculation was more likely, the vision formed in my mind
of Louisa lost, beaten, robbed, insensible, her golden hair
lying in an arc beneath her limp, pale body. The vision
would not release me.

I toyed with the idea of persuading Milton Pomeroy, the
Bow Street Runner, to, as a favor to me, keep an eye out
for Louisa. Runners, in addition to solving crimes—often
they were hired by the victims of those crimes—also
helped track missing persons. Those hiring them offered a
reward, and the Runner, if he obtained a conviction or
found the missing person, reaped it.

I did not have the means to offer a reward, but I might
convince Pomeroy, who was not as thick as he pretended
to be, to help me. But I disliked revealing what might be
Louisa's personal quarrel with Brandon, did not like to set
the tenacious Pomeroy on her.

I posted my letters then went to Covent Garden market
to purchase the necessities of life, including more candles,
made easier because my half-pay packet had been recently
released to my bank. I had paid Mrs. Beltan for my rooms
the previous day, but I had to make what little was left last
for another quarter.

Many officers came from wealthy families—even second or third sons might have a generous allowance—and
their army pay was a secondary income. Then there were
officers like me, gentlemen, but destitute. My father had
been furious with me when I'd run off with the army, following Brandon, who was then a captain, to the 35th Light
Dragoons. My father had cut me off from whatever funds
he possibly could.

Which was laughable to me, because my father had already managed to squander away most of the Lacey
money before I even reached my majority. He had disgraced himself with debts and spent his days scrambling to
pay them. He'd sold off every scrap of land that was not

entailed, and allowed the house we lived in to fall into ruin. I'd gone to school only because my mother, before her death, had put money in trust for my education, a trust so firmly set with traps that my father had not been able to touch the money, no matter how he'd tried.

After I'd arrived on the Peninsula, my father, who had celebrated my desertion by going into yet more debt, went into a decline, and died the day I was promoted from lieutenant to captain, the morning after the bloody battle at Talavera.

The creditors had stripped the house of everything before they'd at last declared the debts satisfied. Nothing was left of the estate now except the house, which was entailed to the son I doubted I would ever have. I could let the house, but either I or a zealous tenant would have to spend an enormous amount of money to repair it and make it livable. So far, I had not found that zealous tenant. So it sat, forlorn in its corner of England, waiting for the last Lacey male to come home.

Absorbed in these thoughts, I wandered through Covent Garden market. Golden peaches like pieces of sunshine mounded on stalls, and carts overflowed with bright greens from fields beyond London. The sky held clouds, some of them still gray with last night's rain, but Covent Garden shimmered with an air of festivity. The summer day was warm, riots of blue, red, and gold flowers overflowed baskets, women in cool linen haggled prices like the best of fishwives, game girls in bright reds and blues and greens sashayed about, darting into dark corners with gentlemen or hiding behind carts when a watchman strolled by.

I touched a peach, letting my fingers find joy in its downy softness. I paid the seller with a coin as bright as the fruit and bit into the peach's delight.

As I savored the fruit, sweet as a summer day, I thought again of Lydia Westin.

Her husband, who had been headed for disgrace and notoriety, was now conveniently dead. Lydia's foremost thought was to clear his name and save her daughter and herself from the stain of it, and to punish those she held responsible. She claimed she wanted justice, but I'd seen the look in her eyes, heard the note of fury in her voice. What she wanted was revenge.

I wondered anew if she had loved her husband. I did not believe I had witnessed a widow's grief at losing her heart mate; rather, I had seen wounded pride and great determination. She wanted her husband's name respected, but the relief she had exhibited when she spoke of his death had been true.

I also realized I felt more than mere curiosity, even my form of curiosity, which liked to pick apart events to find their cause or their source. Lydia Westin was deeply beautiful, and that beauty, even marred with dirt and blood and fear, had struck a responsive chord within me. I recognized that, and I recognized the danger.

Behind her agitation lay a woman of profound serenity, as calm and clear as an unruffled lake. A man could close his eyes and lose himself in that beauty.

Wrapped in these thoughts, I emerged into crowded Russel Street and halted when a carriage door was nearly flung open in my face. The stopped carriage was opulent, with varnished wood inlay outlining the doors and windows. The wheels were picked out in gold, which matched the trim of the horses' harness. The coachman wore red livery with a brush in his hat; the footman who leapt from his perch and reached in for the passenger was dressed in blue satin.

I had seen the carriage before. Had ridden in it—once. And I was acquainted with the man who descended from it not a foot in front of me.

He saw me, and stopped. A fairly young man, he was lean of build, though as tall as I. His face might have been called handsome, but his blue eyes were cold as the depths of the Thames.

His name was James Denis. I had met him in the spring, and I loathed him. What he thought of me, I had no idea, for his habitually cool eyes betrayed nothing. They were soulless eyes, eyes of a man who cared for nothing, and no one. ·

James Denis procured things for people, for wealthy men who wanted something unobtainable through ordinary means. They made an appointment with Denis at his elegant Curzon Street house, and the item was made available to them for a high fee. Once, Lucius Grenville had hired him to help a French aristocrat recover a family painting that Napoleon had commandeered. Denis and his associates had managed to purloin that painting from under the emperor's nose. How, Grenville had declined to ask, and had advised me to do the same. Grenville thought it likely that much of the Prince of Wales's lavish collections of art had been obtained by James Denis.

Denis had not been guilty of the human trafficking I'd first suspected him of, but that fact did not relieve my qualms about him. The last time we'd met, he'd coolly dispatched a servant who'd had a hand in the murder of a young girl—not because of the heinous crime, but because the servant had acted without Denis's permission.

I had been enraged with the servant in question, and I had not tried to stop Denis meting out his own style of justice. Denis had afterward claimed that I owed him a favor. I had no intention of ever letting him call it in.

Now the two of us stared at one another in tense silence. His eyes glittered, cold and dispassionate. I did not bother to hide my dislike.

We regarded one another for a long moment, then he ever so slightly tilted his head in the ghost of a nod.

I cut him dead. Turning my back, I marched back across the street, my stick ringing on the pavement. A cart swerved to miss me, but I made it to the opposite side without mishap.

I longed to look back to see how he took my insult, but that would have ruined the impact of the cut direct. I strode on toward Grimpen Lane, the remains of the peach dangling from my nerveless fingers.

•   •   •

I returned to my rooms, tired and churning with mixed emotions. I had not slept at all the night before, so I locked my door, stripped off my clothes, and lay on the sheets Lydia Westin had occupied. Her perfume lingered on them.

The day was sweltering, and I thought to lie awake contemplating all Lydia had told me. I scrubbed at my face, feeling prickly beard beneath my palms. Lydia had great faith in me. One did not lightly accuse a lordship of a crime. They could stand trial and be hanged, just like the rest of us, but one would have a hard fight on one's hands to get them to trial at all. These gentlemen and their families would never allow me, a nobody, to topple them, and well I knew it.

I did not lie awake as I'd expected. A few moments after I stretched upon the bed, I sank into slumber, my lack of sleep finally punishing me. I woke to the sun low in the west and someone banging on my outer door.

CHAPTER 5

BECAUSE I'd slept in my skin, I had to dress before I could limp to the door and open it.

Lucius Grenville stood on the threshold, with Bartholomew, his tall, bulky footman, behind him. Grenville was resplendent in buff breeches and boots and immaculate black coat, and wore an emerald stickpin in his snowy cravat.

He had dark brown hair, as I did, though his contained no threads of gray, possibly because he was a few years younger than I, or because his valet took care to remove or dye the offending hairs. His face was not handsome, being a little too plain and too sharp in the chin, but not one of his admirers seemed to note that. His eyes, as though to compensate for his plainness, were sparkling and lively. Grenville lived life to the fullest and took an interest in everything, great or small.

He seldom visited me in my rooms. Most of the time, he waited in his luxurious carriage at the end of the lane and sent his footman for me, or simply sent the empty carriage across London alone. Now he stood on my doorstep, his dark eyes alert with curiosity.

"Yes?" I snapped, not fully myself.

"Are you all right?"

I must have looked frightful, face unshaven, hair rumpled, eyes bloodshot. I raked my hand through my hair. "Sleeping. I beg your pardon. Please come in."

He stepped into my sitting room and looked about him as though I'd just invited him into a grand palace in Saint Petersburg. Across the lane the curtains of my opposite neighbor, Mrs. Carfax, stood open to catch the last of the daylight, allowing us to see right into her always painfully clean parlor. A table stood in her window in the same position it had occupied for the year and a half I'd lived here. A book rested in the precise center of the table, edges in perfect alignment. I had witnessed both Mrs. Carfax and her faded companion carefully dust this book, but I had never observed either of them lift it, open it, or read it. Mrs. Carfax liked to leave the curtains open as long as possible, she had confided to me one day in the bake shop, because she was forced to be very frugal with her candles. She would have hated living downstairs from Marianne.

Grenville peered through the dusty panes until Bartholomew had bowed and departed, then he pulled a newspaper out from under his arm and handed it to me. "You have become famous, my friend. I congratulate you."

I stared at him, nonplussed. "Famous?"

"Fresh this evening."

I took the paper from him and looked where he pointed. A caricature of myself, or at least a cavalry officer in dark regimentals brandishing a cavalry saber, accosted a frightened-looking man who was backing hastily away, dropping pencil and notebook. The head of the officer was overlarge, the saber too long. A ribbon of words from his mouth proclaimed: "A flogging! A flogging, I say, sir! Forty lashes will teach you to keep a foul Tongue in your Mouth, sir!"

In the background stood a man who could only be

Grenville. The artist had given him an exaggerated athletic body, a huge cravat, and a high hat. He was smiling and nodding to an audience of anonymous but obviously upper-class ladies and gentlemen. His ribbon read: "Excellent, excellent, Cpt. We're to Drury Lane next, then on to Gtlmn J—'s."

Beneath this ran the words. "A soldier of Honor, who took to shooting his *Fellow Officers* when he felt peevish—is dead and gone. His widow grieves—and another Gallant Dragoon leaps to the side of this most Fortunate of Women."

More of this drivel followed, but I flung it away. "Good God." If ever I saw that fellow Billings again, I would thrash him good and hard, making certain I rendered him unable to write. "I am sorry. They had no right to drag you into it."

Grenville waved it away. "I have appeared in far less flattering cartoons, believe me. But this coming hard after your letter made me wonder very much. As you intended me to."

In the dim light of the dying day, his dark eyes glistened like pieces of onyx. His curiosity upon receiving my letter must have been insatiable, because he'd not been willing to wait for his carriage to convey me to him. I did not like him here, which was why I never invited him. My lodgings were pitiful in contrast to his sumptuous mansion, where every luxury imaginable was at his disposal, including hot water pumped in for his baths.

But there was nothing for it now, and besides, I truly needed his help. I would have to swallow my pride and live with the bitter aftertaste.

I gestured him to my wing chair. "Sit, then. I will fetch some coffee."

"No need," he said quickly.

I opened the door again. "There is need. *My* need."

I left him alone and made my way downstairs to Mrs. Beltan's bake shop. She saw me and bustled to get my coffee. She did not normally sell coffee to her customers, but she'd started doing so for me, learning that I craved the stuff. She made a few extra coins by it, and she gave it to me cheaper than I could have obtained it at the coffee-houses or from street vendors.

Today I asked to borrow a second cup so Grenville could share if he chose. I'd drunk coffee at Grenville's mansion, and I'd drunk Mrs. Beltan's coffee, and I would be surprised if he chose.

When I entered my rooms again, balancing pot, tray, two cups, and half a loaf of bread, Marianne and Grenville were facing each other across the space of my hearth rug.

Neither noticed me. Grenville was very red in the face, and Marianne was smiling at him.

I clanked the tray to my writing table. Grenville nearly jumped out of his skin. Marianne gave me a languid look, as though she'd known I'd been there all along. "After-noon, Lacey. I came to ask if you'd share your dinner. I'm hungry and I already owe Ma Beltan for the last two days."

I motioned to the bread. "Take it." I was hungry, too, but I had a pay packet, and Marianne's irregular income was far more meager than mine.

Grenville scowled at her. "I gave you twenty guineas."

"You did. Right gentleman you are." She reached for the bread.

Grenville seized her outstretched wrist. "She will not tell me what has become of it."

I poured coffee. What influence he thought I had with Marianne, I could not imagine.

"Was it drink?" Grenville asked, his voice strained.

I answered for her. "Not likely." I breathed in the wel-come aroma of coffee, and the world brightened a bit. "She does not like it."

"Thank God for that."

"Gave it to my sick mum," Marianne said. "What do you think I did with it?"

Grenville's eyes were wary. "Did you give it to a man?"

She looked offended. "None of your business what I did

with it. You're plenty rich enough to spare a girl twenty guineas without worrying about where it goes."

I took a sip of coffee. The rich bitterness rolled across my tongue, and suddenly even Marianne's insolence became easier to bear. "It was an enormous amount of money, Marianne," I remarked. "A maidservant does not even make that much in a year."

She gave me a lofty glance. "I am not a maidservant."

Grenville released her. "No, Lacey, she is right." He drew a silken purse from his waistcoat. "I can spare it." He fished out a handful of gold coins.

Marianne shot me a look of triumph. She held out her hand, taking care to hold her fingers daintily—a woman receiving her dues, not a beggar desperate for coin.

Grenville dropped at least ten gold guineas into that slim palm. She smiled in a satisfied way and closed her fingers around them. "Mr. Grenville is a gentleman," she informed me. Her look told me I was not.

She reached again for the bread, her thin gown sliding across her hips. Grenville could not look away from her, though I saw him try.

I lifted the tray away. "Buy your own."

A final glare and curl of her lip, and she waltzed out. Downstairs, not up. Off to spend her newfound wealth.

Grenville stood looking at the door long after I'd closed it. "I cannot help it. She *was* hungry, Lacey, she trembled with it. I felt her trembling. But she would never have admitted it."

I sipped more coffee, my nerves finally settling. "She will trample you."

Grenville gave a little shrug, still staring at the door.

I offered him coffee and refrained from pointing out the folly of pinning his hopes on Marianne. She would use him until he refused to hand her money and then dismiss him. I could not condemn her for being a parasite, because she had to survive, but I had the feeling that Grenville, though he'd traveled the world, had finally met his match.

He drank his coffee absently, and I began to tell him the

tale. He listened, his eyes growing sharper as I told him everything, omitting only the fact that Westin had been murdered. I disliked lying to him, and I think he sensed I did not tell him the entire truth, but he did not remark upon it.

As I talked, my feeling of futility grew. Lydia Westin had compelled me to help her, but as I explained the situation, I realized that proving her husband's innocence might be nearly impossible.

Grenville was quick to point this out. "How can she be so certain he did not kill Captain Spencer? She was not with him on the Peninsula. He must have done a number of things that she knows nothing about, and even a moral man can falter in the heat of battle." He leaned to me, seemingly relieved to have something to occupy his thoughts other than Marianne. "When I spent time in America, I witnessed a few of the native uprisings, both massacres of natives by the colonials and massacres of the colonials by natives. I saw upright, honest, and moral men commit depraved acts, and then be horrified afterward. Perhaps Westin was simply so amazed at what he'd done that he believed in his own innocence."

I shook my head. "She believes it as well." I remembered the conviction in her eyes, her utter belief in him.

"Is a wife ever truly certain of her husband?" Grenville mused. "I have no idea; I have never been married. The married women of my acquaintance rarely speak of their husbands at all, except as a nuisance to be borne."

"Hmm," I said. "Nuisance" at least sounded affectionate. My wife had been alternately terrified of or furious with me. My clumsy attempts at affection had been abject failures.

"Even if she is right," Grenville continued, "I cannot understand his actions. I am acquainted with Lord Richard Eggleston and Lord Breckenridge, and I would not cover up a grass stain for either of them, let alone a murder. So either he is guilty, or—"

"Or they offered him something," I finished. "Something so important he was willing to go to the gallows to obtain it." I thought a moment. "Or they threatened him, had some hold over him. Threatened his family, perhaps." I did not like that idea at all.

Grenville gestured with his cup. "Perhaps Westin had ruined himself, with gambling debts or bad investments. Perhaps he was afraid to tell his wife. His three friends promised him they would pay his debt, and Mrs. Westin would never need know."

"But could he trust them to do it?"

Grenville shrugged. "Suppose they made a contract. No, perhaps they would not risk anything written. But if Westin was as fond of honor as his wife believes, perhaps he took their solemn words as binding."

"Now he is dead," I said slowly. "So all bargains are off?"

"Possibly. I can easily discover if he had been in too deep." He smiled a little. "It is supposed to be bad form to talk about money, or the lack of it, but the clubs are full of gossip. Everyone knows how much everyone else is into the money lenders for. We are all hypocrites." He chuckled. "What will you do?"

"What I did in the affair in Hanover Square. Apply to you for introduction to the upper classes."

He grinned. "Always happy to help."

"Only because you have an insatiable curiosity and thirst for adventure," I remarked. Life in upper-class London with unlimited funds at his disposal often grated on him, the unfortunate man.

His grin increased. He'd once told me he admired me because I faced what was real, and was not misled by what others perceived to be important. On days when my rooms permeated with chill and I had spent the last of my pennies on bread, I would have traded my reality with the trappings of his artificial world in a trice.

"I am not acquainted with Connaught," Grenville was saying, "but I do know the other two. Not the most genial of companions, I must warn you."

"Nevertheless an introduction would be a great help," I said. "I will also ask Mrs. Westin if I can look through her husband's letters and journals. They might shed some light on what really happened that night at Badajoz. John Spencer searched the papers of his father and Colonel Spinnet; it might be worth my while to try to look at those as well. I do not know John Spencer, but perhaps I can convince him we are both on the side of truth."

"I am not acquainted with him, either," Grenville said. "Eggleston I see often enough. He is rude and sulks when he loses at cards, though he pays up like a gentleman. I have heard whispers that he is a sodomite, but if so, he is very discreet. He boasts loudly of affairs with actresses and courtesans, on the other hand." He drained his cup. "He and Viscount Breckenridge are the oldest of friends, but it is an odd friendship. They disparage each other behind each other's backs—and face to face, for that matter. I once saw them nearly come to blows right in the middle of the card room at White's. And yet, they have been constant companions for years."

I looked a question, but Grenville shook his head. "No, I do not believe they are lovers. Where Eggleston boasts of his female conquests, Breckenridge is dead silent. But I once attended a house party with them, and in one weekend, Breckenridge had quietly fornicated with every woman in the house from the scullery maid to the hostess."

I grimaced. "I believe I understand why Mrs. Westin wishes to lay the blame at his door."

"Yes, he is rather vulgar." Grenville set down his empty cup. "I will cultivate my acquaintance with them both in the interest of justice." He rose and looked at me seriously. "Take care with the newspapermen, Lacey. They can destroy your character so quickly. And Mrs. Westin's."

"Yes," I answered, thinking longingly of my next meeting with Billings.

He seemed to read my thoughts. "Ignoring them utterly is best. If you confront them, they only write with more glee."

I nodded. I supposed he was right, and the famous Grenville had far more experience with prying journalists than I ever would. I still wanted to break Billings in half.

He left me then, summoning Bartholomew from downstairs. The two of them walked off down Grimpen Lane. The street was far too narrow for Grenville's opulent conveyance, so he always left it around the corner in Russel Street. Blond Bartholomew towered over his master, but they chatted amicably as they ambled along.

I never knew quite what to make of Grenville. I had heard tales of him reducing a gentleman to quivering tears simply by raising his brows. And yet he'd come to my barren and run-down rooms and behaved as though I'd received him at Carlton House.

I thought, however, that I'd have far better luck discovering the murderers of Captain Spencer and Colonel Westin than I would unraveling the mystery that was Lucius Grenville.

I decided to begin my investigation with a chat with the man who had dined with Westin on the fatal night in Spain. I shaved and washed and brushed down my clothes, then departed for Brook Street to visit Colonel Brandon.

He received me with ill grace. The servant left us in the downstairs reception room; Brandon was not even allowing me in the more comfortable rooms upstairs.

He looked terrible. He had obviously not slept. The skin beneath his eyes was bruised and puffy, and the corner of his mouth twitched uncontrollably.

I was reminded of Brandon's temper tantrums of old, of an irritability that only Louisa could soothe. I had the feeling he restrained himself from bodily flinging me from the house only because his servants would report his behavior to Louisa.

"I am quite busy, Lacey, what is it?"

I began without preliminary. "I have come to ask you a question or two about Colonel Westin."

His lip curled. "Why ask me? You had his wife in your bed."

I bristled. "I told you that you dishonored her with your speculations. You continue to at your peril."

"Do not insult me by threatening to call me out, Gabriel, even if you have the great Mr. Grenville to second you."

We faced each other, the tall former commander and the captain he had made and ruined. I had difficulty remembering that once upon a time I had admired this man. I had wanted to emulate him in all things. Now he stared at me with open belligerence, his handsome face mottled.

It struck me on a sudden that if Louisa truly did leave forever, there would be no more buffer between Brandon and me. Nothing to keep our hatred from coming to the fore. We would destroy each other.

I fixed him with a cold stare. "May we keep to the point? I want to know what happened the night that Colonel Westin took supper with you at Badajoz."

"Why? He already admitted he killed Spencer. Besides, he was the ranking officer."

"You were ready enough to accuse Westin of drunkenness," I said. "Was he truly?"

"Good lord, it was four years ago. How am I to remember how much a man drank on one certain night that long ago?"

"Yet you were prepared to say he had been so excessively drunk that he joined in the raping and pillaging."

Brandon flushed. "Please, Lacey. You do have a bald way of putting things."

"And you are excellent at evasion. Were you asked to tell the world that? To lead the blame to Westin?"

Brandon's flush deepened. "You go too far, Lacey. Westin is dead. He killed the man, drunk or no. Let it lie."

"I made a promise to Mrs. Westin to discover the truth," I said. "I intend to keep it."

"You are a bloody fool. If his widow has any sense, she will go into mourning and quietly withdraw from society. It would be the decent thing to do. You stirring it all up again is in poor taste, I must say."

"Does she not have a right to clear her husband's name?"

"Leave it be, Lacey. The thing's done. What is your interest, by the by? She certainly did not waste any time transferring her clutches to you, did she?"

I took a step forward.

He went on recklessly. "She was in your bed, plain as day. If you had the least amount of shame, you would at least not try to deny it. Good God, he has only been dead a week."

I stood carefully, keeping myself from lunging at him. "I am not Lydia Westin's lover. She is an unfortunate woman, and I am trying to help her. That is all."

His hands curled to fists. "Where is Louisa?"

"I told you, I have no idea."

"You are so anxious to help the wives of other gentlemen. Perhaps you helped her to run away from me."

I took another step forward. "Damn you—"

"No, Gabriel. Damn you. I offered to reconcile, and you were pleased to throw it in my face."

He spoke the truth. I had rejected his attempts at forgiveness, because I knew it was not absolution he offered, but penance. He would take on the role as the wronged party and would forgive me and forgive me and forgive me until I ground my teeth with it.

I tapped my left boot with my walking stick. "I do believe you already had your vengeance."

As usual, when I made any reference to my injury, he grew furious. "God damn you, Lacey. Get out of my house."

"I am pleased to."

If Louisa did not return soon, we certainly would murder each other.

As I turned away, I nearly stumbled into the little cabinet house, called a "baby house," that Brandon had commissioned a cabinetmaker to construct for Louisa. It was a miniature replica of a fine mansion and opened at the front in two doors. The interior was bisected by a hall with a tiny, elegant staircase that led to a tiny, elegant drawing room and bedchamber. Cabinetmakers had fashioned the small furniture, perfect replicas of full-sized chairs and tables, in exact detail.

The thing had always fascinated me. Louisa delighted in showing me any new piece she had obtained for it. Her eyes would light as she demonstrated a miniature highboy's working drawers or the cunning sliding panels in the tiny secretary.

Nearly smashing the house now brought me up with a cold start. Louisa had gone. Forever? If she abandoned her husband, he could divorce her, disgrace and leave her. He had contemplated such a step once before, and I knew it was not beyond him.

My heart chilled as I thought of the possibility of my life without her cool presence. That event would be much like the breaking of this precise little house—something precious and unique destroyed.

I swallowed hard, avoided looking at Brandon, and went away.

CHAPTER 6

GRENVILLE wrote to me the next morning that he had succeeded in discovering a manner in which to slip me into aristocratic society. Lady Mary Fortescue, sister of Lord Fortescue, a minor baron, had invited Grenville to her brother's house, Astley Close, in Kent, where both Breckenridge and Eggleston were to stay. Grenville had had no trouble persuading the lady to allow him to bring me down with him.

I was not surprised. Any house party that contained Grenville would likely be the most fashionable of the summer. Other hostesses would gnash their teeth in envy. We would leave on the morrow.

I replied that I would gladly accompany him. In happier times as a lad—which meant whenever my father was away or I visited a mate from school—I had reveled in the country. I remembered long, rambling walks through orchards and over gentle hills, fishing barefoot in the streams between grassy banks, following a buxom maid who would entice me with her smile before her father ran me off with a stout plank.

Retrospect made it more idyllic than it had been, but even so, the English country evoked the happiest memories of my life. I looked forward to sampling it again, even if I would be cross-questioning two former army officers, and even if a buxom maid's offerings would pale beside the cool, elegant beauty of Lydia Westin.

I also received a reply to the letter I'd penned to Lady Aline Carrington. In it she told me that she knew perfectly well where Louisa was, but had no intention of telling me. She said that Louisa was fine and well and that I should leave her the devil alone.

I felt a little better upon reading this. Lady Aline was a fifty-year-old spinster, a firm disciple of Mary Wollstonecraft who believed women should involve themselves in politics and champion artists and writers. She had never married, but she had many male friends—friends only; she preferred a good gossip to any other activity. She had taken Louisa under her wing, and I knew she would protect her like the fiercest mastiff. Though it frustrated me not to know where Louisa was, at least I was reassured that she was in no danger. If Lady Aline was looking after her, all would be well. Probably.

I wrote a polite note back thanking her, then I wrote to Lydia, asking leave to call and look through her husband's papers. She granted permission by return messenger. I gathered shillings to pay for a hackney and set off for Grosvenor Street.

William the footman met me at the door. Yesterday he'd watched me in cool suspicion; today, he readily ushered me into the house and showed me into Colonel Westin's study on the first floor.

I did not see Lydia at all, to my disappointment, but William gave me the keys to Colonel Westin's desk and left me to it.

I settled myself and for the next few hours studied the recent life of Colonel Roehampton Westin. I learned two things about him that day. First, the colonel had been a very meticulous and careful man, noting in his diary the routines of a cavalry officer, most of which were quite familiar to me. Second, he had borne affection for his wife, but seemed to have regarded her as a comfortable family partner, not as a lover. His letters were warm, but never touched upon intimacy.

He spoke only once of the Badajoz event.

"I was sickened," he wrote, "as I have never been before, even through the carnage I have seen since I began soldiering. Spinnet was shot, poor fellow, in the face, by a marauder in an English uniform. Breckenridge raised a toast to him, which makes him a hypocrite; they had never liked one another."

After Badajoz, Westin's mood became black, and the letters for the remainder of 1812 were depressed. "I find home and peace so far from me in these times. Why have I traded walks through the dusk over the farms for this slaughter of men like cattle?"

He grew more hopeful later, as Wellesley and the English army began to push the French from Spain, but his letters still held formality: "Millar sends his respects. It is hard for him, poor fellow, to be far from home—and he is French, of course, which makes him the butt of many cruelties, though I try to prevent them. You did right not to open the Berkshire house this year. It is too much time and expense for only a few weeks. Give dear Chloe my warmest regards and my letter for her enclosed."

I sat back when I'd finished and neatly piled the letters together. From them I had seen that Westin had been an ordinary man caught up in a war he did not like, in a profession he had taken to satisfy the pride of his father and grandfather. Nowhere did I a find a man who would dream of drinking himself into a frenzy and gleefully rushing about a fallen city looting homes and raping its inhabitants. Unless he had painted a very misleading portrait in these letters to his wife, I had to agree with Lydia. It was unlikely that Westin had murdered Captain Spencer in a fit of drunken madness.

Lydia herself entered the room as I laid the letters back in the desk where I'd found them. I sensed her presence before I looked up, or perhaps her faint perfume had alerted me.

Rest and food had erased the ravages of the last few days, though she was still pale, and her eyes bore smudges like bruises beneath them. She wore a black silk gown trimmed with dark gray piping and a white widow's cap fixed to her carefully curled hair. Against this monotone, her blue eyes stood out like patches of sky on a cloud-filled day.

"Have you found anything?" she asked.

I rose to my feet. She motioned me to sit again, but I remained standing, manners beaten into me long ago winning out.

"Only what you told me I would find. The letters of a moral, conscientious man who abhorred violence. He makes no mention of Captain Spencer, by name or otherwise."

She pressed her slim hands together. "I do wish he had confided in me."

I mused. "Who *would* he have confided in? A friend, a colleague? Millar, perhaps?"

She shook her head. "He was not one for confidences. Or even for conversation, for that matter. At least not with me." She laughed a little.

Not every man made a friend of his wife. I had not, to my own shame. I had always found it easy and natural to speak to Louisa Brandon on almost any subject, but speaking to my own wife had been most awkward. I had tried, but Carlotta had only regarded my speeches with glazed-eyed boredom if not trepidation.

"I dislike to ask this," I began. "Do you know if your husband had a mistress?"

I waited for the icy scorn that she did so well, but she did not look offended. "Because he might have confided in her?" She shook her head. "I have not seen any hint of one. But then, Roe was not a man who enjoyed pleasures of the flesh. He believed in moderation in all things."

I began to grow irritated with the man. He had been married to one of the loveliest women I'd encountered in my lifetime, and by all accounts had taken little interest in her. He had been either mad or blind.

But Lydia championed him. Perhaps he'd had some redeeming quality after all.

She left the room with me and saw me to the front door. It was all I could do not to linger, not to hold her hand longer than was proper when I said good-bye.

As I left, William nodded to me. "Good luck, sir," he whispered. I would need it.

IN the morning, I composed a letter to Lydia to thank her. I had thought to pen it and then dress and wait for Grenville, but two hours later, I had to hastily sign the seventh draft and shrug into my coat as a knock sounded at my door.

It should have been simple to tell her that I appreciated her letting me look through her husband's correspondence and that I would keep her informed of my inquiries in Kent. Such a note should have taken ten minutes to write, and the ink should have long since dried.

But I could not get the words right, no matter how often I tried. My hand would tremble over the paper, a drop of black ink would tumble from the nib onto the white, and I would just stop myself from writing, *When may I see you again?*

The knock startled me and ink blotted the paper yet again. I muttered colorful curses as I swiftly scribbled my name, sanded the page, and rose to open the door.

The large man who filled the doorway was not Grenville's footman. He was tall and wide and hard-eyed, and I'd seen him before, inside the subdued and richly appointed library of James Denis.

"What do you want?" I asked unceremoniously.

"Mr. Denis would like a word, sir."

I had suspected the man had not come to invite me to dance. "Mr. Denis can go to the devil."

His face darkened. I imagined Denis had given the man instructions to bring me, willing or no. Once upon a time, Denis's minions had lured me into a stupid trap, to teach me a lesson, to cow me, to show me my place. I had never been one for keeping to my place.

"Mr. Denis wants only to speak to you. He gives his word."

I had no idea what the word of James Denis was worth. Likely, he would keep it, at least when it suited him, but I was not moved.

"He is too late. I am leaving London on the moment."

The man glared at me. I knew he did not want to return to Denis empty-handed, but that was not my concern.

"Sir?" A blond head looked over the beefy man's shoulder, not an easy feat, but one that Grenville's footman, Bartholomew, could perform. Grenville had the best in footmen, two very tall, very blond, Teutonic-looking brothers who possessed intelligence as well as strength. I suspected the two brothers lived a far more comfortable and civilized life than I did.

"The carriage is waiting, sir," Bartholomew said. "Do you require assistance?"

I saw by the gleam in his blue eye that he would enjoy tossing Denis's man down the stairs, but then said minion might call for a constable and delay me, so I shook my head.

Denis's man glowered. I should pity him, returning to Denis alone and confessing he could not shift me, but I did not.

"Convey my apologies to Mr. Denis," I said coldly. I told Bartholomew, "My case is in my chamber."

I snatched the letter from my writing table, walked past Denis's man and down the stairs. Bartholomew's brother Matthias waited below. He escorted me down the narrow lane to Grenville's carriage. "Post that for you, sir?" he asked as he opened the door for me.

I dropped the letter into his hand and let him assist me into the carriage. Grenville waited for me there. He was correctly dressed for traveling—well-fitting trousers and square-toed boots topped with a subdued brown coat and a loose cravat.

I had few suits to my name, so I simply wore breeches and boots with a threadbare brown frock coat. The dust of the road could hardly render it worse for wear.

Bartholomew arrived with my case and secured it in the compartment beneath the coach. Denis's minion was nowhere in sight, and Bartholomew had a slightly satisfied look on his face. He joined his brother on top of the coach, and our journey began.

As we made for the Dover road, I told Grenville what I had discovered in Westin's letters, which had not been much. He listened with interest then related that he had made inquiries about John Spencer and found that the man and his brother had left London. This was not surprising; most families departed the hot city for cool country lanes in the summer. The Spencer brothers apparently made their home in Norfolk. Grenville suggested we travel there after we found what we could in Kent.

The Dover road led through pleasant countryside, the most pleasant in England, some said, although I, used to the rugged country of Spain and Portugal and before that, France and India, found the endless green hills, ribbon of road that dipped between hedgerows, and emerald fields dotted with sheep and country cottages a little tiring.

But it was high summer, and the soft air, cooler than the baking heat of London, soothed me. I watched farm laborers bending their backs in the fields, hoeing and raking, following strong draft horses behind plows.

Grenville confessed to me as we started that he did not travel well. We had journeyed together in his coach as far as Hampstead that spring, but a longer journey like this one, he said, brought out his motion sickness. I offered him the seat facing forward, but he declined it as manners dictated. I thought this damn fool of him because as soon as we began rocking along the country road, he turned green and had to lie down.

He smiled weakly and assured me that it mattered little whether he sat facing front or rear; his illness was not particular. Besides, he had fashioned his carriage to cater to his malady—the seat pulled out to offer him a cushioned platform upon which he could lie.

"Odd thing in a gentleman who enjoys travel as much as I, is it not?" he observed shakily.

"How do you fare aboard ship?" I asked.

"I moan a great deal. Strangely, though, a ship in storm does not affect me as much as a ship on waters calm as glass. Odd, I think, but there it is."

He spent most of the day lying on his back with his hand over his eyes. I perused the stack of newspapers provided for us and served myself the smooth and velvet-rich port contained in a special compartment in the paneled wall. Silver goblets and a crystal decanter reposed there, along with snowy linen and a box of sweet biscuits. Everything the pampered gentleman traveler could want.

I wondered, uncharitably, how Grenville would have fared crossing water in the naval ships I had boarded that transported my regiment across the Channel and down through the Atlantic to our destinations. Officers fared only slightly better than the men on these trips—which was to say, we had room for a hammock and a box and had first choice of rations.

Many times, what we ate and where we slept depended entirely on the competence and charity of the ship's captain. I'd voyaged with captains who were intelligent and competent; then again, I'd sailed with those who spent the time drunk and dissolute, locked in their cabin with their whore of choice, while their lieutenants ran the ship like a pack of petty tyrants.

As we rolled onward, I regretted my speculations. Grenville did not sleep but remained still, breathing shallowly, obviously miserable. I supposed a strong stomach was something to be thankful for.

The newspapers I read contained several more spurious stories about Mrs. Westin and her new devoted dragoon, the friend of society's darling, Mr. Grenville. How long would Mrs. W— remain a widow? they wondered.

I threw the newspapers aside, the country air spoiled for me.

We paused for lunch at a wayside inn near Faversham. Grenville hired a private parlor, and we were waited on by the publican himself. I feasted on a joint of beef and a heaping bowl of greens, while Grenville watched me shakily and took only brandy and a few sweet biscuits.

Grenville wanted to rest before we departed again, so I took a short walk through the village to stretch my cramped leg. The publican's daughter, a plump young woman with a space between her front teeth, sent me a hopeful smile, but I resisted her charms and simply enjoyed the country air.

In the village square I indulged myself in a few fresh strawberries, picked that morning, then strolled back to the inn, hoping Grenville was ready.

As I entered the yard, I spied a furtive movement, as though someone had ducked back out of sight behind the wall. As a light dragoon, I had become very familiar with signs that someone wished to observe without being seen.

Silently, I retreated through the yard gate and moved as quickly as my bad leg would let me to the corner of the wall. I stopped and peered around it, then made a noise of annoyance. I had thought the inn wall connected to the end house of the village, but closer examination showed me a narrow passage between house and inn, one of those crooked, windowless, paths between buildings. I heard a step at the far end, but by the time I hurried through and emerged on the other side, no one was in sight.

Trying to suppress my feeling of disquiet, I returned to the inn yard. I might simply have disturbed a stable lad who was shirking his duties or the publican's daughter, whose smile may have won her success elsewhere. But I did not think so, and I could not shake my feeling of foreboding the rest of the day.

CHAPTER 7

※

GRENVILLE was on his feet and looking slightly better by the time I gained the parlor again. He gave me a weak nod and marched down the stairs to the carriage like a soldier preparing to face battle.

I looked warily about as we climbed aboard the carriage, but saw no shadowy figures or furtive persons watching. Still, I could not shake the feeling, born of long experience, of being watched.

We turned south here and made for the edges of the North Downs. The second part of the journey was quite similar to the first except that the woods became a little thicker on the edges of the hills.

We reached Astley Close, the Fortescue manor house, at seven o'clock that evening. It being high summer, the sun still shone mightily, though it was westering. We rolled through the gates and past the gatehouse to a mile-long drive that curved and dipped through a park and over an arched bridge to the main house.

The house itself extended long arms from a colonnaded

façade. A hundred windows glittered down on us like watchful eyes, their eyebrow-like pediments quirked in permanent disdain.

A butler wearing a similar expression stalked from the house and waited silently while Grenville's two footman sprang down from the roof.

Bartholomew placed a cushioned stool in the gravel while Matthias opened the door and reached in to help his master. Grenville descended, put his hat in place, and tried to look cheerful. He greeted the stoic Fortescue butler, who merely flicked his eyebrows in response. Grenville's own majordomo always greeted guests by name and made it a point to inquire as to their health or other events of that guest's life. The Fortescue butler looked put out to have to receive guests at all.

Matthias assisted me out in such a way that an observer would think I needed no assistance at all. In truth, my leg was stiff with hours of riding, and the ache when I unfolded it made my eyes water.

The butler did not even bother with an eyebrow flicker at my greeting, and turned and led us silently into the house.

The cool foyer swallowed us, and we emerged into a three-storied hall that ran the depth of the house. Far above, octagon-framed paintings of frolicking gods and goddesses radiated across the ceiling from a central point. A staircase rose to a railed gallery that circled the hall below.

The butler took us up these stairs and then into the left-hand wing. The house was strangely silent, with no sign of any other inhabitants. I wondered when I would meet my hostess.

The butler showed us to our bedchambers, mine next to Grenville's. He announced that a light supper would be served in a half-hour's time and departed. Grenville stumbled into his room with a look of relief, and I left him to it.

My chamber was only slightly larger than the one in

which I'd stayed in Grenville's Grosvenor Street house that spring. His guest chamber had been quietly opulent, but this one contained so much gold and silver gilt—on the panel frames, ceiling moldings, chandelier, and the French chairs—that it was almost nauseating. I hoped Grenville's stomach calmed down before he looked hard at his surroundings.

I washed the grime of the road from my hands and face and changed into my dark blue regimentals, the finest suit I owned. I returned to Grenville's chamber and found him, to my surprise, in his dressing gown just settling down with a book and a goblet of port.

"What about the light supper?" I asked. "Shall we go down?"

He took a sip of wine. "No. We let them wait. And descend when we are ready."

"Is that not a bit rude?"

He gave me a wry smile. "Rudeness is in fashion, my friend. Hadn't you noticed? They expect it of me. And I think it a bit rude to have supper at the boorish hour of half past seven. I am certainly not going to hurry down like a schoolboy called by the headmaster."

He seemed out of sorts and ready to sit there all night. But I was hungry, and I could not bring myself to snub my hostess after she had so graciously invited me. Grenville raised his brows, but bade me go and enjoy myself.

I left him alone and descended into the cold gaudiness of the front hall. The servants seemed to have deserted the place, forcing me to make my own way to the dining room. I at last found it in the rear of the house, a huge, darkly paneled room lined with portraits of frowning Fortescues.

Three gentlemen sitting at the long walnut table broke off their conversation and looked up when I appeared in the doorway. They were the only inhabitants of the room; Lady Mary, my hostess, was nowhere in sight.

I seated myself after murmuring a greeting. A spotted-faced footman appeared, plunked cold soup into my bowl, and shuffled out.

The gentlemen at the table seemed already to have dined. Two of them noisily slurped port, the third merely toyed with the stem of his glass and watched the others with amused eyes.

The man across from me leaned forward. He had dark, rather wiry hair that fluffed about his flat face. His eyes were light blue, round like a child's, and he watched me, slightly pop-eyed, as I proceeded to eat the tasteless soup.

"Where's Grenville?" he asked.

"Resting," I answered truthfully. "He felt a bit unwell from the journey."

The man jerked his thumb at the gentleman at the head of the table. "Breckenridge here brought along a tame pugilist. Wants to know what Grenville thinks of him."

The gentleman referred to as Breckenridge looked already far gone in drink. His hairline receded all the way to the back of his head, but a mane of hair, thick and dark, curled from there to his neck. His jaw moved in a circular motion, even after he swallowed, almost like a cow chewing cud. The movement was not overt, but it was distracting. He wore a fine black suit and a cream-colored waistcoat, and he regarded my regimentals with an obvious sneer.

The third gentleman said, "Jack Sharp, beloved of the Fancy."

My interest perked. I had heard much of Jack Sharp as well as the Pugilist Club, the members of which were often called the "Fancy." The club sponsored boxing exhibitions and helped pugilists gain fame and fortune. True prize fighting had been outlawed long ago, but wagering at exhibition matches remained just as fierce.

"Lady Mary's got him set up in the kitchen," the first man said. I concluded he must be Lord Richard Eggleston, the second of the men that Lydia wished me to investigate. "Except for bed. She's put him in old Farty Forty's room."

"Really?" the third member asked. "Where is Lord Fortescue sleeping?"

Eggleston looked blank. "Devil if I know. In a bed, I suppose. He's in Paris."

"Lord Fortescue is not at home?" I asked, surprised.

The blue-eyed man shook his head. "He don't care what Lady Mary gets up to. Hell, she is one of the cards." He cackled.

What he meant by this, I could not fathom.

Eggleston lost interest in me and turned to the topic of women. His childish eyes shone with the enthusiasm of a Methodist preacher as he described the gyrations in his bed of a lady he'd met in London before his journey down.

I tried to ignore him and concentrate on my soup. I had at last recognized the third man. His name was Pierce Egan, a journalist whose specialty was pugilism. He'd written scores of articles on boxing and horse racing and generally was hailed as the most knowledgeable of men on the subjects.

I disliked journalists, like Billings, but I made an exception for Egan. I appreciated his dry, observant style that painted pictures of boxers and the men who watched them. He seemed to find London an endless parade of fascinating characters. He fixed his attention now on the two aristocrats, rather like a member of the Royal Society might observe two particularly intriguing insects.

"Damn me, but she was a big-arsed whore," Eggleston concluded, then stumbled to his feet. "Bottle's empty. Why the devil do they not bring more?" He marched to the door, wrenched it open, and staggered through, calling for the butler.

Breckenridge took a noisy gulp of port. "Talks about women like he actually beds them."

I remembered what Grenville had said about Eggleston's proclivities, and about how he and Breckenridge often disparaged one another in public. Breckenridge certainly gave the door Eggleston had disappeared through a derisive stare.

Egan lifted his brows at me, then went back to study-ing Breckenridge. I finished the lukewarm soup and hoped more courses would follow, but the footman did not reappear.

Eggleston shuffled back in, a bottle under each arm. He poured another glass for himself and shoved the bottle at Egan. Egan studied it a moment, then quietly passed it to me. My glass had stood empty the entire time.

I poured for myself and drank thirstily. Fortunately, though the soup had been less than palatable, the port was rich and smooth. Lady Mary had obviously allowed us the best of her brother Lord Fortescue's cellar.

Eggleston leaned across the table as I drank and began asking me questions about Grenville, his blue eyes glitter-ing. Did he truly change his suit twelve times a day? Was there truth to the gossip that he'd thrown a valet down the stairs when the man had slightly creased his cravat? Was it true that he and George Brummell, the famous "Beau," had been the deadliest of enemies? That once at White's they'd met in a doorway and had, for the next eleven hours, each waited for the other to give way?

Grenville, I knew, had been on quite friendly terms with Mr. Brummell, and each had regarded the other as the only other man in London with dress sense. Brummell had fled England for France earlier this year, his extravagant spend-ing and debts at last catching up to him.

Eggleston rose suddenly, tottered to the sideboard, opened the lower right-hand door, and pulled out a cham-ber pot. So might a gentleman at a London club who could not bear to leave his games too long. I turned my head quickly as he unfastened his trousers and sent a stream of liquid into the pot. The sound competed with the noise of Breckenridge clearing his throat.

"When do we join the ladies?" I asked quickly. I'd had enough of male company that night, and I still wanted to greet my hostess.

"Ah, yes, the ladies," Eggleston said, buttoning his trousers. "We must draw."

He returned to the sideboard and came back with a deck of cards. I pushed away my empty soup bowl and watched as he leafed his way through the pack, pulling out cards as he went. I wondered what game he meant to play, and why here on the cluttered dining room table that the footman had not cleared.

Eggleston set the deck aside, and flourished the four cards he'd pulled out. "Gentleman," he intoned. "I give you—the ladies."

CHAPTER 8

❦

HE slapped the four cards face down on the table. Breckenridge, without preliminary, reached out and drew
one. I watched, puzzled, as he turned over the queen of
hearts. He grunted.

"Mrs. Carter," Eggleston announced. "Lucky man.
Lacey?"

Following Breckenridge's example, I drew a card and
turned it over. The queen of clubs.

"Ah," Breckenridge said. His jaw moved. "Mine."

I looked at him. "Yours? I beg your pardon?"

"My wife. Lady Breckenridge."

Egan's hand darted forward, and he turned over the
queen of spades. "Hmm. The lovely Lady Richard."

Eggleston grinned. "Best of luck to you." He flipped the
remaining card, which was the queen of diamonds. "And
Lady Mary for Mr. Grenville. You'll tell him, will you not,
Captain?"

"What about you, Lord Richard?" Pierce Egan inquired.

Eggleston made a dismissive gesture at the cards. "I do not play. Bad for my health."

Breckenridge made a noise like a smothered laugh and Eggleston shot him a sharp look.

The soup sat heavily on my stomach. I looked at the queen of clubs with an uneasy feeling. It did not go well with the soup.

"Have a walk, Captain?" Egan said, rising. He tossed his card into the pile. "The weather's cooled a bit."

Anything was better than sitting here with Brecken-ridge and Eggleston. The smell from the chamber pot that Eggleston had left on the floor was not pleasant, and his aim had been a bit off.

I rose and followed Egan from the dining room. He led me to the French doors at the back of the house and out into the long stretch of garden.

We strolled silently together, our feet crunching on the gravel to the brick path that led through well-tended flower beds and trimmed topiary. A fountain trickled quietly in the center of the garden surrounded by scarlet geraniums and deep blue delphiniums. However rude Lady Mary's guests, her gardeners were of superb quality.

"What do you think of them?" Egan asked. He was gaz-ing at a pair of trained rose trees that climbed through a trellis set over the path. I had the feeling, however, that he did not mean the roses.

"I have only just met them," I said diplomatically.

He snorted. "You think them vulgar, and I agree with you. The only reason they let me sit at table with them is because they are anxious for me to write all about their pet pugilist." He fixed me with a knowing look. "Why do they let you?"

"Because I came with Grenville," I answered.

"Exactly. The pugilist is the prize exhibit. Mr. Grenville is the other prize exhibit, unlooked for. Happy chance for them that he came along. You and I are tolerable second choices while the prizes are elsewhere."

I had to agree. I asked tentatively, "What was the business with the cards?"

"Ah. Their game. They have been playing it for years. Each card represents a lady in the party. You are to devote yourself entirely to the lady you drew."

I was puzzled. "A gentleman should devote himself to all ladies present, especially his hostess."

"Not that kind of devotion. She is yours for the duration of your visit. To do with whatever you please."

I stopped. "That is deplorable."

"A bit disgusting, yes."

"You knew about this? Why did you not refuse?"

He shrugged. "I refuse, they might ask me to go. Bring in another journalist in my place. I must write about Jack Sharp and what they get him up to. All else is unimportant."

I did not find the honor of a lady unimportant, and I told him so. He took my admonishment with good nature. But after all, I myself had not departed in high dudgeon. I stayed because I needed to investigate Breckenridge and Eggleston, and I would have to bear with their idea of entertainment for as long as it took. Like Egan, I had come here for my own purposes.

Egan wanted to walk farther, but I was tired from the journey and decided to retire. We parted, he strolling away through the flower beds, and I turning back to the house.

As I neared the garden door, I glimpsed a movement in the shadows near the south wing. I was strongly reminded of what I'd seen at the inn near Faversham, and my senses came awake.

I walked toward the shadows, loosening the sword in my walking stick as I went. I wondered briefly if James Denis had sent one of his trained thugs to drag me back to London. I had the feeling, however, that Mr. Denis would be somewhat more direct than hiring someone to skulk about the gardens.

I walked purposefully toward the darker shadows under

the trees, but when I reached the spot where I thought I'd seen the movement, no one was in sight.

I waited a few more minutes, listening hard, but I heard nothing, saw no one. Still, the space between my shoulder blades prickled, as it had in Faversham, and did not stop until I reached the house and closed the door behind me.

GRENVILLE made his grand appearance early the next afternoon, after closeting himself with his valet for hours. When at last he emerged into the drawing room that opened out to the garden, the gentlemen of the party, including me, had been assembled for several hours. I still had not met the ladies.

What there had been of conversation—Breckenridge and Eggleston had been exchanging insults, I had been pretending to read, and Egan had stared at paintings—ceased when Grenville strolled into the room. He wore trousers and boots, a casual black frock coat, a brown and cream striped cotton waistcoat, and a simply tied cravat. Eggleston stared with his overly round eyes, running his gaze over every crease of fabric that hung on Grenville's body.

Grenville sauntered past us all, murmured a vague "Good morning," then opened the French door and went out. As one, the party followed him. I brought up the rear.

I had never yet seen Grenville submerge himself into the role of the famous fashionable dandy. I decided, watching him now, that if I had witnessed it, I possibly would never have accepted his overtures of friendship.

He ignored his train of followers and wandered to a stand of rosebushes. He drew out his quizzing glass and peered through it at a half-blown bud for at least five minutes. He raised his eyebrows at it, then said, "Lovely."

Eggleston giggled. "I will tell Lady Mary you said so."

For one moment, Grenville blanched. When I had informed him this morning, over breakfast in his chamber,

that he'd drawn Lady Mary's card, he had shot me a look
of horror. "Good lord, I ought to have gone down."

"You knew about this game?" I asked in irritation.
"Why did you not warn me?"

"Truth to tell, I forgot about it. I do apologize. You are
of course not obligated to do anything more than escort
your lady and make certain she has her fill of macaroons
and lemonade. Breckenridge and Eggleston will disparage you, of course, but I have the feeling this will not of-
fend you."

"I drew Lady Breckenridge," I said.

His brows shot up. "God help you. She is—well, interesting. But I do not pity you too much. I have Lady Mary.
She loves only one thing, and that is her roses. I am
pleased she has found a pleasant pastime, but she *never
stops talking* about the bloody things."

Grenville, now recovered, turned to Eggleston. He
lifted his quizzing glass again, frowned through it at
Eggleston's cherry red and lavender striped waistcoat, then
shook his head and dropped the glass back into his pocket.
Eggleston paled. Breckenridge gave one of his snorting
laughs.

Grenville ignored him. "Where is this pugilist?"

Eggleston, still white-faced, summoned a servant, who
presently returned leading what Mr. Egan had termed the
prize exhibit.

Jack Sharp was a smaller man than I'd thought he
would be, standing only as high as my chin. His arms,
however, bulged with muscle and his shoulders and back
filled out his frock coat. He greeted us all cordially and
shook hands with me in a friendly manner. He showed no
awe of the great Grenville, and Grenville betrayed no awe
of him.

The match, or exhibition, so I understood, would be
held later that afternoon. Eggleston expected crowds to
come from miles around to watch. He boasted of Sharp's
prowess, punctuating his sentences with giggles. Brecken-

ridge laconically asked Sharp to remove his coat and
demonstrate a few moves.

I soon grew weary of standing about admiring Sharp's
muscles, though I found little in his character to object to.
Sharp had a cheerful good nature and an intelligent eye. I
would have been far happier talking to him in a public
house over a warm ale, but he, like Grenville, was doomed
to exhibit status here in this beautiful garden.

The advantage to being a nobody was that the company
did not notice when I drifted away and reentered the house.
The morning had turned hot, and the sun beat through a
white haze that made my eyes ache. The echoing coolness
of the house, however gaudy, was welcoming.

But I seethed with frustration. I had spent the entire
morning attempting, without success, to turn Breckenridge's and Eggleston's conversation to the Peninsular War
and happenings there. A handful of veterans of the Peninsular campaign finding themselves together would invari-
ably discuss the English victories at Salamanca, Vitoria,
and San Sebastian, usually with some anecdote of what
they had done during the battle.

Yet Breckenridge and Eggleston seemed to have forgotten that the entire Peninsular campaign had ever happened.
When I tried to broach the subject, they stared as though
they'd never heard of any of the places and events I mentioned. I began to wonder whether they'd been Belemites,
officers who'd contrived to miss every battle, every dangerous encounter with the enemy. They could do it, volun-
teering to transfer prisoners or carry messages to
headquarters or other jobs that would take them away from
the lines of battle. The 43rd Light had done little during the
siege of Badajoz so the two gentlemen could have been far
from it, but I knew they had at least returned to the town
after it had been conquered. Westin's letters and Spencer's
investigation put them there.

The only reference to army life came from Breckenridge, who made comments on officers who could barely
afford their kit. He also told the tale of a handsome cavalry

saddle he'd bagged from a downed French officer. Breckenridge used the saddle for his early rides every morning,
never missed since the day. He'd boasted of the pilfering
as though he'd won some great battle, but likely he'd come
upon the officer and horse already dead and had simply
stolen the saddle.

My errand was beginning to seem for naught. My mind
turned over possibilities for wringing information from the
two gentlemen as I made my way toward the front of the
house in search of my elusive hostess.

What I found—or rather heard, as I approached open
double doors to a sunny drawing room—were violent,
choking sobs and a shrill female voice endeavoring to
shriek over them.

A slap rang out. "Shut up, you impertinent slut!"

The weeper screamed. "Cow! Skinny cow! He don't
love you, never did."

I halted in the doorway. Two women stood in the middle of a grand room whose high ceilings were covered with
the same sort of gods and goddesses that adorned the main
hall. The weeper was a large-boned young woman in apron
and mobcap. Her face was scarlet, and the white outline of
a hand showed stark on her cheek.

The young woman who faced her hardly deserved to be
called a cow. She was a slender, birdlike girl with soft
ringlets of brown hair and large blue eyes. She could not
have been long out of her governess's care, and I wondered
if she were the daughter of one of my fellow guests.

She could rightly be termed *skinny,* however, because
her slenderness was most pronounced. The fashion these
days was for women to have very little shape at all, but I,
always out of date, preferred females with a bit more
roundness. This girl's body was as narrow as that of a
twelve-year-old boy's.

The maid saw me. Covering her face, she rushed out of
the room, bathing me in a scent of warm sweat.

The young woman transferred her gaze to me, unem-
barrassed. "Who are you?"

I made a half-bow and introduced myself.

"You are Mr. Grenville's friend," she announced, looking me up and down. "Did you draw my card?"

Since I had no idea who she was, I did not know. "I drew Lady Breckenridge."

"Oh." She looked neither disappointed nor elated. "She is in the billiards room. She is mad for everything billiards. I hate her."

The gods and goddesses above us seemed to laugh. I stood silently, at a loss as to how to respond.

She went on, "Did Mr. Grenville draw me, then?"

"Mr. Grenville drew our hostess."

"I wanted Mr. Grenville." She toyed with her lower lip. Her white summer frock was thin and wispy, and she looked far too young to be playing the gentlemen's wretched card game. "It was not Breckenridge, was it?"

"He drew Mrs. Carter."

She made a face. "I hate her, too. She is fat, like Lady Breckenridge. Do you know how I stay so slender, Captain?"

Of course, I had no idea. I'd had conversations with eight-year-old children that had baffled me less.

"I eat what I like," she explained. "Then I put my fingers down my throat and bring it up again. Lady Breckenridge could do that. Then she would not be so fat."

I wondered what she wanted in response. Praise that she was so clever? Admonishment for a disgusting practice? I was beyond my depth.

I assumed, from process of elimination, that this young woman must be Lady Richard Eggleston. I found it difficult to believe that the oily Eggleston had been paired with this flower-like creature, but marriages in the ton produced some odd bedfellows. She could not have been more than seventeen years old.

"Can you direct me to the billiards room?" I asked.

She did not even blink. She pointed with a small, bony finger. "The north wing. Last door along. She will be there. I hate billiards."

I was not certain whom to feel sorrier for, Eggleston or his bride. I supposed I should give Richard Eggleston's young wife my compassion. She had no doubt been thrust into marriage to fulfill her family's ambitions.

My own father had wished me to marry the daughter of a nabob—those businessmen who made their fortunes on the plantations of Jamaica and Antigua and returned to England to live in high style. I suppose the woman in question had been no better or worse than any other, but I had defied my father and married a pretty girl of poor gentility with whom I'd thought myself madly in love.

I turned from Lady Richard after a polite leave-taking, at least on my part, and sought the north wing.

CHAPTER 9

❧

THE windows in the billiards room at the end of the wing faced west. Sunlight dazzled me when I entered, and the character of the room became clear only after I'd blinked a few moments. Every flat surface of the pale green walls and white ceiling was filled with plaster motifs of rams' heads. Two billiards tables stood in the center of the room, and gilded armless chairs rested against the walls where players could lounge while they awaited their turns.

A woman bent over the far table, cue poised in competent fingers. She had a mass of dark brown hair pulled under a lace cap and wore a dark blue, high-waisted, long-sleeved gown. She was thankfully older than Lady Richard Eggleston; I put her age to be close to thirty.

She had a long, sharp nose that did not mar her face but drew attention to deep-set dark eyes, which showed hard intelligence. Lady Richard Eggleston had called her "fat," but this was a misnomer. Lady Breckenridge was plump of arm and leg, but her rounded physique was much more pleasing than Lady Richard's starved appearance.

A thin string of smoke rose from the lit black cigarillo that rested on the varnished edge of the table. Lady Breckenridge glanced at me once, then her cue moved expertly forward, connecting with the ball with a sharp *crack*.

She lifted the cigarillo and inhaled from it for a long time, all the while watching me. "Well, come on then," she said, smoke mixing with her words.

I hesitated. A game with Lady Breckenridge could provide me the perfect opportunity to quiz her about her husband, but no one played without wagering on the outcome, and I could not afford to lose.

I resigned myself. I chose a slender cue from the rack at the end of the room then returned to the table. Lady Breckenridge watched while I gathered the balls and positioned them for a new game.

She handed me the cigarillo. "Be useful."

I took it. A wisp of smoke curled into my eyes, stinging them.

She leaned over the table again and quickly shot. Her balls rolled into precise position. "Is the commotion over?" she asked. "I mean Serena shrieking at that damned maid."

I took Serena to be Lady Richard. "It seems to be finished."

Lady Breckenridge lined up another shot. "They were rowing over my husband, if you want to know. Lord knows why. The little bitch can have him."

I wondered if she meant Lady Richard or the maid. I leaned against the table as Lady Breckenridge went on with the game. The cigarillo burned steadily and a bit of ash floated to the floor.

Balls clacked. "She's already put an heir in the nursery," Lady Breckenridge went on, "and Eggleston does not want her. Breckenridge does not really either, but the silly fool believes herself enchanting."

She missed her shot. She straightened and almost snatched the cigarillo from my hand. She drew a long breath of it. "Oh, do not look so shocked, Captain. Are you a Methodist?"

"No," I answered.

I leaned down and sighted along my cue. Three balls plus one cue ball occupied the table. We would generate points for ourselves by sending balls into the six pockets about the table, or by caroming the cue ball from the table's side into one of the other balls. A simple game, but one that took some skill.

I shot. Balls clacked to the corner of the table, and one disappeared.

As I leaned down for another shot, Lady Breckenridge said suddenly, "Why are you here?"

As she probably had intended, I started, and my cue slipped. I straightened it, not taking the shot, and answered, "I came with Mr. Grenville."

"I thought you were a journalist. Like Egan."

"No," I said.

But like Egan, I'd come to pry. I shot, and missed. She gave me a triumphant look and handed me the cigarillo.

"You do not say much for yourself," she observed.

I leaned on my cue. "Grenville is more interesting."

"Of course he is. My husband worships him like a god. Lord Richard wants to sleep with him."

I hid a start, but upon reflection, I was not terribly surprised. Grenville had attracted such attentions before, though he did not return them. Such were the hazards, I supposed, of a raging popularity.

Lady Breckenridge was staring at me again. She glanced at the cigarillo, then at me, and her lip curled derisively.

I preferred my tobacco in the form of snuff, but under Lady Breckenridge's dark stare, I lifted the cigarillo to my lips and drew its smoke into my mouth. She watched me with calm dispassion until I exhaled slowly, then she lifted her cue and shot both cue ball and secondary ball into a net pocket.

She won that game and suggested another.

Fortunately, though she was obviously prepared to trounce me at billiards, she had no qualms about discussing her husband, not even when I asked a direct question about the incident with Captain Spencer on the Peninsula.

"I suppose you are asking because Westin managed to kill himself last week and so escape a trial," she said. "Serena told me. Full of glee she was. But she is sordid and likes sordid things to happen."

"And do you?"

She gave me an amused smile as if my fishing delighted her. "The entire incident was entertaining. Mrs. Westin holds herself above everyone else, and yet, her husband was about to be arrested for murder. Happy escape for her when he died, was it not? Her marriage was cold, Captain, very cold. That is why she is so brittle."

"She has borne much," I pointed out.

"As have I, married to Breckenridge. Pity me that the war ended and he came home." She carefully sighted down her cue, then shot. The cue ball slammed into the table's side then hard into another ball. "Do you know what happened when the Westins stayed at Eggleston's in Oxfordshire? Lord Richard proposed the card game. Mrs. Westin grew so upset when she learned what it was all about that she nearly swooned. She begged her husband to take her away, which he meekly did. The silly idiot might have had the Duke of Devonshire or Granville Leveson Gower."

She leaned over the table again and proceeded to gather up ten more points. At long last, she missed and I took my turn. I lined up my cue.

A sudden flake of hot ash landed on my hand. I jumped. Lady Breckenridge gave me a malicious smile. "So what do *you* think of her?" she asked.

"Of who?"

"Lydia Westin, of course." The smile broadened. "Oh, come, Captain, it is all over the newspapers. You and the wife of the deceased colonel. It is the delight of Mayfair."

I ground my teeth, silently cursing Billings.

She touched the lapel of my coat. "You are a gallant

gentleman, leaping to her side. And not without ambition, I wager."

I stared at her. "Ambition? I beg your pardon?"

"You are penniless, Captain. Mrs. Westin is a wealthy woman. It is natural, but do not expect warmth from her. Gentlemen have dashed themselves to pieces on those rocks before."

I was rapidly tiring of Lady Breckenridge. "What are you suggesting?"

"I am suggesting that you are in want of a bit of blunt." She traced her finger down my coat. "To pay your tailor's bill, to settle your billiards losses. Not to mention a soft bed to lie in, a comfortable chair at supper. What gentleman would not want this?"

Of course, she was saying, any man would rather make a whore of himself to a wealthy woman than live the way I did. "I would not take such a thing from Lydia Westin."

Her smile deepened. "You would, Captain. I read it in your eyes. If she offered, you would, in an instant."

She drew on the cigarillo. "But she will not," she said through the smoke. "I've told you. Gentlemen have dashed themselves to pieces against her. You will do the same." She touched my lapel again. "But against another lady you would not."

Her breath, scented with acrid smoke, touched my face. Her eyelashes were clumped, sharp points of black.

I decided I very much disliked her.

WE finished that game, her smiling, me uncomfortable. After that, commotion began in the drive as guests and observers began to arrive for the exhibition match of Jack Sharp. Lady Breckenridge announced that I owed her five guineas, which I doubted, but I led her from the billiards room and to the pavilion set up for the fighting at the end of the garden.

A flock had descended upon Astley Close to witness

Jack Sharp's fight. Boxing attracted men from all walks of life, from landed peers and wealthy nabobs to publicans and ostlers. These same gentlemen could be seen in the studios that enterprising pugilists set up to teach the fine art of boxing. I had accompanied Grenville to Gentleman Joe Jackson's rooms in Bond Street more than once, where we watched dukes eagerly strip down to shirtsleeves to fight Gentleman Joe.

Today they arrived in fine carriages or in hired hacks, on elegant blooded steeds or on broken-down cobs. They streamed from the road and across Lady Mary's brother's park, intent on obtaining their fill of boxing satisfaction.

Grenville shot me a weary look as I entered the pavilion. A woman who must be Lady Mary—this was the first I'd seen of her—clung to his arm and chattered loudly in his ear, no doubt about roses. A woman in her fifties, she wore a fantastic cap puffed like a Yorkshire pudding festooned with ribbons. Her chin sank into her neck, and she seemed to have plucked out all of her own eyebrows and drawn in new ones. The hem of her white gown was coated with mud and grass stains, as though she'd busily dragged Grenville all over the grounds.

Lady Richard Eggleston entered on the arm of Pierce Egan. Mrs. Carter, the fourth woman of the party, appeared now with Lord Breckenridge. I recognized Mrs. Carter from the stage—I had recently seen her in a production of *As You Like It* in Drury Lane. I had not gone with Grenville to sit in his elegant box, but paid my shillings and watched from the gallery. I had enjoyed her performance as Rosalind, and she looked as Rosalind should—tall and straight, with hair a natural yellow, an elegant face with a long and straight nose, and a pair of shrewd gray eyes.

That she had been won by Breckenridge was a crime. He paraded her about as though she were a prize mare, sleek and groomed and beautiful. That his wife stood not five feet from him while he whispered in Mrs. Carter's ear and nearly drooled on her neck seemed to bother him not at all. At one point, he slid his broad hand down to cover her backside and squeezed.

She reddened, then burst into forced laughter. I gave him a cold glare. If he did it again, I would begin a boxing match of my own.

Lady Breckenridge did not seem to notice or care about her husband's behavior. She slipped from my side and made for the center of the ring with Lady Mary. They, like Egan, had eyes only for Jack Sharp.

Sharp waited in the center of the pavilion, dressed in shirtsleeves and knee breeches. His brawny arms stretched out his linen shirt, and his tanned legs bulged with muscle. A bench waited for him to one side, along with a pail of water and a fold of sacking. Here he would rest between rounds, attended by his seconds. He smiled cheerily, his round face beaming at all assembled.

I stopped next to Grenville. "Whom will he fight?" I asked. I saw no second pugilist, and Eggleston had not mentioned the name of Sharp's opponent.

"I haven't the faintest idea," Grenville replied. He sounded tired. "Lady Mary forced me to view every one of her roses. She has thousands."

I could not hide my smile, and he gave me an irritated look.

Another gentleman, older, but with the same physique as Sharp—probably a former pugilist—stepped to the center of the pavilion next to Sharp. He rubbed his hands. "A treat today, friends. An exhibition by one of the most lauded pugilists of all time. Mr. Sharp will defend himself against all comers. Come along, gentlemen, who is willing?"

There was a moment of surprised silence, then a clamor began that grew to a roar. Gentlemen shouted that they would be first and pushed and shoved their way to the ring. The retired pugilist pointed them out in turn while Jack Sharp stood still and grinned.

The first to fight was a boy of about twelve. He ran at Sharp and pummeled him repeatedly in the stomach. Sharp lifted the lad by the shoulder, one-handed, and held him there while the boy flailed futilely. The crowd screamed with laughter. Sharp gently tossed the boy away, smiling hugely.

The matches began in earnest then and the wagering started. I heard numbers that made me nervous, and I inched my way to the back of the crowd.

I watched from there, enjoying the display of Sharp's skill. He did not land every blow, and sometimes he was hit, but he knew how to assess his opponent's competence and adjust accordingly. He won bout after bout against the array of men thrown against him—local bruisers, farmhands, coachmen—to the joy of the crowd.

"Do you not like it, Lacey?"

I looked around. An hour had passed, and I had moved beyond the circle of the hooting, cheering crowd as they shouted for Sharp.

Lord Richard stood at my elbow. His flat face gave him a squashed look, and his nose looked as though it had been pressed against his cheekbones. The mirth in his bright blue eyes made me wary. He looked like a child who had done something naughty, and was just waiting for everyone to find out. "Not your sort of thing?" he asked.

"Indeed, I enjoy a good match," I answered neutrally.

Breckenridge stopped next to his friend. Where Eggleston looked like a child, Breckenridge regarded me with the hard eyes of a man who did as he pleased and damned anyone who got in his way.

"Wager on Sharp," he grunted. "You cannot lose."

"I imagine every man here is wagering on Sharp," I said mildly. "Whom would I find to oppose me?"

Eggleston rocked back on his heels. "Wager how long it takes Sharp to lay someone out, then. That is what most are doing. I will see you."

He gave me a fairly nasty smile. He knew I dared not lose a bet, and the inability to wager made me persona non grata in these circles. I should wager anyway, and take my losses like a gentleman.

"You can always take him on yourself," Breckenridge suggested. Eggleston cackled.

I stared in surprise. "I could not stand against him." I gestured to my walking stick. "I would be foolish to try."

Breckenridge only looked at me. His dark eyes held a coldness that I sensed was far more dangerous than Eggleston's boyish pranks. "Fight him, Lacey."

I stared him down. "I said I shall not."

They arrayed themselves before me like a pair of inquisitors. Breckenridge gave me a steady look. "It is no good, Lacey," he said. "We know why you have come down. Best if you take your pet dandy and hie back up to Town. Yours is a fool's errand. You've come for nothing."

From under the canopy came the sound of a fist hitting flesh, and the collected company roared their approval.

"I came to accompany Grenville," I said.

Breckenridge pointed a large finger at me. His breath smelled heavily of brandy. "You are the Westin's lover. She hates us and makes no secret of wanting to bring about our downfalls. As though anyone gives a horse's ass about a captain dying in the war. Westin killed that captain, depend upon it. End of the tale."

"What about John Spencer's investigation?" I asked. "He has found witnesses to the event."

"He found a Spanish whore," Breckenridge said. "And drunken soldiers. Who will believe them?"

"I might," I said.

"Take your example from your own colonel," Breckenridge went on. "He knows what is what."

I nodded. "I'd wondered whether you had instructed Colonel Brandon what to say. A colonel's word counts for much, am I right?"

Breckenridge's gaze was chill. "It no longer matters. Westin is dead. Did us all a favor."

"Did you visit him the night of his death?" I asked.

Eggleston looked puzzled. Breckenridge turned brick red. "What has that Westin bitch been telling you?"

"Did you visit him?" I asked evenly.

"*I* did not," Eggleston broke in, a little breathlessly. "I stopped at home that night."

Breckenridge fixed me with a glare. "The Westin is quite comely, is she not? A gentleman who has poked between her thighs might believe anything she tells him. That is, once he's broken through the bitch's wall of ice to get there."

Anger seeped through me, blinding me to anything but Breckenridge's lined face and small eyes. I knew he deliberately provoked me, but I no longer cared.

I punched him full in the face. I had not visited Gentleman Joe's boxing rooms for nothing. My knuckles contacted neatly with his jaw, and I held my elbow bent just right to absorb the shock.

He rocked back, his mouth popping open in surprise and pain. He swung his fist in a sloppy, roundhouse strike. I blocked it and delivered him another blow. He ducked back, blood running from his nose.

Those in back of the crowd turned. A cheer went up. "A match, a match! Go to, gentlemen!"

My blood was up, though I realized that I was behaving like a fool. I tried to step away, end the fight, but Breckenridge came at me again. I defended myself, fists raised. The crowd surged around us, hemming us in, calling wagers.

Breckenridge swung blindly at me, like the little boy had at Jack Sharp. Blood ran down his face in scarlet rivulets and dropped from his chin. His eyes were wide, his lips pulled back into a snarl. I blocked his blows and struck back.

The crowd cheered first me, then Breckenridge. I fought on, letting my anger at him and men like him flow through me and into my fists.

I landed a blow on his face, and his cheek split open. Blood gushed from the new wound. I stepped back, waiting for him to recover himself. He staggered forward, then suddenly his eyes rolled back in his head, and he dropped to the ground like a felled ox.

I drew a long breath. Blood ran from my nose, and my knuckles were raw and bloody.

"Gentlemen." Jack Sharp stood with fists on hips at the edge of the pavilion, looking at us. He was breathing hard, but grinning. "You're spoiling me match."

"Your pardon," I croaked. "I believe we are finished."

CHAPTER 10

I arrived in the supper room on time that evening, and at least got to eat. Breckenridge did not appear, but the rest of the house party was there, as well as several additional gentlemen who had attended the match. Pierce Egan and Jack Sharp were notably absent.

I had expected Grenville to ply me with questions about the fight, such as why the devil I had let Breckenridge provoke me at all. But he had said nothing, only watched speculatively as his valet, a small dandified man called Gautier, had washed and bandaged my hand as though he patched up bare-knuckle boxers every day.

Lady Mary thanked me for livening up the day. A pugilist who won every match was dull, she said, but a spontaneous bout between her guests was always entertaining. She'd pinned a half-blown white rose to my coat.

Jack Sharp had, in fact, at last lost a match. Bartholomew reported to Grenville while I was being bandaged that Sharp, after standing against all comers, had finally fallen, his face a bloody mess, to a burly farm lad.

Upon inquiring, Bartholomew had learned that Eggleston had hired the farm lad to take Sharp on once the man had been thoroughly tired out from the rest of the exhibition.

Eggleston giggled now about the incident, praising himself for his own cleverness. "Should not have missed it, Lacey. It was a sight to see, the famous Jack Sharp flailing under a whirlwind of blows. Blood spattering the crowd four deep." He took a large swig of wine.

Across from me, Eggleston's child bride ate with gusto. I remembered her telling me that she would rid herself of her meal not long after she ate it. She seemed determined to enjoy herself and spoke very little. Lady Breckenridge sat on my left and spent the meal gliding her slippered foot up and down my leg. I ate steadily and pretended not to notice.

Tonight, at least, I was served every course and my port glass kept full at all times. I consumed more port than usual, trying to deaden the fact that my right hand hurt like the devil. The company was maddening, and I was frustrated with my ineffectualness. By the end of the meal, I was well on the way to being foxed, and the brandy I consumed after the ladies went up to bed completed the process. Four snifters' worth set up a pleasant buzz in my ears that at last drowned out Eggleston's voice.

He suggested cards, but he had a sly gleam in his eye, and I bowed out. I'd had enough of his card games.

Grenville had already gone upstairs, his politeness strained. I decided to follow him, and said good night to the company, who behaved as though they cared not one whit whether I stayed or departed. The world was fuzzy about the edges as I made my way upstairs; the gods and goddesses above me writhed and whirled in obscene frenzy.

I stopped in Grenville's chamber and he and I spent another hour in companionable silence, both of us relieved at not having to make conversation. When he began to yawn, I sought my own bed.

I reached my chamber and opened the door.

Lady Breckenridge lay on my bed, propped up by my pillows. The skirt of her nightdress was hiked above her hips, and her fingers played busily between her thighs. Her eyes glittered; her face was flushed.

"Captain," she panted. "I am almost there. Come and catch me."

I stared at her for a frozen moment, then turned my back and closed the door.

I slept that night in an empty chamber far down the corridor, making my bed on an uncomfortable divan. I awoke at dawn, both my head and my hand competing for which could throb the most, but I was alone.

Though it was barely light and very early, I decided upon a dose of fresh air. Coffee would have done me better, but I disliked to wake a servant for it. I rose, shrugged on my frock coat, and let myself out.

I hobbled along the path that led from the house, drinking in the welcome chill of morning. I speculated whether Lady Breckenridge had given up and gone back to bed, or if she was still there waiting for me.

I wondered suddenly what Louisa Brandon would make of all this nonsense. I realized I missed her deeply. She would have found some joke or quip to steady me and we would have laughed together. Also, I could have told her everything, all my fears and frustrations. She would have lent me some hint or suggestion of how I could proceed. She had helped me in the past and I longed for her help now.

I found myself turning toward the stables. Stables had a comforting smell about them, horses and leather and grain and dust. I had never realized how much a part of my life horses had been until I'd given up the cavalry and could no longer afford to keep a horse of my own.

A ride would soothe me, I decided, more than a walk. I let myself into the stables. Quietly, so as not to disturb the lads sleeping above, I chose a steady-looking bay gelding and in a trice had the horse bridled and saddled.

I did have a devil of a time making the horse stand still next to the mounting block. My injury made it impossible for me to climb onto a horse from the ground. A leg up was best, but a mounting block or a box helped much—from there, I could simply swing my right leg over and quickly transfer my weight to the saddle.

The horse proved immune to my bad language, but at last, I got mounted and rode quietly out of the yard.

Once on horseback, my lameness mattered little, and I could ride with only small discomfort. Within a matter of minutes, I was moving at an easy trot toward the paths in the woods.

I had been right; the ride did soothe me. I put Brecken-ridge and Eggleston and their odd wives behind me, and simply enjoyed a gallop over the downs. I thought of nothing but the horse moving beneath me, of my shifting balance, and the feel of the horse's mouth through the reins.

After some time of this, I felt much better. I slowed the horse and turned him back for the house, letting him breathe while I ordered my thoughts.

Eggleston and Breckenridge were proving difficult to question. I would have to pin them down or abandon the attempt. I wanted to talk again with Lydia Westin. She must know some reason why Eggleston and Breckenridge would blackmail her husband into taking the blame for Captain Spencer's death at Badajoz.

Truth to tell, I simply wanted to see her again. I wanted her to look upon me and thank me for helping her.

I sighed. I had a long way to go before she would thank me for anything.

The curious prickling between my shoulder blades suddenly returned, just as it had at the wayside inn, just as it had in the gardens the night we'd arrived. Someone followed me, someone who lingered in the trees in the bend of the road. I could taste it in the air, breathe it in the scent of dewy grass.

I abruptly wheeled the horse and plunged back the way I'd come. Startled doves fluttered from the underbrush and a rabbit dashed away across the field. Nothing else moved.

I slowed the horse and peered among the trees. The damp brown and green of the woods showed no signs of human life, and I heard nothing but early birds in song. I hesitated for a long time, disquiet settling upon me. I knew someone followed me, someone who knew how to mask his footsteps and hide himself with skill.

I looked for a long time, holding the horse still, but I saw no one. At last, I turned the horse again and rode back to the house, looking about me, unnerved.

The stable lads were still not stirring when I entered the yard, so I removed the saddle and bridle myself and led the horse back into his box. I was too conscientious to leave the horse without rubbing him down, so I did this quickly, with a curry comb and brush I found in the tack room. The saddle and bridle, on the other hand, I left for the stable lads to clean.

Despite the unknown person tracking me, the ride had settled my nerves somewhat. I entered the house through the garden door I'd left unlocked and trudged back upstairs. I paused at my bedchamber door then bravely opened it.

To my immense relief, the room was empty. I closed the door and locked it behind me. Tired now with my short night and long ride, I removed my boots and lay down on the bed.

I felt blissfully drowsy. The ride, the port and brandy I'd imbibed the night before, and the horse care combined to send me to sleep in a trice.

So hard I slept that I did not awaken until nearly ten, which, as it turned out, proved to be most unfortunate.

ONCE awake, I performed my usual ablutions—washed, shaved, cleaned my teeth with tooth powder, and combed my hair. I donned my regimentals, since I seemed to have

left my coat in the stables. I had a vague memory of sliding it from my shoulders as I rubbed down the horse in the
morning heat.

I made my way down to the dining room, hoping to
scare up a servant to bring me a large feast for breakfast.
And coffee. Plenty of coffee.

When I reached the dining room, I heard raised voices
on the other side of the door. One was Grenville's. Odd,
because he prided himself on never shouting or losing his
sangfroid in public.

The other voice was—My eyes widened in astonishment and I opened the door.

"How the hell should I know?" Grenville was snarling.
"You and your wife are the closest thing . . ." He broke off
and swung around as I entered.

The man facing him was Colonel Brandon. When Brandon saw me, his expression performed a powerful transformation from astonishment to relief to disappointed
dismay.

I had witnessed the identical transformation one day a
few years ago when I'd returned from a mission he'd sent
me on. I had been dragged, half-dead, back to camp on a
makeshift litter, and when Brandon had first seen me, he'd
assumed me dead. His face had betrayed triumph, guilt,
remorse, and behind that, glee. And then when I'd opened
my mouth and called him a bastard, his look had changed
to one of horror. He had wanted me dead, and against all
odds, I lived.

His look now was little different. This morning, Brandon had once again thought, for some reason, that I was
permanently out of his life.

Grenville, on the other hand, gaped at me, white-faced.
"Lacey! Good God."

"What the devil is the matter?" I snapped. My headache
had returned.

Grenville took two strides to me, relief lighting his
eyes. "Good God, Lacey." He clapped both hands to my
shoulders. For a moment, I thought he would embrace me.

I frowned. "Tell me what has happened."

His fingers clenched my shoulders, hard, once, then he stepped back, his Adam's apple moving. "We thought you had gone and died, my friend," he said lightly. "I knew it had to be a mistake."

I looked from one man to the other. "Died?"

Grenville turned and strolled to the decanter on the sideboard. His hands were shaking. "Brandon here rushed in and told me he'd found you dead in the woods. Frightened me half to death."

My gaze switched to Brandon. His face suffused with blood. "I thought it was you," he said. "He was dressed in that brown coat of yours, or so I thought. He was face down in the brush, and obviously dead. Hair the same color as yours, too." He glared at my head as if it were to blame for this deception.

"Did it not occur to you to roll the poor man over and discover who he was?" I demanded.

Brandon looked peevish. "He is down the side of a hill. I could not get to him through the mud and the saplings without help. Looks as though he was thrown from his horse and slid there. And a stable lad told me he'd seen you go riding in the wee hours of the morning. Sounded like a damn fool thing you would do."

"I did go," I answered. "But I returned. I even rubbed down the horse and left the furniture in the middle of the tack room. Did they not reason I'd returned?"

Grenville broke in. "Apparently not. Colonel Brandon came to rouse the house. And found only me. No one else is stirring."

Brandon sneered. "At ten o'clock on a fine summer's day. I do not think much of your friends, Mr. Grenville."

Grenville held up his hand. "They are not my friends. Believe that." He drank down a measure of brandy and clicked his glass back onto the sideboard. "Well, shall we go and see to this poor gentleman?"

Brandon led us to a lane that lay near to where I had been riding that morning. The stable lad who accompanied us called it Linden Hill Lane. Tortuous and narrow, the road climbed toward a low ridge that encircled the valley. To either side of the lane, the land fell away in steep, wooded banks. Trees grew thinly here, but the underbrush was dry as tinder in the summer heat.

About a quarter of a mile along, Brandon stopped. "There."

He pointed. A body was caught halfway down the brown hill, the brush and branches broken in a path to it. He lay face down, very still. I could see why Brandon had thought him me. He was a tall, lean man with thick, dark hair and no hat and wore a brown coat, the one I had mislaid that morning.

We stood in a semicircle, staring down at him. In addition to the stable lad, Bartholomew and Matthias had accompanied us.

"If he rode a horse up here," I began, "then where is the horse? Has it returned home?"

The stable lad shook his head. "Lad" was a misleading appellation—this man looked to be about fifty. A stable lad was simply a man, of whatever age, who looked after the tack and helped the grooms care for and exercise the horses. "Unusual, that," he said. "A horse will run right back to his own stable. Knows where the grub is, don't he?"

Grenville poked at the brush with his walking stick. "Bartholomew, can you get down there?"

The energetic young footman promptly began crashing through the dried scrub toward the body. His brother followed. I came after them, using my walking stick to bear my weight.

I slid and scrambled down the two dozen or so feet between the road and the body, arriving just as Bartholomew put out a large hand and turned the body over.

Matthias whistled.

"Who is it?" Grenville called down.

I straightened. "It's Breckenridge."

CHAPTER 11

BRECKENRIDGE'S eyes were open to nothing, unseeing and glassy, pupils fixed. His mouth was open as well, as though he'd been drawing a breath to shout. His face had been slashed by the dozens of branches he'd crashed through, not to mention bruised where I'd hit him the day before. His knee-high boots and buckskin breeches were likewise scarred by his descent. My coat and his gloves were in ribbons.

Bartholomew slid his huge hand beneath Breckenridge's head. "Neck's broken," he informed us.

Grenville cupped his hands around his mouth. "Can you bring him up here?"

Bartholomew stooped beneath the branches. Breckenridge was a large man, but Bartholomew was larger. He rolled the older man onto his shoulder. With his brother's help, Bartholomew began climbing back toward the road, brush crackling and breaking under his onslaught. I followed slowly.

Bartholomew laid Breckenridge out at Grenville's feet.

"Must have fallen from his horse, sir," he said, dusting off his hands. "Broke his neck tumbling down the hill."

Questions spilled through my mind. Had Breckenridge truly fallen or had someone broken his neck for him and tossed him down the hill? What had Breckenridge been doing up here at all? And why dressed in my coat?

I also wondered why Brandon had suddenly turned up at Astley Close, and why he'd just happened to have been taking a walk this morning in Linden Hill Lane. I thought I knew the answer, and beneath my stunned surprise at Breckenridge's death, anger seethed.

Something caught my eye and I moved away from the others. The soft earth at the side of the lane showed two shallow furrows. They began about ten yards from where Bartholomew had dropped the body and led straight to the edge of the road where Breckenridge had gone over. The tracks were intermittent, sometimes disappearing altogether, sometimes appearing for only an inch or so.

I followed the trail back. "Look at his boots," I instructed.

They stared at me collectively. Impatiently, I bent over Breckenridge and turned the sole of his boot upward. The edge of the heel was crusted in earth. The other was the same.

I straightened. "He was dragged here, and thrown over the side. He did not fall from a horse."

"But there's a horse gone," the stable lad said. He removed his cap, wiped his forehead, and replaced it. "And the tack. Someone rode out." He looked at me. "Thought it was you."

"Which horse is gone?" I asked.

"Chestnut gelding."

"I rode a bay," I said. "I put him away when I returned. Was the chestnut Breckenridge's own horse?"

"He was that."

I mused. "Even if he did ride up here in the first place, someone dragged him from there to here." I pointed.

"Here, the brush is not as heavy. Easier to throw him down the side. He would slide most of the way."

Grenville frowned. "But why, if he'd broken his neck falling, would someone push him from the road? Why not lay the poor man over the horse and bring him home?"

"Because I think the person deliberately killed him and wished it to look as though he'd had a bad fall."

Brandon snorted. "Who would do such a thing?"

"A very strong man," I said. "Or a very angry one. Or perhaps it was an accident. Perhaps they quarreled, Breckenridge slipped and fell and broke his neck, and the second man panicked."

"Seems unlikely they'd come all the way up here for a quarrel," the stable lad pointed out.

I considered. "An appointment, perhaps."

"Or a footpad," Grenville said. "Tried to rob him, broke his neck, and pushed him over."

I closed my mouth. I sensed strongly that this had been murder with a purpose, but Grenville's suggestion was logical, and arguing with it at present might look strange to the others. It might have been simple robbery, but I did not think so.

We all did agree about the need to search for the horse. The stable lad and Matthias easily found the chestnut gelding not a mile down the road, in a pasture of the farm that the lane skirted. Whether he had wandered through an open gate on his own, or someone had retrieved him and led him there, we could not tell.

The horse seemed displeased at being found, having had its pleasant meal of lush grass interrupted, but once caught he was docile enough. He was about sixteen hands high, fine-boned, and expensive. The head stall and saddle he wore were the very ones I had ridden out with and left behind to be cleaned.

Bartholomew and Matthias agreed to stay with the body while the rest of us returned to Astley Close. The magistrate would need to be informed and a cart sent to retrieve Breckenridge. There would be an inquiry, and an inquest.

I imagined the coroner and jury would happily let the horse be the culprit, but I was not so certain he had been.

We followed the lad into the stable yard. I looked into the tack room, which was simply a horse box on the end of the row used for the purpose. Saddles on pegs lined one wall, and bridles and halters hung opposite. A wooden shelf filled with curry combs, brushes, hoof picks, and cloths occupied the wall opposite the door.

"Why would he use the saddle I had left to be cleaned?" I asked as the lad unfastened the cinch and dragged the saddle from the horse.

The stable lad shrugged. "It was nearby."

"It was dirty. In the middle of the floor, where I left it. Why not use a bridle with a clean bit? Besides, Breckenridge had his own saddle, a French cavalry saddle. He boasted of it."

I pointed. The saddle rested on a peg at the end of the row. Both pommel and cantle curved high, making the seat, covered with a quilted leather pad, deep. The English saddles had been similar. On campaign, we had strapped sheepskin to the saddle for more comfort, the cinch wrapping across the top of the sheepskin and fastening beneath the horse.

Breckenridge's stolen French saddle was a fine thing, obviously the property of a high-ranking officer. I knew in my heart that if he'd saddled his own horse and gone off riding early, he would have used the cavalry saddle, not the one I'd left, damp and dirty, on the stone floor.

The stable lad shrugged again, and moved off to care for the horse. Grenville was watching me curiously, Brandon impatiently. I sensed I would learn no more here, and the three of us left the stable and trudged toward the house.

"I will inform Lady Mary," Grenville said as we walked. "And tell her to send for the magistrate." He slanted me a glance. "I think for now you should keep your murder theory to yourself, Lacey. You would have difficulty convincing a magistrate without more proof."

"We have proof," I said. "He would not have used that

saddle, and he was dragged down the road to a convenient place to be tossed over the hill."

"What about my idea of the robber?" Grenville asked.

I shook my head. "He still had his watch. I saw it in his waistcoat. A robber would have taken the watch, not to mention the horse."

Grenville deflated. "That is true."

"For God's sake, Lacey," Brandon broke in. He had been striding along Grenville's other side in silent anger. "A man has just died, and his wife waits in the house to learn of it. She will not want to hear you going on about murder. Leave it be."

I stopped. We stood halfway between the house and the stables. The stable and yard lay beneath the curve of a hill, the roof just visible from our position. The house sat a good fifty yards ahead of us, rising like a sphinx from the green lawns, arms extended.

"If he was murdered," I said doggedly, "it was not done up on that road. He was killed in a place such as this, where they would not be heard from house or stable. The killer fetched the horse, saddling it with the tack I'd left, and led it back to Breckenridge. He laid Breckenridge across the saddle and led him up to the woods until he found a likely spot to dispose of him. Then he slapped the horse on the rump and sent it on its way. When the horse was found, the assumption would be that Breckenridge had fallen from it."

"He did fall," Brandon said. "Why make things complicated? If a man could know which horse was Breckenridge's, why would he not know which saddle belonged to him?"

"Perhaps the murderer was not staying at the house. Breckenridge rode out at an early hour every morning by habit. Anyone staying at the village would have grown used to seeing him on the chestnut, and assume the horse was his, or at least the one he liked always to ride. But they might not have noted the saddle."

Brandon still looked annoyed, but Grenville nodded.

"You may be right. I admit, if Westin were not dead, I would not be as quick to agree with you. But two of the four gentlemen involved in the incident on the Peninsula are dead, seemingly by accident. Strange, is it not?"

He was closer to the truth than he knew. Brandon did not stop scowling, but a worried light entered his eyes.

Grenville nodded to us. "I will go break the news to Lady Mary."

"Do you want me to come with you?" I offered.

Grenville considered. "No. Best I do this alone. I dislike Lady Mary, but Breckenridge was her friend. She will doubtless take it hard."

He pivoted on his heel and marched away, shoulders squared.

When he was out of earshot, I turned on Brandon, other questions troubling me. Brandon had mistaken the fallen Breckenridge for me; Breckenridge was dead. I feared, I very much feared, that the idiot had done something irreversible.

"What brings you to Kent?" I asked him sharply.

He met my gaze, his eyes chilling. "I like the country."

My anger rose. "Balls. You followed me down here. It was you skulking about the inn and the gardens, watching me, and then again this morning, was it not?"

He did not answer, but his ice blue stare told me I'd guessed right.

"Good God," I exploded. "Why?"

"Why the devil do you think?"

I balled my hands. To think I'd fretted about the tracker, wondering if it were Westin's killer. All this time it had been Brandon. It fit. He knew better than most how to follow someone about without being seen. Hell, he had taught me.

My hands tightened. "You thought I knew where Louisa was. You thought I'd come down here to see her."

"Can you blame me? Why else would you gallivant down to the country? You do not even know these people."

"They were at Badajoz," I said. "Did it not occur to you

that I was still poking into the question of Captain Spencer's death?"

"Of course it occurred to me. You can never let well enough alone. But one conclusion does not preclude the other."

I stared at him. "Did you think I'd brought her with me? How damned stupid do you think I am?"

We faced each other, fists clenched. The sun shone down on us, the bright, soft morning belying the storm that ever roiled between us.

Brandon was speaking again, rapidly. "I would have thought you'd had enough of scandal. If you have her hidden somewhere, I swear I will have you arrested."

"You are an idiot. I do not know where she is."

"Damn it, Gabriel, do not lie to me. I am surprised it is not all over the scandal sheets along with all your other adventures."

I leaned to him. "It will be if you do not stop making such a pig's breakfast of it. You can follow me all over England and make scenes and look overjoyed when you think me dead, but I still do not know where your wife is."

I watched him lose strength. A warm breeze stirred his hair, brushed a loose brown lock across his cheek. "Then where did she go? If she did not go to you, then tell me where she went."

That question still troubled me as well. Lady Aline's letter had only told me she was safe, and I trusted Lady Aline to know that. But I wanted to know myself. I wanted to see her, to hold her hand, to reassure myself that all was well.

"Louisa's note said she needed time alone," I reminded him.

"Alone, where? Do you think she has gone to the Continent?" He paused and would not look at me. "Or to a lover?"

"She would not disgrace you like that. If she wanted to abandon you for another, no doubt she would look you in the face and tell you so."

He did not appear convinced. But I knew that Louisa had no slyness in her, no deceit. She would rather face her husband with the truth than resort to trickery. She had left him for some other reason, a reason he could not see beyond his fear and jealousy.

A dart of pain laced my heart. On the Peninsula, when Brandon had cast her out, Louisa had come to me. I had been dreaming of that hot night when I'd walked down to the bridge the night I'd saved Lydia Westin. Louisa had come to me, ill with weeping, and had thrown her arms about me. Her golden hair had tangled on my shoulder, and for the first time since I'd met her, I dared furrow it with my fingers.

This time, she had not turned to me. Whatever Louisa had needed or wanted, she had known I could not give it to her. This time, she had left me as well.

I ended the futile quarrel by turning from him and walking back to the house in silence.

THE inquest of Viscount Breckenridge was held the next day at the public house, the Crow and Cross, in the village. The local magistrate had called in a magistrate from London, Sir Montague Harris, a rotund man obviously fond of his beefsteak and port, but one with a shrewd eye.

Colonel Brandon stood up and described how he had found the body. He had been staying in the village, he said, in fact, here at the Crow and Cross. He had decided the morning in question to walk along Linden Hill Lane. He had wanted a brisk walk and thought it would be just the thing.

This caused the coroner to ask why he was in their corner of Kent at all. To take the country air after the hot closeness of London, he replied. The Londoners in the crowd nodded in commiseration.

Had he attended the exhibition of the pugilist, Jack Sharp? No, Brandon replied. He did not like blood sports.

This caused a murmur of disapproval from all those who had flocked down for their fill of the blood sport.

So far Brandon had delivered his answers in a strong, matter-of-fact voice. But when he began to describe how he had found the body and what he had done, his hands clenched into hard fists, and he kept his eyes firmly fixed two feet to the right of the coroner.

He had gone walking, as he'd said, about nine o'clock that morning. Upon reaching the crest of the hill, he'd notice that branches to the right of him had been snapped and broken, as though someone had tried to force a path through the undergrowth. Upon investigating, he had spotted the body of Lord Breckenridge lying face down in the brush. The man had been dressed for riding, but no horse was about.

Had he gone down to the body? No? Why not? Because, Brandon said, he could see at once that the man was dead and Brandon would likely need help to lift him back to the road. Thought it more sensible to go at once for help.

The coroner shrugged, but Sir Montague Harris leaned forward. Why had Brandon made for the manor house rather than the village, which was closer? Brandon, reddening, answered that he had been acquainted with members of the house party there and naturally turned to people he knew.

Sir Montague sat back, satisfied. Then Brandon, as if suddenly remembering, said that of course he had sought out Astley Close because Lord Breckenridge had been a guest there and of course his friends would want to know if he'd been hurt.

The coroner, looking uninterested, nodded. Prompted, Brandon continued that he'd entered the stables where the grooms and stable hands had been readying horses for exercise. Brandon had reported the death and asked to be taken to the main house. Upon reaching the house, he'd found the only guest awake had been Mr. Grenville, to whom he had repeated the account of the accident.

The coroner carefully noted all this and dismissed him.

Brandon visibly relaxed as he walked back to his chair. He hated to lie, and was bad at it, just as I was. And he was certainly lying about how he'd found the body. Not about all of it, but about a good part, if I were any judge.

Grenville and the stable lad and I all concurred with Brandon's story of his first going to the stables and then to the main house. We each related how we'd gone up the hill with Brandon and found Breckenridge together. Neither Brandon nor Grenville mentioned Brandon's certainty that the dead man had been me, and I did not volunteer the information.

I did mention the saddle. I explained my reasoning, that Breckenridge would have used his own cavalry saddle, which he'd said he preferred, when it was so close to hand. Sir Montague listened, his eyes fastened on me, taking in every word. I used the opportunity to mention the marks I'd found on the road, and concluded that, in my opinion, the death warranted further investigation.

The coroner eyed me in dislike. He was sitting on the body of a viscount—a peer, not an unfortunate farmhand. He wanted a simple accident, and here I was trying to complicate things.

Once all statements were made, a doctor was consulted who agreed that Lord Breckenridge had died when his neck was severed early on the morning of his death. The coroner finished his note-taking, and then instructed the jury.

Notwithstanding Captain Lacey's remarks, he said, they must decide whether they thought this a clear enough accident. There was nothing to stop a man from changing his mind and using a different saddle if the whim took him. The marks on the road could have been made at any time. The horse was found, Lord Breckenridge had been dressed for riding, and for what other purpose could he have gone up the hill?

The jury did not deliberate long. To the coroner's obvious relief, they returned with the verdict I expected—Lord

Breckenridge had died while accidentally falling from his horse.

Everyone in the hot room, from the coroner to Eggleston to Brandon to the stable lads, looked pleased with the conclusion.

I kept my feelings to myself.

When we returned to Astley Close, Lady Mary closeted herself with her brother, whom she had summoned home, and left her guests to fend for themselves. The house party over, Grenville ordered his carriage made ready to take us back to London.

I encountered Lady Breckenridge in the downstairs drawing room—entirely by accident; I had been looking for Grenville. I had not seen her since finding her in my bed two nights before. But much as I disliked her, Breckenridge's death had been sudden and shocking. I paused.

"Please accept my condolences on your husband's death," I said. "I am sorry."

She studied me with eyes as glittering and hard as any magistrate's. "My son is now Viscount Breckenridge. Why be sorry about that?"

While I searched for a way to respond, she went on, "Tell your friend, Mr. Grenville, that *his* company was most pleasing."

I supposed this meant mine had not been. Somehow, I could not feel disappointment that she had not liked me.

"I will." I bowed. "Good afternoon."

CHAPTER 12

GRENVILLE and I left Astley Close half an hour later. We talked little on the journey to London because Grenville, though manfully remaining upright for the first few miles, soon had to drink a brandy and lie down again. He spent the journey up much as he'd spent the journey down, flat on his back on his makeshift bed, eyes closed.

I had not had the chance to speak to Brandon after the inquest. He had avoided me when we left the inn, and disappeared shortly after. But I did not need him near to speculate. The half-truths he'd told the coroner and magistrate worried me. I spent the journey deep in thought about his actions and about our past and present, while Grenville alternately dozed and woke, pale and preoccupied.

Grenville's carriage deposited me at the top of Grimpen Lane just at sunset. He bade me a feeble good-night and rolled away to be tended by his footmen. I returned to my rooms and spent a restless night worrying about Louisa, Brandon's lies, and Breckenridge's death.

The next morning's post included a letter from John

Spencer. I perused it eagerly. Mr. Spencer informed me that he had returned from Norfolk and invited me to meet him and his brother on the morrow at a tavern in Pall Mall. The tone of the missive was rather cold. Mr. Spencer said that he did not see the point of such a meeting, but his brother had convinced him that we should speak.

I wrote a reply that I would attend, and turned to my other mail.

Someone, I did not know who, had sent me a page from the newspaper tucked into a blank letter. The page featured a another caricature of an overly lean-legged, overly broad-shouldered dragoon captain who pointed at a dead dog that had just been run down by a cart. The balloon from his mouth proclaimed: "It is murder, sir. We cannot let it lie." In the picture, a fancy carriage was just passing, and women in exaggerated bonnets stared out of the windows, open-mouthed, at the scene.

Beneath the picture ran the caption: "The Shortcomings of England's policing, or Murder not Recognized."

I tore it to pieces and tossed it on the fire. The journalists who'd attended Breckenridge's inquest must have found it a perfect opportunity for more levity. I wondered if Billings had sent the cutting to make certain I'd see it.

Lydia Westin had also written. It was a simple note asking me to call on her the following evening, but I savored it a long time. At last laying it aside, I penned a reply that I would be delighted to attend.

I went out to post my letters, then turned my steps to Bow Street and the magistrate's house. The tall, narrow Bow Street house had been lived in by the famous Fieldings—Henry, the author, who had first established the Bow Street Runners, and Sir John, his blind half-brother, who had succeeded him. From what I understood from Pomeroy, Henry Fielding had taken the post for the money, since he rarely had any, but had grown interested in keeping the peace and detecting crime. The half-dozen men he recruited to help him were at first referred to simply as "Mr. Fielding's People." Then Sir John had built his brother's Runners into an elite machine that now assisted in investigations across England. The magistrate lived in private rooms at the top of the house, with the jail and court below. I often wondered how easily he slept in his bed of nights.

I asked for my former sergeant, Milton Pomeroy, and a clerk led me through the hall, where the day patrol were bringing in their catches for the morning, to a small private room where he offered me muddy coffee.

I waited on a hard chair while Pomeroy finished his report of his previous night's arrests. He wrote slowly, his pen squeaking, his tongue pushed against his large teeth. A copy of the *Hue and Cry* lay at my elbow, and I idly studied the reports of various criminals or supposed criminals lurking about England.

Pomeroy shuffled out to deliver his report, then returned with more coffee. Pomeroy was a big man with bright yellow hair and blue eyes that twinkled. He seated himself heavily and sent me a grin. "I heard, sir, that you twitted the magistrate in Kent about Viscount Breckenridge. Ha. I'd have liked to see that. Why were you so certain it was murder?"

I explained my reasons and my speculations. Pomeroy nodded over his coffee, his round face serious. "Could be. Could be. I know you, sir, sometimes you're right. What did you come to me for? Hiring me to investigate it? Have to talk to the magistrate."

I shook my head. "I came to ask you about Colonel Westin. You were investigating him for John Spencer. I want to know what you found."

His eyebrows climbed. "Do you, sir? That's interesting. I stopped at his death, saw no reason to go on. Can't prove anything one way or another, but I found eyewitnesses that put Colonel Westin at the shooting at Badajoz." He grimaced. "That was a bad time, eh, Captain? Nasty goings-on."

I had to agree. "Do you think Westin was the true culprit?"

Pomeroy shrugged. "Couldn't say. He was there, all right, but I found little more than that. Truth to tell, Colonel Westin was a fine and quiet-spoken gentleman. When I first asked him about Captain Spencer and Badajoz, he behaved like he'd never met the man. And then one day he asked me to call on him." Pomeroy leaned forward, eyes bright. "He said he'd thought it over, and he believed that he had, in fact, shot Captain Spencer. He'd been drunk after the siege, he said, and couldn't remember, but now he was having flashes of it in his mind. He was upset like, sorry he'd caused Spencer's sons so much pain."

"And what did you think?"

He pursed his lips. "Ain't paid to think, am I?"

I eyed him severely. "Yes, you are. You are a Runner, an elite investigator."

"Fancy names for sergeanting. All right, sir, yes, it sounded a little too easy. But the magistrate says, we gather some proof, and then we go and arrest him. And then, before we get there, Colonel Westin up and falls down the stairs."

He sat back, thick hands cradling his cup of coffee, his eye on me.

"Conveniently avoiding the dock," I finished. "And what truths he might tell there."

"I thought of that, sir. Bit too convenient, eh?" He slanted me a glance. "Think his wife pushed him? Would have gotten him out of her life and just in time, too."

"No," I said sharply.

But the possibility that Lydia herself had killed her husband had occurred to me, much as I disliked the idea. Westin had died quickly, by Lydia's account, without struggle, and she'd found him in bed. We assumed the murderer had killed him then put him there.

But what if Colonel Westin had already been in bed, perhaps with his wife in his arms. She could have stabbed him in the neck and rolled him onto his back once he was dead. Or he might have been lying beside her, and she had risen up, her dark hair snaking about her, her body naked and beautiful, and killed him with a thin knife in her slender hand.

I tried to banish this idea, but I could not. It had been she who had decided that her servants should not report the murder, she who had decided to tell the world it had been an accident, she who'd pointed the finger at Breckenridge and Eggleston and Sir Edward Connaught, the third member of the "triumvirate."

"His fall was witnessed by the footman and the valet," I said carefully. "He slipped and fell."

"Could be." Pomeroy grinned. "Widow's a bit of a stunner, eh, Captain?"

I eyed him coldly. "Keep your remarks respectful, Sergeant."

His grin was wide. "Might have known you'd have noticed. You're always one for the ladies."

I ignored him. "What about Westin's colleagues, who were with him at Badajoz? Breckenridge, Eggleston, Connaught? Did you discover anything interesting about them?"

He shook his head. "Not much, except they were present when Captain Spencer was shot. But they're lordships. Didn't like a Runner poking about their business, did they? No, Colonel Westin was a gentleman about it, but the others did everything but set their dogs on me."

This information did not surprise me. Breckenridge and Eggleston might have continually insulted each other, but I remembered how they had closed ranks to confront me at the boxing match. I had not yet met Connaught, but I would not be surprised to find him cut from the same cloth. "Poke some more," I suggested. "If you cannot speak to the gentlemen themselves, speak to their servants or friends, or even their enemies. I want to know everything about them, where they go, who they meet, what they eat every day." I was certain Eggleston had plenty to do with Captain Spencer's death, and Colonel Westin's, and I damn well wanted to prove it. Breckenridge's death I had different ideas about.

Pomeroy grinned. "A tall order, sir. You want me to do this as a favor?"

He knew bloody well I could not pay him. "Yes, Sergeant. As a favor to your old captain."

He was laughing at me. "'Twill be a pleasure, sir. I always like the look on your face when I tell you something interesting. I'll be sure to let you know."

I left Bow Street deep in thought and returned to my rooms.

A note from Grenville had been hand-delivered in my absence to say that he felt much better and would send Bartholomew with the carriage for me that evening. His note was short, only four lines on an entire sheet of heavy white paper.

Did I envy a man who could afford to throw away an expensive piece of paper on a short note, or think him a fool? In any case, I carefully tore the clean end of the sheet from the written area and tucked it into my drawer to save for my own letters.

I spent the day thinking about what Pomeroy had told me, and about the character of Colonel Westin. When Bartholomew arrived later that afternoon, I was dressed and ready. We arrived at the Grosvenor Street house just as clocks were striking eight. As Bartholomew helped me descend and led me to the house, I was very aware that Lydia Westin reposed only ten doors down.

Grenville greeted me and informed me I was to take supper with him. After we had enjoyed a few glasses of excellent port, he led me to the dining room.

"Anton is experimenting again," he said as we entered. "I have no idea what he will offer us, but please tell him you like it, no matter what you truly think."

Anton was Grenville's celebrated French chef. The man was an artist with food, as I had come to know to my delight.

"He has been doing this all summer," Grenville informed me in a low voice. "He spends the day creating a dish then brings it to me to sample. If ever I say it is not his best, he crumples into tears and refuses to cook for a week." He put a heavy hand on my shoulder. "So praise him and swallow it, even if it tastes like sawdust."

I assured him I would dissemble, though, as I suspected, he needn't have worried. Anton brought us a delicate mussel bisque, so smooth and light it flowed like silk on the tongue. He followed this with grouse in a wild raspberry sauce, then a salad of cool greens, and ended with a lemon tart, not too sweet, and a rich chocolate soup.

I ate every bite and sang his praises without compunction. He beamed at me and glided away, back to his sanctum to no doubt create more delectable feasts.

Once left on our own with brandy, Matthias entered the room bearing a tray stacked neatly with papers and two ledgers. He set this down before his master, bowed, then departed.

To the questioning look on my face, Grenville said, "I did not invite you here simply to soothe Anton's temperament. I managed to procure Colonel Westin's financial papers, in hopes that they might tell us why Eggleston and Breckenridge might have blackmailed him into confessing to Spencer's murder."

I leaned forward, my interest quickening. "How did you get them?"

He gave me a modest look. "I know people. Some of whom owe me favors. Shall we begin?"

We divided the stack between us and sorted things out across the dining room table. Matthias and Bartholomew kept us in brandy and also brought in black coffee as rich as chocolate.

For the next several hours, we leafed through papers, passed ledgers back and forth, and discussed our findings. The Colonel Westin I found here had been as meticulous as the one I'd come to know in his private papers in Lydia's house. He or his man of business had kept strict accounts for everything: for the country house and the London house, for servants' wages and clothing, for food, for fuel, for horses, for his wife's clothing and jewelry.

My fingers felt a bit sticky as I turned over the pages describing Lydia's personal finances. These were none of my business, and yet, I desperately wanted to discover anything that would point away from her and to Eggleston or Breckenridge or the elusive Connaught as her husband's murderers.

I found that Lydia was just as careful as her husband in the matter of finances. Her bills for her dressmaker, her glovemaker, her milliner, and her shoemaker were high, but not extravagant, and well within Colonel Westin's means. Likewise her household budget bore the marks of a woman who could spend wisely and still manage to live in elegance.

The Westins appeared, by all accounts, to have been a model couple of moderation, good taste, and financial sense.

Grenville sat back as the clock struck one. "Well," he said. "We have learned that Westin had no heavy debts, gambling or otherwise. Pity."

"Yes," I answered, subdued. "It seems that he led a blameless life."

Grenville sighed and tossed down the sheet he'd been perusing. "So why would he suddenly sacrifice this blameless life for Breckenridge, Eggleston, and Connaught?"

"He would sacrifice his family as well," I remarked.

Grenville nodded. "Perhaps Breckenridge and Eggleston were instrumental in persuading Allandale to propose to the daughter. Then Allandale could look after both daughter and Mrs. Westin after Westin had been tried and executed."

"Is Allandale such a catch?" I asked. The opinion I'd formed upon meeting him in Lydia's house had not been high.

Grenville thought a moment. "I would not have chosen him for my own daughter, but yes, Geoffrey Allandale is, from what I have heard of him, a catch. He has money and he has connections and the beginnings of a political career. Everything a father could want for his daughter."

What about a mother? I wondered. Lydia disliked Mr. Allandale. I read that in her tone when she spoke of him and in her face when she'd looked at him. And yet, she'd not opposed the match. Or perhaps she had, and had been overruled. I wondered if the daughter, Chloe, had been happy with the choice.

"Providing an excellent marriage for the daughter would fit," Grenville speculated. "Westin let his friends set up the marriage knowing he would go to the gallows. His daughter and wife would simply be absorbed into Allandale's family."

I could sincerely hope not. Perhaps another reason Lydia had expressed relief at her husband's death was that she would no longer be at the mercy of Allandale. Westin had died technically a free and innocent man, and she would come into whatever money and property he had left her absolutely. His sudden death had saved her from the fate of living in Allandale's household.

"We should find a copy of the marriage settlement," I said, "before we draw a conclusion."

"Agreed. But I cannot imagine what else it could be. Westin certainly was a man without vices . . ." He broke off, his dark eyes riveting to an entry on a ledger page. "A moment. I spoke too soon. This is interesting."

Nothing else had been all night. I waited impatiently.

"I am not certain whether this counts as a vice," Grenville said. "But at one time in his life, our Colonel Westin was in the habit of purchasing *cantharides*." He sat back and looked at me.

"Spanish fly?" I asked, surprised.

"On more than one occasion. But this was a long time ago. 1798, to be precise." He turned back a page. "No, wait, a few years before that as well."

"Anything more recent?"

Grenville flipped forward through the book. I took up the other ledger and gently turned its pages. We had been looking for things of recent memory, but perhaps we ought to examine the man's deep past as well.

"I looks as though he gave it up," Grenville said presently.

I frowned. "Why on earth would a man married to Lydia Westin need an aphrodisiac?"

Grenville shot me a thoughtful look. "Some take it for the stimulation. It adds a spice, shall we say, to the performance. Though one must have a care not to poison oneself with it."

I leafed through the ledger, baffled. Westin did not seem the type of man to try something as dangerous as Spanish fly simply for the adventure of it. Especially in light of Lydia's assertion that her husband had disliked pleasures of the flesh. Were I married to Lydia Westin, I certainly would not need a dose of Spanish fly to convince myself to take her to bed.

I searched for another explanation. "I have heard that it is sometimes used for the skin, as well." I touched an entry. "This ledger shows he was seeing a doctor for an unnamed affliction in the past. Perhaps he used the *cantharides* for that."

"Possibly. But I hardly believe B and E would convince Westin to go to the gallows to keep the secret of a skin condition."

I did not either, but I needed something. "He made payments to this Dr. Barton for a number of years."

Grenville suddenly came alert. "Barton? Jules Barton? Of Bedford Square?"

"Yes. Why?"

He gave me a curious look. "There is only one reason a gentleman consults Dr. Barton of Bedford Square." He watched me as though I should know damn well why without being told.

"I have never heard of the man."

His eyes flickered. "Hmm. Well, I doubt any gentleman would confide to you he'd made a visit to Dr. Barton. At least not in another's hearing."

"Why? Who the devil is he?"

Grenville pressed his fingertips together. "One consults Dr. Barton when . . ." He paused, and flushed. "Well, to put it bluntly, one consults him—discreetly—when one cannot make one's soldier stand to attention."

My brows rose. Lydia's faint smile, her rueful look when she explained why she doubted her husband had a mistress, became suddenly clear. "So," I said, "you believe Westin was not so much unattracted by pleasures of the flesh as unable to enjoy them."

"That would explain the Spanish fly," Grenville said. "Perhaps Dr. Barton suggested it. Poor beggar. To be married to such a lovely woman, and not be able to—"

"They had a child," I pointed out. "Miss Westin is of marriageable age now, so could well have been conceived near to 1798. Perhaps he was cured."

Grenville seemed determined to throw cold water on everything. "One child. A girl. Most gentlemen would keep trying until his wife produced a son. Did he continue to see the doctor after her birth?"

I examined the page of payments to Dr. Barton. Several were dated a mere nine years previously, shortly before the Peninsular campaign began. "Yes," I answered.

"A lucky shot, then. Or . . ." Grenville paused. "This is not a nice speculation, but perhaps . . ." Again he hesitated. "Perhaps Miss Westin is not Westin's daughter at all."

Silence fell. I traced a pattern on the ledger page. My finger shook once. "What are you suggesting?"

"Something sordid and vulgar, I am sorry to say. But we are looking for reasons that Breckenridge and Eggleston or Connaught might have blackmailed Colonel Westin."

"If we were speaking of Lady Breckenridge," I said, keeping my voice quiet, "I might agree with you. But Mrs. Westin does not seem the type to have a sordid affair and then force her husband to accept her child. I do not believe it is in her character."

"I know." He studied me for a time. "But perhaps when

she was young, and wanted a child, and her husband could not give it to her . . ."

"She sought it elsewhere?" My fingers tightened on the ledger. "Colonel Westin's letters are filled with great affection for his daughter," I pointed out. "Would he have doted on her if she were another man's child?"

Grenville shrugged. "We live in odd times, Lacey. I know men who grew up in nurseries with half-brothers and -sisters and the illegitimate by-blows of either parent. Lady Oxford is rumored to have borne children by a number of different fathers, and yet her husband keeps the pretense that they are his own, and no one says a word. Hell, my own father brought home a little girl he called my cousin, and we both discovered much later he had fathered her with his mistress. It happens. Mrs. Westin may simply have wanted a child too desperately."

I looked at him. "This line of speculation is distasteful."

"I know. It is a distasteful business, all of it. But such a secret might be enough for Westin. Breckenridge could have threatened to reveal that shame to the world."

I let out my breath. "Such a predicament would certainly give Breckenridge, Eggleston, or Connaught hold over Colonel Westin." I took a draught of my now-cold coffee. "But dear God, Grenville, I do not want it to be true. I pray we find a better explanation."

I pictured Eggleston's glee at knowing a sordid secret about the impeccable Colonel Westin. But would they have loosed that hold by murdering him?

Grenville rested his elbows on the table. "Even if what we have speculated is true, that still does not prove who killed Captain Spencer at Badajoz. This is a most baffling problem you have become tangled in, Lacey."

Well I knew it. Lydia Westin had asked me to clear her husband's name. So far, I was only succeeding in tarnishing it.

As much as we tried, we could find nothing else that night to explain why Colonel Westin might have offered to die on the gallows. Defeated, we closed the ledgers, and

Grenville called his carriage to take me the long way back home.

GRENVILLE had asked leave to accompany me to my meeting with the Spencer brothers and I had agreed. He had an uncanny knack for asking the right questions, and his head was a bit clearer on the entire Westin affair than was mine. The next afternoon I met him at Pall Mall and we made our way to the appointment together.

The façade of the tavern had been refurbished to complement the modern buildings surrounding it, but the interior remained dark with age. The paneled walls and spindle-legged tables were nearly black, the beamed ceiling bowed, and the floorboards creaked. A blurred sign in one corner proclaimed that the house had stood since 1673. I felt surprised that it had not burned down at least once during that time, but perhaps it had, and the sign reposted to reassure patrons that it was as traditional as any other tavern.

Only a few men sat about sipping thick coffee or eating beefsteak this afternoon. We were in Saint James's, where clubs had become far more the fashion than taverns or coffeehouses. But political liaisons were still cultivated here and old friends still met. I was pleased to see, however, that no journalists lingered here today.

As we halted just inside the doorway, blinking to adjust to the dim interior, two gentlemen rose and advanced upon us. One was slight of build and had thin brown hair, a fringe of which hung limply on his forehead. The second man looked much like him, but larger, and his hair was thicker.

I advanced to shake hands, but Grenville stopped, staring. "A moment," he said in an odd voice. "I remember you. You were in Kent, at Astley Close, four days ago. I saw you there, at Jack Sharp's boxing match."

CHAPTER 13

I looked from the two of them to Grenville. Grenville was scowling at them, and the large man scowled back. The other wet his lips, his gaze flicking to me and back to Grenville.

"You must be mistaken," he said.

"I'm not," Grenville said flatly. "I saw you both. You watched the match. I did not know who you were, but I remember you."

I did not recall seeing either one of them in Kent, but then, I had backed out of the crowd, and later been distracted by Breckenridge and Eggleston. My pulse quickened with my speculations. These men certainly had motive to murder the officers from Badajoz, and now we knew they had been on the spot for Breckenridge's death.

The smaller man shot his brother an anxious glance. "Shall we sit down, gentlemen? And discuss this?"

He pulled back a straight-legged chair with trembling hand and sat down. Grenville took the seat next to him. His larger brother waited until I'd seated myself, then he joined us. I noted he chose a chair with the least obstructed path to the door.

The smaller gentleman offered his hand. "I am Kenneth Spencer. My brother, John."

I shook his hand. John Spencer did not offer his. He sat with arms folded, regarding us in deep suspicion. He certainly looked strong enough to break a man's neck, even a man as muscular as Breckenridge had been.

Keeping my expression neutral, I said, "So you did not go to Norfolk, after all."

"We did," Kenneth answered. John shot him a glare, but Kenneth plunged on. "But John discovered that Lord Breckenridge was traveling to Kent and decided we should go there to speak to him."

"Why?" I asked.

John Spencer unfolded his arms. "By all accounts, Lord Breckenridge was present at my father's death. That makes me interested in him."

"And did you speak to him?"

His lip curled. "No. Their lordships do not take kindly to being approached without introduction."

And the two of them had no doubt closed ranks against Captain Spencer's sons, just as they had against Pomeroy.

Spencer fell silent as the proprietor brought port for Grenville and coffee for the rest of us. We sipped in tense silence for a moment, then Kenneth took up the tale. "We left Kent immediately after Mr. Sharp had fallen at the end of his match, and reached London that night. We found Mr. Grenville's letter, sent on from Norfolk, waiting for us. I believed that meeting Captain Lacey would be a good idea." He glanced at his brother, who scowled back. "Perhaps together we can see an end to this matter."

"There will be no end until my father's murder is avenged," John said fiercely. "Colonel Westin escaped justice, and now Lord Breckenridge has as well."

"I consider Colonel Westin's death a blessing," Kenneth

said quickly. "It saved us all from being dragged through the courts. The newspapers were bad enough."

John frowned at me. "If you gentlemen have come here to convince me to give up my search for the truth, save your breath. I am not satisfied that Colonel Westin killed my father, much as he was ready to admit to it." He shot his brother a stony look.

"I agree with you, Mr. Spencer," I broke in to what sounded like a long-standing argument. "I think the conclusion too pat, and it does not tally with what I have learned of Colonel Westin's character."

John lifted his brows in surprise. "You share my assessment? I assumed you friends of their lordships."

Grenville gave a half-laugh. "Good heavens, no."

I looked at John. "I would be interested to know how you discovered that your father's death was murder at all. That he was not a random and unfortunate victim of the rioting at Badajoz."

"Colonel Westin himself," Kenneth said.

I stared at him. "I beg your pardon? He told you?"

John sipped his coffee, face dark. "He wrote a letter to our mother. Just after my father's death. We did not know; she kept it to herself, and I found it among her papers after she died last winter. In it, Colonel Westin apologized profusely for our father's death at Badajoz. As though an apology could ever suffice."

His brother broke in. "Colonel Westin was kind to write. He said the incident had been unfortunate, and those men who had caused it deserved to be punished, but he was powerless in the matter. He was trying to console her."

John snorted. "It was not kindness. Guilt, rather. I wondered why the devil he had chosen to write at all. He was not my father's commanding officer; they were not even in the same regiment. I concluded that he must have been present at my father's death, and had known how utterly wrong it had been."

I watched him pensively. The remorse that moved

Colonel Westin to pen the letter fit with what I'd learned of his character so far.

"The letter made me decide to discover just who had actually killed my father," John continued. "I asked questions of officers I knew and then of the soldiers and officers they directed me to. I even advertised in the newspapers. I at last found one man and a woman who had been eyewitnesses." He took another sip of coffee. "The man, an infantry corporal, told me that he had seen my father at Badajoz, running toward a group of officers who had been drunk and shouting. There was much smoke and glare of fire, and he could not see precisely what happened, but he heard a shot and then saw my father fall dead to the ground."

His voice was flat, toneless, as though he had recited this story time and again. "The woman told a similar tale. She saw my father peering through smoke at a group of officers. According to her, he went suddenly still, looked horrified, then began running toward them. Just before he reached the officers, he fell dead. Where the shot had actually come from, neither could say, but they were certain one among the group of officers had fired it."

I wondered what Captain Spencer had seen. I was ready to believe that with Eggleston and Breckenridge, anything was possible.

"I at last pieced together the identities of the officers," John went on in a hard voice. "Westin, Breckenridge, Eggleston, Connaught, and a Colonel Spinnet, although Spinnet died there himself. Colonel Spinnet's journal told me much about the others, most of which I found disgusting. I hired a Bow Street Runner, and began to investigate them."

Kenneth fingered his cup nervously. "I expected them to bring suit against us."

John frowned at him. "They would not have dared. The Runner could not discover much, but then suddenly, Colonel Westin offered to confess. The newspapers took up that sensation, and the other gentlemen faded back into the moldings."

His brother broke in gently. "I was pleased he came forward. He was ready to pay for what he had done."

"Kenneth is too quick to finish the business," John said to me. "The more I learned about the other gentlemen, the more I decided Colonel Westin was unlikely to have pulled the trigger. He may have been about to tell us the entire truth of the matter himself."

I fingered the handle of my cup. "Why do you say that?"

"He made an appointment with us. One he never kept."

I came alert. "Appointment?"

John nodded. "The night before he died. He wrote to me and begged to see us."

"For what purpose?"

Kenneth said, "We will never know. He asked us to meet him at a coffeehouse in Conduit Street at an early hour of the morning. We appeared and waited. He never arrived."

Because he'd likely been dead by then, I thought. Tucked up in his bed waiting for Lydia to find him.

"We assumed he had changed his mind," John continued. "Too cowardly to tell us the truth. And then the next day, we heard he'd fallen to his death. I could not help but think it served him right. If he knew the truth, he ought to have told it at once."

He looked grimly satisfied. His brother sent him an uneasy glance.

"Colonel Westin was an honorable man, by all accounts," I said. "He did not deserve to die."

"Neither did my father," John snapped back.

I had to agree. "I, too, am interested in the truth. And now Breckenridge is dead."

"And can tell no tales?" John asked. He lifted his cup, his dark eyes glittering. "Well, all we need do is wait and see which is the last man standing."

Kenneth shot him another look, worried and nervous.

"I hope it will not come to that," I said. "If you discover anything more, please write to me."

John nodded tersely. Kenneth tried to be pleasant.

After an uncomfortable leave-taking, Grenville and I left the tavern.

"Interesting," Grenville said as we walked up Pall Mall, past shops and booksellers. "I noted that Kenneth Spencer made bloody certain we knew he and his brother had departed Kent before Breckenridge died."

"Yes," I mused. "I wonder if that is the truth. Did you notice them after the match?"

He shook his head. "I was busy watching you get bandaged. I wish I had known who the devil they were then, because I could have kept an eye on them." He looked glum. "I can always send someone back to Astley Close to nose about the village and discover when they did depart, I suppose. Of course this widens the range of suspects, rather than narrows it."

I greeted this fact with relief, because it lessened my worry about Brandon.

Grenville stopped. "What do we do now?"

I considered. "Do find out when the Spencer brothers departed Astley Close. I would be interested to know also if their appointment with Westin was in fact at his house rather than a coffeehouse. He could have let them in himself, unknown to the servants. I can quite imagine John Spencer killing Westin in anger. He does not strike me as the most self-controlled of men."

"I agree with you." We reached a hackney stand, and Grenville shook my hand in parting. "On with the investigation, then. Here is to swift results."

We said good-bye, and I hired the hackney to return me home to prepare for my evening call on Lydia.

I thought over what the Spencers had said, as well as what I'd discovered in Kent, as I brushed my dark blue regimentals and asked Mrs. Beltan for a bit of thread to repair a torn silver braid. I fussed more than usual about my appearance, wishing for a fine suit of clothes and hair that lay flat, but at last I left my rooms and took myself back to Grosvenor Street.

To my great disappointment, I found Lydia in the company of her daughter's fiancé, Geoffrey Allandale.

CHAPTER 14

ALLANDALE greeted me cordially enough, his too-handsome face arranged in polite lines that expressed nothing.

I had been invited to take supper. We sat at the long table in the dining room, the three of us, Lydia at the head, with Allandale and I across from each other, I on her right hand, he on her left.

Lydia wore a dull black mourning gown that covered her bosom and circled her throat with thin, pale lace. Long black sleeves fastened at her slim wrists with onyx buttons. She wore a widow's cap, a small lawn piece that fitted snuggly. Her dark hair peeped from beneath it.

She wore the costume like a uniform, the outward shell of it reflecting nothing of the woman inside. Behind her thick lashes, her eyes smoldered with anger and impatience, whether at me and my lack of news, or at Allandale, or at both of us, I could not tell.

Allandale led the discussion and Lydia let him. He talked of conventional things, like the controversial novel *Glenarvon,* published that year. In it, Lady Caroline Lamb had satirized most of London society in retaliation for her failed, very public love affair with the poet Byron. Byron,

sensibly, Allandale said, remained on the Continent and ignored it. Allandale professed disgust for the book and
those who had flocked to buy it, but I noted that he seemed
to know many of its details.

I could not contribute much to the conversation because
I had not read the book, nor was I likely to. Lydia only ate
in silence.

As supper and Allandale's monologue drew to a close,
I inquired after Lydia's daughter. She was well, Lydia answered, still in Surrey with her uncle and aunt.

"Better that Chloe remains there for a time," Allandale
interposed. "Let the newspapers calm down before she returns. What trash they do print. I have forbidden William
to bring them into the house." He shot me a look that said
he blamed me for the scurrilous stories.

"She will not return here at all," Lydia said. She broke
off a tiny piece of bread and lifted it to her lips. "My husband left this house to me, and I plan to sell it."

"Now, Mother-in-law." Allandale began. He took on a
look of patience. "We have discussed this. You should do
nothing in haste."

Lydia's eyes flickered. She returned her gaze to her
food, but not in submission. I had seen her flash of temper
at Allandale's impudence. Allandale was overstepping his
mark, trying to slide in as man of the house before he'd
even married Lydia's daughter. I was pleased to note that,
because she'd mentioned selling the house, Colonel
Westin must have left it to her outright. I hoped he had left
her everything absolutely, as a man with no entail and no
son might do. Doubtless she held any money left to her
daughter in trust. It would be in Allandale's best interest to
ingratiate himself to Lydia, but the fool obviously did not
know how to do it.

I carefully clicked my knife to my plate, interrupting
them. Allandale shot me a rueful smile.

"Forgive us, Captain, for bringing up family business."
He dabbed at his mouth with a napkin. "But as long as we
have broached the subject, I do so hope that you will help

me persuade my mother-in-law to give up this business about Captain Spencer. It is agitating her greatly."

"My husband did not kill him," Lydia said calmly.

Allandale's tone was all that was pleasant, but I sensed in him the quiet, unthinking stubbornness of a limpet. "It is over and done with, now. No need to worry about it any longer."

"It will be over and done with," Lydia answered. "Once Captain Lacey and I have unraveled the truth."

Allandale shot her a glance. She returned the look, un-cowed.

Allandale laid down his knife. "Captain, would you speak to me a moment in the drawing room? Mother-in-law, please excuse us."

Lydia said nothing. I looked a question at her, and she inclined her head slightly. I hoped she trusted that I would oppose him on her behalf, but her gaze told me nothing.

Allandale led me to the next room, which was Lydia's private drawing room. Candles had been lit here. The light brushed the pianoforte and gently touched Lydia's portrait.

Allandale closed the door. His expression held annoy-ance, but he spoke in the soft, careful voice of a man who suppressed his annoyance because the person he addressed was a fool. "Captain, I truly must take you to task. When I heard that Mrs. Westin had invited you here tonight to dis-cuss Captain Spencer, I was most distressed. I insisted I at-tend as well, so that I could speak to you." Behind him, Lydia's portrait looked down on him, cold and haughty. "You must cease speaking to her of the incident on the Peninsula. It upsets her. Colonel Westin is dead, and that is that."

He sounded like Kenneth Spencer. "Her husband was accused of murder," I said dryly. "That would certainly be upsetting."

For one instant his affable expression vanished. Be-neath it I glimpsed something ugly and hard, a glittering sharpness. It was a flash only, then his fatuous smile re-turned.

"Even so," he went on, "I do not like what the events of the past month have done to her. I will ask you to please have done discussing it with her." He clasped his hands. "I have asked her to go to her daughter, but she refuses. You can certainly see that such a thing would be better for her."

"On that point, I can concede." When Lydia had lifted her glass, I was alarmed to see how much her too-thin hand had trembled. The country air could only do her good.

"Excellent," Allandale said. "I do appreciate your interest, but really, Captain, this business must stop." He gave a decided nod, as though he expected his word to be final on the subject.

I opened my mouth to tell him that not talking of it did not mean the deed had not been done, but William, Lydia's footman, opened the door on us. "Forgive me, sir."

Allandale swung on him, then quickly rearranged his expression. "Yes, William. What is it?"

"Message for you, sir." The boy advanced across the carpet, a folded paper in his hand.

Allandale took the note, unfolded it, and read the two lines penned there. He blew out his breath. "Devilish nuisance. Forgive me, Captain, but there is business I must take care of. William, please send for the carriage to take Captain Lacey home. I will hire one for my errand."

He shook my hand, his polite mask returning. "Pleased that you should dine with us, Captain."

He crumpled the paper, his brow creasing even as he turned away.

He marched from the room. I followed more slowly. Lydia had not dismissed me, and I certainly would not rush to obey the upstart Mr. Allandale.

I looked in at the dining room, but Lydia had gone. Disappointed, I proceeded downstairs, and reached the ground floor just as Allandale was gathering his hat and gloves from the young footman.

Allandale looked up at me. "Good night, Captain," he said firmly. He went out. The front door closed.

William's expression performed an instant transformation. The deferential footman's mask vanished, his young eyes twinkled, and he almost smiled. He raised his finger to his lips.

On the other side of the door, Allandale tramped away, his footsteps soon lost in the noise of traffic. William turned, nearly quivering with glee. "Please come with me, sir."

He led me back upstairs and to the drawing room I had just vacated. I followed, puzzled, and hopeful.

"Just wait here, sir," William said, then vanished.

I waited for about twenty minutes, pacing the room beneath Lydia's portrait. She gazed down at me, serene, calmly beautiful. She'd had no troubles at the time the picture had been painted—she'd had a young daughter and a husband with a solid and distinguished army career.

I had just decided William had forgotten about me, when, to my delight, and answering my hope, he opened the door again and ushered Lydia inside.

She smiled at me as William closed the door and left us alone. "The cocklebur has become unstuck at last."

I smiled back. "Happy chance that took him away."

She flushed. "It was not chance, truth to tell. I caused that message to be sent. It will take him to Essex, and by the time he discovers the ruse, it will be far too late to reach London again until morning. But I wanted to speak to you, uninterrupted."

My heart quickened. "I forgive you your deception. I, too, find him a constraint to conversation."

She sat down in her usual place on the divan. "You mentioned selling this house," I said. "Where will you go after this business is cleared up? That is, if it ever is. I feel devilish ineffectual, I must say."

"You believe in Roe's innocence. That is already a great help."

"I want to do so much more."

Her eyes softened. "You do not know how it feels to have someone on my side, Captain, such a relief to speak openly. I so long to know the truth. The newspapers—what

they print is horrible. Those cartoons about you are ludi-
crous. How can you bear it?"

I smiled. "I thought Mr. Allandale had forbidden newspapers in the house."

She made a derisive noise. "He might have told William
to throw them away, but William is loyal to me, not to Mr.
Allandale. Yes, I have seen the stories. They do not upset
me, they make me quite angry. They have no right to
ridicule you."

"I am a convenient target. It will pass." Or else I would
break all Billings's teeth.

"They are hashing out the entire Badajoz incident over
again." She sighed. "I am so tired of all of this."

I sat forward, wanting to comfort her and not knowing
how.

She sent me a wavering smile. "Please, Captain. Tell me
what you discovered in Kent."

"Little, I am afraid. I discovered that Lord Richard
Eggleston and Lord Breckenridge are vulgar and irritating,
but you did not need me to tell you that. And that they were
Belemites."

She raised her delicate brows. "Belemites?"

"Officers who manage to be assigned posts nowhere
near the fighting. Even if their regiment is heavily involved in battle, they somehow have been assigned to
transport prisoners or look into a supply problem."

"My husband was not fond of them," Lydia said. "They
liked a pretty uniform, but nothing more. Lord Breckenridge plied Roe for a long time to raise his rank, but fortunately Roe had the resolve not to let him become a
colonel."

"I can believe that. Breckenridge might have served in
the Peninsular campaign, but he was not a soldier."

I then gave her the full account of my visit to Astley
Close. I omitted the shameful game of cards and my boxing bout with Breckenridge. I did tell her of Brandon's un-
expected appearance and Breckenridge's suspicious death.
While I spoke, she toyed with a heavy gold and garnet ring

on her right forefinger, twisting it round in a distracted
way.

"So I really learned nothing," I concluded. "Except that
Eggleston and Breckenridge were most put out that I
should be investigating them. I have not yet made acquaintance with Connaught, though Grenville is trying to
contact him."

"He is much the same as the other two, I am afraid."

I tapped my fingers to the arm of the chair. "I wonder
that your husband did not cut his acquaintance with them
after the war. They are thoroughly unpleasant, and not men
whose company I would have thought your husband would
seek."

She opened her hands in a helpless gesture. "I asked
him why myself, but he never would tell me. He only said
that they had shared the camaraderie of battle, and so they
must remain friends. I knew he did not much like them, but
he refused to break the connection."

I remembered Lady Breckenridge describing how
Lydia had begged her husband to take her home when
Breckenridge wanted to play his disgusting card game.
"He ought to have spared you."

She shrugged. "It no longer matters."

It mattered to me.

I continued, telling her what I'd learned from the
Spencers and from Pomeroy. She listened attentively, the
garnet on her ring winking as she twisted the band again.

"What this means," I said carefully, "is that not only
could Breckenridge and Eggleston or Connaught have
killed your husband, but the Spencers could have also. And
they might have killed Breckenridge as well."

She looked surprised. "But why should they?"

"Because John Spencer longs for revenge against those
connected to his father's death. He reeks with it. And Kenneth Spencer worries much about his brother. He might
have murdered your husband believing that John would be
satisfied once Colonel Westin was dead. He seemed much

distressed that John wanted to continue his search for the truth."

Her eyes widened, pupils spreading to swallow the blue. "Could they have gained the house?"

"Indeed. The same way Breckenridge or Eggleston could have. I have toyed with the idea that their two lord-ships had an early morning appointment with your husband, that he let them into the house himself. But suppose the appointment had been with the Spencers? They admit-ted he'd asked to meet them at a coffeehouse, but what if he had told them to meet them here instead? He goes downstairs and lets them in. They murder him and leave."

She watched me in growing dismay. She had wanted the three aristocrats to be the culprits, wanted it with her whole being. The possibility that Breckenridge or Eggle-ston or Connaught had nothing to do with it meant that she might have made a grave mistake.

"I must agree with Mr. Allandale on one point," I said gently. "Perhaps you should go to the country. Stay with your daughter and brother. I will write you of anything I find."

She shook her head. "I am not ready yet. I would go mad in the country, waiting."

"Your daughter might need you."

She raised her hands in supplication. "Do not ask me, Captain. I cannot go. Chloe's uncle will look after her well."

"But the country might be safer for you. There is real possibility that someone closer to home killed your hus-band, as I suggested before. You should face that. William, for instance."

She stared at me in baffled outrage. "I have told you, that is impossible. William refuses to kill even insects. The idea that he might have hurt my husband is preposterous."

"But he is large and strong and could easily have struck your husband down. Or Millar could have done the same."

She shook her head, her eyes sparking anger. "Millar had been my husband's manservant for twenty years. He grieved and still does. And he and William are both devoted to me."

"Perhaps too devoted," I suggested. "Perhaps William saw that your life would be eased if your husband died."

She sprang from her chair and paced in agitation to the pianoforte. "No. Please stop this. He cannot have."

"Forgive me. I simply want no harm to come to you."

"I did not ask you to investigate my husband's death, Captain Lacey. I asked you to clear his name."

"I know. I cannot help myself. I want to be certain."

She swung on me, her head high. "Certain of what? You have no right to accuse my servants. How dare you?"

"I accuse them to stop myself from speaking something still more repugnant, from drawing a conclusion even Sergeant Pomeroy leapt to without prompting."

"What conclusion? What are you talking about?"

"Good lord, Lydia, have you not seen it? That you killed him yourself."

Her face flashed white with shock. "What?"

I went on remorselessly. "You most easily of all could have crept into your husband's chamber and stabbed him while he lay abed. The servants were asleep; who would notice you move from your bedroom to his? And then in the morning you pretend to find him and swear your servants to silence on the matter."

She stared. "How can you say these things to me?"

"Because they might just be true."

Her look turned furious. "They are not."

She moved as though to flee the room. I stepped in front of her.

"No? What was he to you? You had no marriage; you admitted so yourself. He was about to bring disgrace to you and your daughter, and his friends disgusted you. If he died, you would be spared an ordeal, and if you could push the deed onto the foul Breckenridge, so much the better."

I could not still my tongue. My fears were pouring from me, words spilling into the still room.

"If I am so clever," she flashed, "why on earth did I tell you all?"

"Because when I helped you on the bridge, you saw a chance to move your plan along. You saw that you could stir me to pity, that you could make me do anything you pleased. That I would scramble to cast the blame on your husband's disgusting colleagues, anything to keep them from you and the taint from your name. You must have seen how easily I'd promise you anything."

I ran out of breath. She stared at me, lips parted. A slight draft of air stirred the tapes of her cap.

I eased my hands open. "You see," I said, lowering my voice. "You are barely a widow, and I make declarations that I should not. I take the unpardonable liberty of speaking your name, uninvited. And who am I? A nobody, here on your leave, hardly better than a servant."

She continued to stand still in shock, her gaze fixed on mine. "No." Her whisper was cracked. "Not a servant. A gentleman."

"Hardly, at this moment. I am ready to ask for what I do not deserve."

Color climbed in her cheeks. "And if I say you may have it freely?"

"Then I will count myself most blessed of men." I shook my head. "But I cannot ask it. I will go."

"No," she said quickly. "I was willing once before to grant it. Do you remember?"

How could I forget? I recalled her warm lips against mine, her arms about my neck. I had thought of the incident every day since it had happened.

"You were ill, and frightened. And a bit foxed, as I recall." I made a slight bow, my throat aching. "Forgive me. I will go."

"Please do not leave me alone, Gabriel." She held her hand palm out, as if pushing me away. "Not yet."

"Lydia." I could not stop myself saying her name again. The word filled my mouth, liquid and light. "If I stay . . ."

"Stay. Please."

She stood motionless until I came to her and gathered her into my arms. She leaned to my chest, and the clean scent of the lawn cap drifted to me as I pressed a kiss to it.

Her hold tightened, and she raised her face to mine. I kissed her. I tasted her lips, her brow, her throat, the lace at her neck.

"Gabriel," she whispered. "Please stay."

I kissed her again. I threaded my fingers into her dark hair, and her white cap loosened and fluttered to the floor like a fallen bird.

THE warmth of her bed wrapped me in a comfort I had not known in many a year. I learned her that night in her chamber beneath silken bed hangings, learned the cool brush of her fingers, the scent of her skin, the taste of her mouth. I had not realized how starved I'd been; I was like a man who hadn't known he was thirsty until given clear water to drink.

I sensed from her inexperienced caresses, her unpracticed kisses, that she'd not had a lover in many years. I scorned her fool of a husband as I gentled my touch for her. Even a man who could not complete the act could have pleasured a woman in myriad ways. Colonel Westin seemingly had not bothered to do so.

I liked the way we fit, her head tucked beneath my chin, my arm about her shoulders. She brushed her fingers over my face, smiling at the stiff bristles there. We lay together far into the night, warm and contented. I drifted in and out of sleep, not dreaming, simply dozing in blissful warmth.

At last in the cool hours of the morning I rose and dressed. She smiled sleepily as I kissed her good-bye and departed into the gray dawn.

Happiness settled over me. I knew it would not last, but I drank it in, savoring it for the time I could.

•   •   •

COVENT Garden was quiet when I reached it, though a few street ladies still paraded. Black Nancy, a game girl Louisa had taken in to reform, was no longer there, but the others recognized me and greeted me raucously. I tipped my hat to them, my mood still sunny, and moved on to Grimpen Lane.

I reached the bake shop and let myself into the stuffy staircase hall.

Light footsteps hastened down to me. "Lacey!" Marianne said in a hoarse whisper. A wavering taper, likely one of mine, lit her face. Her eyes were wide. "Where the devil have you been?"

"Out," I answered laconically.

"There are men in your rooms, looking for you. Came banging on my door, asking where you were, about two hours ago. As if I take your particulars."

I glanced up the stairs. All was quiet. The painted shepherds and shepherdesses wavered under the glare of Marianne's candle.

I clasped the head of my cane. "They are up there now?"

"Yes. I tell you, you cannot fight all three, and they looked well able to throw you down the stairs."

"Who are they?"

"How the devil should I know? I have never seen them before."

"Let us find out, shall we?"

I moved past her. She stared at me as though I'd run mad but made no move to stop me.

I quickly and quietly ascended to the first floor. My door stood closed. Long ago, it had been painted dove gray and its panels outlined in gold. The handle was fancifully shaped like a maiden who'd sprouted great long wings from her back. Once she had been gold, but now she was only the tarnished brass that had lain beneath the gold leafing.

I opened the door.

Two large footmen stood to either side, waiting for me to come bursting in. I foiled them by simply swinging open the door and remaining in the hall. Across the room, James Denis rose from my worn wing chair.

CHAPTER 15

HE wore a black evening suit of superfine, as though he'd just arrived from the theatre or opera. A sapphire ring glinted on his third finger, and a diamond sparkled coldly on his cravat. He or his toadies had lit every one of my candles. The light tinged the flaking ceiling plaster the delicate red-gold of rose petals.

"What do you want?" I asked unceremoniously.

"A moment of your time," Denis replied. "Since I could not convince you to visit me in my home, I have traveled to yours. Please come inside."

"I will when you leave."

He gave me a frosty look. "You will want to hear what I have to say, believe me, Captain."

"I did not ask for your help."

"Yet I give it. And this after my encounters with you last spring. You owe me much."

"There we differ. I say I owe you nothing." I unsheathed my sword. "Please get out. I have no interest in your information."

He paused, his eyes hooded. "Not even in the where-abouts of Mrs. Brandon?"

The words dropped into silence. My heart jumped, then stopped, then began pounding.

"What the devil have you to do with Mrs. Brandon?"

"I know where she is. You do not. I offer the information in fair exchange."

My limbs unfroze. I went for him. The two brutes to either side of me seized my arms. I jerked free, and with two strides I was across the room, my hands locked around James Denis's throat.

His cold blue eyes flickered, but other than that he remained still. Beneath his cravat, his throat was surprisingly warm, and his pulse beat beneath my fingers.

"Tell me where she is," I said, "or by God, I will kill you where you stand."

"Then you would not learn anything."

In a swift, sudden movement, he brought up his hands between my wrists and snapped them apart.

His henchmen closed on me again as he looked me up and down. "I imagine you have heard the term 'loose cannon,' Captain. Aboard a frigate, I believe, a cannon that is not fastened down properly provides for much danger. You are that loose cannon for me. You do not heed counsel to stay out of my way, and wherever I turn these days, I nearly trip over you."

I remembered my encounter with him the day Lydia had asked me to help her. I had wondered what errand he'd been performing in Russel Street. "If I have met you by chance, that is hardly my fault."

"That may be. But I do not trust you not to interfere with my business. I have determined that the only way I can trust you—although 'trust' is not quite the word I would use—is to tame you."

"Tame me?" I almost laughed. "Like one of your trained lackeys?"

"No," he said. "I want you obligated to me. I will appeal to your sense of duty, your sense of fair play. One gentleman does not cheat another."

"But I do not consider you a gentleman."

"I believe that." He gave me the faintest of smiles. "Mrs. Brandon speaks highly of you. She claims you have a good heart, though your judgment is often rash. I believe you a bit misguided myself."

Fury welled up so tight I could barely see. "Where is she?"

"We will come to that in a moment—"

"Where?"

"I will tell you when you meet my price."

I would not encourage him by asking what the price was. I remained stubbornly silent.

"It will be very simple," he continued. "I want you to promise me—your word as a gentleman—that when I call upon you to assist me, in any way or for any reason, you will do so at once, no matter what your situation."

His expression was utterly still, but I did not delude myself that everything he said was not precisely calculated, his thoughts running far ahead of the conversation. He had decided the outcome of this interview before he had even conducted it.

This man bought and sold favors and owned people outright, and he had an extensive network that stretched all over the Continent, perhaps the world. He dressed like a gentleman, lived in a fine house, and drove a fine carriage, but he was as much an underworld figure as the blacklegs who fleeced gentlemen at the gaming hells of Saint James's.

I in no way wanted myself obligated to him. But I thought of Louisa, of her cool gray eyes and warm smile and slightly crooked nose. My blood chilled.

"Why did you come to me and not her husband?" I asked.

"She does not want to see her husband," he replied. "Or so she said."

"She is safe?"

Denis met my eye, cold clarity in his gaze. "That depends very much on you, Captain."

I hated him powerfully at that moment. He had me, and he knew it.

"I want your word," he said.

A candle sputtered in the silence, loud as a pistol shot.

I nodded, my neck sore with it. "I give you my word."

"I will hold you to the bargain. Know that." His voice went soft. "I believe Louisa Brandon is very dear to you, is she not?"

"Just tell me where she is."

He watched a bit of plaster float to the carpet. "She is a clever woman, your Mrs. Brandon. She has hidden herself well." And he told me.

I arrived at a respectable-looking boardinghouse down the Thames in Greenwich at two that afternoon. Denis had told me Louisa had moved into the house under the name "Mrs. Taylor," and had purported to be a widow who had recently lost her husband, found herself cut off by an indifferent son, and had nowhere to go. Her story was not far-fetched; by law, sons were not related to their mothers, and had no legal obligation to care for them. I wondered, on a sudden, what provisions Brandon had made, if any, for Louisa in case of his death.

The landlady who ran the household had a kind face and a softness about her eyes. She told me I'd been expected, and led me to the back of the house to a small, sunny parlor.

Louisa lay on a divan, a shawl over her knees. Her golden hair was loose about her, and a widow's cap similar to the one Lydia had worn rested on her head, verisimilitude for the part of the widowed Mrs. Taylor.

I meant to greet her with a jest about it, but I was struck with how thin she'd grown since I'd last seen her. Her fingers were white and frail, and her gray eyes were enormous in her nearly bloodless face.

My heart tightened. She had been ill, damned ill, if I were any judge. Life could be brutally short in these times, and to be sure, I had already seen a number of childhood acquaintances lost to disease and war, but Louisa had always seemed indomitable, strong, everlasting. The thought that she could be taken from me so easily made my pulse quicken with dread.

But her smile was welcoming. She held out her hands to me. I clasped them in mine and bent to kiss her cheek.

"Gabriel. I am so glad you've come." She squeezed my fingers hard, to the bone.

I went down on one knee beside her. "Louisa, what is it? Are you ill?"

She shook her head. "Not any longer."

"What has happened? Tell me."

She smiled and released my hands. "Oh, do take a chair, Gabriel. The floor must be devilish uncomfortable."

I rose and dragged a rather shabby armchair with ball and claw feet to her side. When I seated myself, I took one of her hands in mine again. Her fingers curled against my palm, but she did not pull away.

"Please tell me what has happened," I repeated.

"Nothing that has not happened before," she said tiredly. "I will weather it."

I looked into her eyes, and I realized that what I read there was not illness, but great sorrow. Her eyelids were rimmed with red, and I saw a woman who had relinquished her last hope.

"Oh God," I whispered.

"I wish I knew why I cannot do what every maid in the street can in a trice," she said. "They even pay to give up what I'd pay a thousandfold to have. It baffles one, does it not?"

"Louisa." I caressed her cold fingers. Three times before, Louisa Brandon had been with child, and three times before, she had lost that child. The first had been born, a tiny little boy. But all too soon, he had began gasping for breath, and then he had died. The others had been born far too early, too weak to live. This one could not have been inside her for more than several weeks. "I am sorry."

Her gray eyes filled as her fingers tightened on mine.

"Does Brandon know?" I asked.

She shook her head. "I said nothing to him. How could I have? It seemed little short of cruel. He would have hoped so much. I decided I'd go away. I'd met the woman who runs this boardinghouse during the Peninsular campaign before her husband was killed and she returned to England. She is a midwife now. We corresponded still, and I thought this would be an ideal place. I could wait here until I was certain all would be well." She smiled shakily. "But all was not well, was it? I do not know why I supposed it would be. I have always failed before."

"It is hardly your fault." My mouth hardened as I remembered a long-ago heated argument with Brandon. "No matter what others might say."

Brandon had once dared complain in my presence that Louisa had sorely disappointed him in the matter of children. He had said bitterly that she could not come up to scratch, and a childless wife was no wife at all. I understood later that he had been as hurt as Louisa by her latest miscarriage, but at the time, all I had seen was the misery in her eyes and the blatant blame in Brandon's. I'd lost my temper and said that perhaps it was not the receptacle that was to blame, but the seed.

That moment, I believe had begun the end of our friendship. Our feud had later taken a darker, grimmer twist, but my words that day had never been quite forgiven.

Louisa toyed with the fringe of her shawl. "I went to Aline," she said. "She advised I go away, somewhere quiet, where I could be alone. I should have nothing that would upset me, she said, and Aloysius was certainly upsetting me." She looked up, a ghost of a defiant glint in her eye. "Agreeing to testify that Colonel Westin had been inebriated and committed murder. Rot and nonsense. I told him no good would come of such lies, but he can be so stubborn!"

She did not need to tell me of Brandon's stubbornness.

"I wondered how you had responded to his promise. I ought to have known you would see the thing for what it was."

"Of course I did," she said firmly. "But he would preach to me about preserving the honor of the regiment. The Forty-Third should not be shamed. Colonel Westin had agreed to take the blame alone so that he could be singled out and punished. Of course Westin did not murder that captain."

"I know."

"I know you know. I have read the newspapers. You are in this up to your neck. I hope you came prepared to tell me everything."

I raised a brow. "If you have read the newspapers, then you already know."

She gave me a deprecating look. "Do not tease me. I am not in the humor for it. The newspapers print what they like, and you know it. I want the truth, Gabriel." She slid her hand from mine and folded her arms. "And I do mean all of it. I read that man Billings's salacious hints about you and Mrs. Westin. Well?"

A day ago, they would still have been lies. Today, I felt my cheeks grow warm.

"So," she said softly. "Not all lies."

"But the truth is not what he makes out," I said. "Fortunately, Billings's stories are so outrageous they can be laughed off as improbable."

She would not let me off so easy. "What is the truth, Gabriel? Stop prevaricating and tell me at once."

I hid a smile. I was pleased that I had sparked her interest. I was willing to let her scold me if doing so would soothe her.

I began my tale with the moment I'd caught sight of Lydia Westin making her way through the rain to the half-constructed bridge. I told of Westin's death, and Lydia's wish that I clear his name. I told her of Pomeroy's investigation, and how Grenville and I had journeyed to Astley

Close and met Lord Richard Eggleston and Lord Breckenridge. I told her about all the events there, not leaving anything out, including the card game. I told her of
Breckenridge's death, Brandon's sudden appearance, and
the inquest and my speculations there.

"Lady Breckenridge seemed not in the least upset by
her husband's death," I concluded. "Almost as though
she'd been waiting for it."

"Some women do spend their marriages waiting for
their husbands to die. Seems a rather uncomfortable existence."

"I doubt she would have had the strength to break his
neck," I mused. "Though she could have caused him to
fall. Or an accomplice might have killed him for her." I
sighed. "I see too many accomplices in this. Lydia Westin
could have stabbed her husband, but she could not have
carried him to bed, were he not already there. Lady Breckenridge never would have been able to fling her husband
over the back of a horse and drag him to the edge of the
rise and pitch him over. No, a man, every time, has done
the brute work of it."

Louisa touched my hand. "But that man was not my
husband."

I ought to have known she would have guessed my fears.
"I am afraid I cannot put the suspicion from my mind."

She shook her head. "No, Gabriel. Aloysius would not
have killed him, even accidentally." She gave me a quiet
look. "You know he would have made certain it was you,
first."

"Hmm. That is comforting."

"But nonetheless true."

"You might be right. That still leaves us with an ap-
palling number of suspects."

Her eyes narrowed. "Yes, Mr. Spencer and his brother,
to name two."

"And Eggleston. And this Major Connaught, whom I
have not yet met."

She levered herself up on the divan, as if determined to

leave her sagging posture behind. "Aloysius is acquainted with him. Ask him to introduce you."

I smiled mirthlessly. "Your husband is more likely to give me a punch in the jaw than help me. If he discovers that Denis told me where you were instead of him, he will have apoplexy." I sobered. "Why did you ask Denis not to tell him?"

Two spots of color appeared on her cheeks. "Because I am not yet ready to face him. My return will be stormy, I know that. I am not yet strong enough for it."

I took her hand in mine again. She rested it there limply. "When you do return, would you like me to go with you?"

"No," she answered quietly. "It must be between me and him."

I nodded. I hated to let her face him alone, but I knew she was right. She would win, but it would take much strength to do it. The last time I'd seen her face him down had been the day I'd lain before them both, drunk with opium, my leg shattered, and she had discovered what he had done. I had laughed, far gone on the drug and pain when she had turned on him, furious and shocked. I had laughed, unable to stop, until I'd wept.

She abruptly withdrew her hand and tried to sound bright. "I was quite pleased to meet your Mr. Denis. An interesting man. I was at last able to tell him what I thought of his treatment of you last spring."

I raised my brows. "Good lord. I would dearly have loved to have heard *that* conversation."

"We were quite civil, do not worry. I found that we agreed that you were often not as prudent as you might me."

"I will not forgive him for dragging you into this," I said.

"I, on the other hand, am pleased he called. I had not realized how much I missed you, my friend, until he offered to send you to me. And then I knew I missed you sorely! To speak to you, to advise you on your latest conundrum, I knew I must do that."

"Thank you for letting me come."

Her fingers were cool on mine. "You comfort me. You cannot know how much."

We shared a look. Her eyes were gray as winter skies.

"You have comforted me so often," I said softly. "How could I not return the favor?"

The clock on the mantel struck the hour. I caressed the backs of her fingers. She looked swiftly away and withdrew her hand.

"About Aloysius," she said.

I sat back. "Please do not lecture to me about reconciling with him, Louisa. His actions this past week have put reconciliation further away, if anything."

"If he did not care for you so deeply, you could not hurt him so much."

I folded my arms. I was not ready to feel great depths of sympathy for Aloysius Brandon. My last encounter with him had all but unraveled our tense politeness. The next time we met, the gloves would be off, much like they'd been when I'd boxed Breckenridge.

"I think you misread him," I said.

"No, I think you do. I still remember what he was like when I first met him. He was a great man, full of fire and able to inspire that fire in others. You felt it."

"Yes," I had to say.

"The fire has dimmed a little, and disappointment has tarnished him. But it is still there, Gabriel, deep inside. He is a man others will live for. That is the man I stand by."

I could not argue with her. When I'd first met Aloysius Brandon, I had been rather dazed by him. I had just reconciled myself to go on living with my martinet father until he died, bearing his tantrums and his beatings, my life bleak and predictable. And then this man, this astonishing man, had told me I could have a life, a career, honors if I wanted them. All I had to do was follow him.

He had compelled me to return to my father, tell him I had volunteered in the King's army, and that I, his only son, was leaving him. That interview had become eight hours of stormy shouting, violent threats, and broken furniture. In the end, I'd flung myself from the house, vowing never to enter it again.

I'd joined Brandon, who had listened with sympathy to my woes. Later, just before we embarked on the ship that would take us to India, he had introduced me to his bride, Louisa.

Life had not been kind to her. I clasped her hand again. As she chatted to me of the boardinghouse and the people she had met here, I wished with all my heart I could change that for her.

CHAPTER 16

I spent the following weeks in an odd mood. On the one hand, I could not shake a feeling that I was ineffectual, a spinning wheel going nowhere. The identity of Westin's murderer eluded me, as did evidence of Captain Spencer's killer. Nor was I any closer to proving who had murdered Breckenridge.

I had not seen or spoken to Lord Richard Eggleston since the incident. I had tried on two occasions to make an appointment with him, but was told firmly by his secretary that he was seeing no one while mourning the death of his friend.

I likewise had no luck questioning Brandon about events in Kent. He refused point blank to see me. He once shut the door in my face himself, and I could only leave his doorstep, muttering choice curses under my breath.

Grenville and I met occasionally to discuss things, while Anton brought us dishes both unusual and delicious. Grenville had tried to meet the elusive Sir Edward Connaught, but he had not been able to find the man. Connaught had left town for the summer, the caretaker of his London house had informed Grenville. Letters to his country house went unanswered.

The newspapers, at least, had tired of taunting me and moved on to bread riots in Seven Dials. London grew hotter still, and I slept with my windows wide open, praying for a breeze or cooling rain.

On the other hand, my mind was much relieved by knowing Louisa was safe. My heart ached for her sorrow, but as promised, I said not a word to her husband, a promise made easier by his refusal to speak to me.

And then, I had Lydia. While part of me puzzled over her husband's past and berated me for not knowing the answers, the rest of me rejoiced in her.

She was a lady like no other. I spent countless time tangled in her black hair, touching her skin, breathing her in. Her smile made all the hurt go away, even deep hurts that had tucked themselves into my heart for years.

I do not know if I soothed her as she soothed me, but when she kissed me, her lips were gentle and warm, and when she slept beside me, her breathing was deep and even, without distress.

William aided and abetted our secret affair. Because she was newly in mourning, Lydia did not go to the opera or theatre or balls, such places that lovers might meet, and in any case, it was high summer and entertainments were few. We met in the afternoons, lying together in the sunlight of her bedchamber, dozing in the white heat while carriages rumbled past in the street. Climbing roses bloomed at the window then wilted in the heat and dust.

William ever made certain that the other servants were well occupied with duties below stairs before Lydia and I ascended to her rooms, or I departed later. He delivered Lydia's letters to me and took mine to her—we exchanged billets-doux like cozy lovers in a farce. He performed these errands with childlike glee, seemingly happy that Lydia and I were conducting a tawdry liaison.

She and I were the tenderest of lovers, even going so far

as to exchange tokens and locks of hair. She had given me a ribbon to wear inside my coat and I had given her one of my handkerchiefs. She wore it about her person, she assured me with a sly smile, but would not tell me where.

She purchased a small enamel snuffbox for me, blushing when she presented it, saying that she had no idea of an appropriate gift for a lover. I kept it with my most prized treasures, and then scraped money together to buy a thin gold chain for her slender ankle.

Even Billings let us alone. I encountered him only once, while hiring a hackney in Hanover Square to take me home early one evening. He emerged from a bakery not far from me, a loaf under his arm.

"Ah, Captain," he hailed me. "Have your feet firmly planted under the Westin table, do you?"

"I will have my foot firmly planted on your backside if you do not go away," I answered. He only laughed and moved on.

My investigation into the murder at Badajoz continued, but slowly. Eggleston refused to see me; Breckenridge was dead and could tell no more tales. Grenville was, of course, making vain attempts to contact Sir Edward Connaught. I met with the Spencer brothers again, but they had not been able to convey much more to me. John Spencer was particularly surly.

But for Lydia, I would have found those summer days hot and frustrating.

I did not return to see Louisa, much as I wanted to. She needed to heal, alone, she'd said, and I would respect that. But I did want very much to ask her advice on one matter. As my affair with Lydia deepened, I seriously contemplated the step of marrying her.

I thought it through during my wakeful nights after I left her afternoon bed. I had found a quiet happiness with her, despite the dark questions that ever hovered round us.

Lydia had given me a second reason to contemplate it. She had quietly told me, four weeks into our affair, that she believed she was increasing. I was not surprised, we had been passionate without much restraint. She looked worried when she had whispered the news, as though she feared I would grow angry, or blame her, or end the affair.

In truth, the news affected me strangely. I was glad, and I told her so. She had provided me with an excuse to face what I had so long refused to face, but once confronting these things, I would be free of them. I told her I would marry her.

I would need Grenville's help in preparing the way, and I made my plans to approach him.

One evening, Grenville took me to a performance of an Austrian lady violinist with whom gossip had begun pairing him. Anastasia Froehm would play at a musicale hosted by a French exile who had decided to remain in England even after Louis XVIII's restoration. Grenville obtained an invitation for me, and we strolled into the Comtesse du Lille's house in Upper Brook Street just as Mrs. Froehm began to play.

Anastasia Froehm was not pretty of face, though she had plump arms and fine brown eyes. But when she played, she filled the air with sweetness. She had loveliness inside her, and it poured through her fingers and through her instrument to entrance us. Grenville's eyes gleamed with pride, and a small smile tugged at his mouth.

At the end of the performance, however, he did not join the throng that greeted her, and instead expressed the wish to depart abruptly for his club. I thought this odd and rude, and told him so.

"Nonsense, Lacey," Grenville said as he sent a footman running for his carriage. "I am hungry. We will go to Watier's. The food is tolerable there."

He did not even offer to introduce me to Mrs. Froehmm so that I could pay my compliments. I held my tongue, but wondered.

Once inside his carriage with cushions at my back and the sweet scent of wax rising from the lanterns, I questioned him. "Do you tell me that you find the charms of

Marianne Simmons far superior to Mrs. Froehm's? I will call you mad and a blackguard if you do."

He frowned. "What the devil has Marianne got to do with Mrs. Froehm?"

"Are you not Mrs. Froehm's paramour?"

He fixed me with a black stare. "I thought you of all people would not believe what you read in the newspapers."

I shrugged. "You escort her everywhere and you have been elusive of late."

He regarded me for a long moment. As I met his enigmatic stare, I realized just how little I knew this man. We had investigated puzzles together, but he showed me only the facets of himself that he wanted me to see.

At last, he spoke. "If I tell you the truth, Lacey, you must keep it to yourself."

"Everything you say to me is in confidence," I said stiffly.

"I mean no offense. It is the lady's secret, not mine. I met Anastasia in Italy a year or so ago, and we became fast friends. When she came to London, she wrote me and asked if I'd be her escort, because she did not want to spend her time fending off offers of protection. She wanted to live quietly, and if she was seen about with me, would-be suitors would leave her alone."

"That is no doubt true," I conceded. "But she does not mind gossip pairing your names?"

"Not in the least. She will return to the Continent soon, and all will be at an end. She did me a good turn in Italy and I decided I would do her one here. That is all."

I studied him a moment, wondering what the "good turn" was. He returned the look blandly, and I knew that tonight, at least, my curiosity would go unsatisfied.

We did not speak again until we arrived at Watier's in Piccadilly at Bolton Street. Grenville called the food here *tolerable,* but only because he employed the best chef in the country. Compared to the clubs that served boiled beef and lifeless greens, Watier's, begun by a chef of that name who had worked for the Prince of Wales, was culinary paradise. Deep play was to be found here, but it was the food that drew gentlemen forth from the sanctums of White's and Brooks's. We dined on tender meat and fish and fine wine and delicate bread.

After supper, to my dismay, we also found Mr. Allandale.

I had managed to avoid him, thanks to William, while making my illicit visits to Lydia. Now, in the card room, he turned to us, a fixed smile on his face, betraying nothing of the flash of temper I'd glimpsed beneath his mild façade on our last meeting.

Mr. Allandale was not alone. Two gentlemen stood with him, one older, one younger, obviously father and son. The son could only have been just down from university; his face was still downy soft and lacked the hardness of experience. His hair was pale yellow and trained into fashionable curls made popular by poets and artists. His expensive suit copied Grenville's tastes, and he seemed quite eager to greet us. As I shook his hand, I beheld in his wide gray eyes a vast innocence, one unprepared for the realities of the world.

The father was a baronet, Sir Gideon Derwent, and I found in his eyes the same deep-seated innocence that dwelled in his son's.

Sir Gideon fastened an awed gaze upon me. "You were a dragoon?" he queried. "Good heavens. Did you see action?"

"India and the Dutch campaign," I replied laconically. "Then the Peninsula. Not Waterloo, I am afraid."

They'd be disappointed. Waterloo made one a hero, even if one had remained behind in camp guarding the water sacks. The Derwents did not seem to mind this, however.

Leland, the son, asked, "Did you lead many charges?"

"A good many more than I would have liked. And then back again after we'd run too far."

I'd hoped my self-deprecating humor would break their intense stares. It did not.

"You must have many stories to tell, Captain," Leland said.

Allandale suddenly interposed, his voice smooth. "Indeed, he is a most entertaining dinner companion. I myself was much delighted with his company several weeks ago."

I was surprised he did not turn purple with the effort of the lie. He had not wanted me there. The room had been palpable with it.

Father and son exchanged a look. "Well then," Sir Gideon said hopefully. "Certainly we would be honored to have you at our supper table, Captain Lacey. Perhaps Monday week?"

I looked at the both of them hovering anxiously upon my answer. It would be impolite to snub them, yet I found their admiring gazes a bit unnerving.

I remained silent a moment too long. Leland looked downcast. "Perhaps he will not be free, Father."

Of course I would be free. I had little to fill my social calendar, I could assure them. But Sir Gideon spoke before I could. "We will write to you, Captain, and fix a date."

I could only agree, and after more exchanges of pleasantries, we parted.

Grenville and I moved from Watier's to a billiards room in St. James's Square. Once ensconced in a game, Grenville remarked, "You have just met the most unworldly father and son in all of England. The entire family is like them. All they know of London and life is what they see between their front door and their carriage door. God help them."

"They seemed kind."

"They are. Unequivocally so. To their credit, they are also the most honest beings you will ever meet. If they professed interest in you, it was not feigned."

"Then it would be rude of me to refuse their invitation."

He smiled. "Be prepared to be questioned to death. But they mean well. And you should cultivate them. The Derwents are acquaintances of Sir Edward Connaught. I should have thought of them at once."

That, of course, clinched the matter. When Sir Gideon wrote to me next day requesting my presence at his table on the following Tuesday, I replied that I would come.

THE day I was to meet the Derwents, William failed us. I strolled downstairs in Lydia's house at five o'clock to find Allandale just coming in.

William, looking distressed, was busily trying to turn him away. Allandale looked up, caught sight of me, and stared in astonishment.

I stopped on the landing. Allandale gaped at me. William helplessly held the door open. A hot breeze filled the hall.

I came out of my standstill and continued down. By the time I stepped off the last stair, Allandale was spluttering.

"I do not understand. William said Mrs. Westin was unwell. What are you doing here?"

I retrieved my hat and gloves from the table myself, William having become fixed to the door handle. "Shall we go out together, Allandale?"

Allandale stared past me and up the stairs. "Where is she?"

I had left Lydia at her dressing table, brushing out her long hair. I had wanted to linger and watch her, but my supper appointment pressed me. I had put my hands on her waist, kissed the nape of her neck, then taken my leave.

"Accompany me, Mr. Allandale," I said firmly. I certainly did not want him waiting at the bottom of the stairs for her like an outraged governess.

Again, his mask slipped. The habitual pleasant expression left him. "How dare you."

I slapped my hat to my head, took Allandale by the elbow, and steered him outside. William gave me an anguished look as we passed. I said to him, "If Mr. Allandale tries to call again tonight, or even tomorrow, do not admit him."

William, wide-eyed, nodded. He closed the door behind us.

Allandale shook off my hold before we'd walked five feet. "Explain yourself, sir. What the devil were you doing upstairs in my mother-in-law's house?"

I set my mouth in a grim line. "I have nothing to explain. And if you question her about it, I will not overlook it. Do you understand me?"

He stopped. A hurrying gentleman, perspiring in the heat, nearly ran him down. Grumbling, the gentleman pushed past and went on.

"Good God, Lacey, you are a cad of the highest water."

"It is not your business," I said.

"Not my business? She is the mother of the woman I shall marry! Shall I let her be ruined by a fortune hunter? I will not stand by and let you deceive her."

I caught his coat lapels, uncaring of others in the street who stopped to gape. I jerked him close, glaring into his flawless face. "I would do nothing to hurt her, you thrice-damned idiot. If you speak one word of this to her, I will—"

"Call me out?" He glared back, his shock overcome.

"No, I will drag you to the Thames and throw you in. Let the watermen fish you out. They will if you offer them enough coin."

He swallowed. "You are mad enough to do it."

"I am. If I discover that you have spoken to her of this matter in any way, I advise you to dress in the suit you most wish to ruin."

I released him. He landed on his feet, looking startled, then he jerked from me and hastily smoothed his coat. "I find it hard to credit that you are a friend of Mr. Grenville's. He would be shocked at your behavior."

"In this case," I said, "I believe he'd agree with me."

I turned on my heel, marched away, and left him red and furious in the middle of the street.

•   •   •

EVERY corner of London had its own characteristic, every street its personality. Rich then poor then rich ran together like water and cream. Mansions could give rise to rook-eries in two streets, and inhabitants of each would not know a thing of what went on not a short walk away.

Not far from Grosvenor Square, where I made my way to the house of the Derwents upon the appointed hour, had stood Tyburn Tree, the infamous gallows where executions had taken place until late in the last century. South of the old hanging place, Mayfair had bloomed a swath of man-sions, some of the finest in London. The Derwents, Grenville had given me to understand, were among the wealthiest citizens in England.

I wondered that I had not heard of the Derwents before, but Grenville assured me they were also among the hum-blest. Sir Gideon had sat in the House of Commons for many years before retiring to spend more time with his family. He had been made a baronet because of services to the realm, mostly philanthropic. No one could claim to know a more disinterested giver of money to the poor than Sir Gideon Derwent, and so George III had been persuaded to honor him.

If he had given away a fortune to the London poor, he must have had much to spare, I thought as I descended from the hackney and gazed up at Derwent's enormous mansion.

Light glowed from every window, as though they ex-pected a crowd. I hoped not, as I was not in the mood to be jovial to dozens of people I did not know.

The hackney driver grinned at me as I counted shillings into his hand. "Someone's got friends in 'igh places," he said. He chortled as he drove away.

Stately columns flanked a grand double-doored en-trance, and a red carpet stretched like a tongue over the small bit of pavement to me. I wondered what exalted guest they were expecting.

I soon learned. A butler met me at the door, bowed formally, and ushered me into the house. A footman, equally stately, though much younger, took my gloves and hat.

The butler led me through a massive hall, equally as large as that in Lady Mary Fortescue's country house, but thankfully, much more tastefully decorated. Gray, white, and gold marbled columns marched along the walls, sheltering niches that bore busts of prominent Greek and Roman scholars. Burgundy hangings framed high windows in the rear, and soft gold panels graced the ceiling.

At the end of this echoing hall stood a tall double doorway, behind it, a gargantuan drawing room, and the Derwents.

They were grouped about a chaise lounge as though posed for a portrait. Lady Derwent reposed on the chaise, and Sir Gideon stood behind her, his hand affectionately on her shoulder. Leland stood next to his father, brimming with delight, his gray eyes fixed hungrily upon my regimentals.

In a chair next to Lady Derwent sat a girl perhaps a few years younger than Leland. Ash-blond hair and gray eyes made her a child of Sir Gideon, and the slightly shy, innocently curious looks she darted at me confirmed it.

The fifth member of the group proved to be a lady I had met earlier that year—Mrs. Danbury, a young widow of the same blond hair and gray eyes of the Derwents. She was not, in fact, Sir Gideon's daughter, I was informed as she was presented, but his niece.

Lady Derwent did not rise, but lifted her hand for me. Her blond hair was darker than her son's and going gray, and her eyes were light blue. The hand she offered me was thin and worn. As I bowed over it, I saw in her face a weariness, a gray tinge that her smile could not disguise.

Melissa Derwent went brilliant scarlet and looked frantically at anything but me when I bowed to her and murmured a greeting. She did not offer her hand, but curled her fingers into her palms so tightly I feared she'd hurt herself.

Mrs. Danbury did profess to remember me. Her smile was crooked, slanting one side of her mouth. "Captain

Lacey and I have met before. At Lord Arbuthnot's, was it not?"

I agreed that it was.

They plied me with Madeira, then we went through another pair of palatial doors, opened by two footmen, to a dining room with a ceiling at least twenty feet high.

As the ambience promised, the food brought in by the deferential footmen on trolleys was on par with what Anton gave me at Grenville's. I ate from fine porcelain plates with a heavy silver knife and spoon, and drank from crystal goblets that never seemed to be empty of smooth, blood-red wine.

I realized as we began that there was no other guest but me. I was the one they had lit the house for, had unfurled the red carpet for, had produced this meal for. Good lord.

By the time we reached the fish course, Sir Gideon had asked me to relate, in detail, my life in the army, from the time I'd volunteered to the day I'd decided to leave the life behind. I could not imagine why they'd want me to tire them with war stories, but they asked many eager questions, and Sir Gideon refused to let me steer the conversation elsewhere.

"Tell us of Mysore," he'd say eagerly. "Did you ride elephants? Was the Tippu Sultan as cruel as they say?"

"I have no idea," I had to reply. "When we at last stormed the city, the Sultan was dead, by his own hand or murdered, who could say. But yes, I did manage to ride an elephant."

I then had to tell them exactly what that had been like. Unnerving, to say the least. The elephants kept in the town of Seringapatam were gentle enough, being generally used as beasts of burden, but to ride atop a creature as large as a house, who regarded you as no more significant than a flea, had been a bit unsettling.

I remembered the hot, baking sun, the smell of vegetation struggling to live in the heat and dense air, the overpowering scent of elephant, and the faint cries of a very young Mrs. Lacey, as white and golden as Melissa Derwent, screaming that the elephant would eat her, or me, or at least kill us in some horrible way. I had laughed at her.

Had I ever been such an arrogant, blind fool? Yes, my conscience whispered to me. You were exactly that.

I was aware I'd paused too long, and hurriedly resumed my narrative.

Mrs. Danbury, seated next to me, listened to my tales as avidly as the others did, but her eyes crinkled in amusement at the rapt attentions of her cousins. But at least she listened. She could have flicked her fingers and sighed and given other signs of growing boredom, but she never did. Leland's stare, on the other hand, fixed and filled with hero-worship, made me most uncomfortable. I hoped to God that tomorrow morning he would not run off to join a regiment.

Lady Derwent ate very little. She toyed with her food, her thin fingers shaking slightly. Her smiles were as eager as her son's and husband's, but I saw her strain to keep her lips still, saw the cough well up in her throat from time to time before she hastily buried it in a handkerchief.

A dart of sympathy pierced my heart. These people, these innocent, kind, genuinely friendly people would soon know grief. I wondered how long it would be. From the waxen tinge to Lady Derwent's skin, I thought it possible she would not live much past Christmas.

I sought to entertain them as I could, pulling their thoughts from sorrows to come. I tried to keep the more gruesome aspects of my stories to a minimum, attempting to relate only the light and humorous. Louisa would like these people, I reflected. I would introduce them, when she recovered from her own present grief. In fact, it might be just the thing for her. She hated to wallow in her own sorrows, and this unworldly, innocent family would tug at her heart.

After we had consumed the elegant desert—a decadent pudding decorated with spun sugar—we moved back to the drawing room. Despite its ostentation, the room was well lived in. Workbaskets rested by chairs, books lay about, a lady's sketchbook had been tucked into a rack near a settee. The Derwents obviously spent every evening here, guests or no. They occupied every inch of this grand house, and with their charming obliviousness, rendering what could be cold and grandiose warm and friendly.

Melissa performed a minuet for us on a satinwood pianoforte. She played competently but nervously. I clapped politely when she finished and smiled when she curtseyed. Sir Gideon and Leland both seemed very pleased with me.

It was very late before I could introduce into the conversation the purpose for which I'd come. I tried to casually lead to the topic of Sir Edward Connaught, Major in the 43rd Light Dragoons, but in the end I had to bluntly ask if he were their acquaintance.

"Of course, my dear fellow," Sir Gideon replied. He handed me yet another tumbler of mellow, sweet brandy. "I do know him. He was one of those involved at Badajoz, was he not? With this killing of the man, Captain Spencer."

"Yes." So they did read the newspapers after all.

Sir Gideon turned an eager gaze on me. "I did not know Colonel Westin well, except from the club, poor chap. Did he really kill that wretched man at Badajoz?"

"No," I answered. "I believe Colonel Westin was innocent."

My words rippled through the room like the faint approach of a summer storm. The four Derwents turned to me, breathless. Even the footman, who had come with a tray of exquisite chocolates, froze to listen.

There was nothing for it then that I should tell them every detail of the Badajoz investigation, as well as about the death of Lord Breckenridge.

Never in my life had anyone listened to me with complete interest, begging me to go on when I slowed. Another man might have been flattered; I realized early on that they simply had very little connection with the outside world. I must have seemed larger than life to them.

By the time I departed—Sir Gideon insisted on calling his own carriage for me—I had made an appointment to meet Connaught in the company of Sir Gideon and Leland four days hence.

I also garnered another invitation for supper in a week. They suggested they make my invitation to supper a standing one once a fortnight. This idea delighted the four Derwents; Mrs. Danbury smiled in the background. I was uncertain whether to be pleased or alarmed.

As we pulled away, I looked back at the warm, bright house that had welcomed me so. They wanted me back. I would oblige them.

I was just settling back when my eye caught a brief movement. I peered past the coach lights into the darkness. Gaslight had been laid here, but in the space between the pale yellow globes the darkness was complete. I had seen someone, a man I thought, duck back into shadows.

It had been Brandon trailing me to and about Astley Close, but he had no reason to do so now. Disquiet settled over me. I asked the coachman to stop, told him what I saw, and to drive back to the spot.

When we reached it, the footman and I climbed down and examined the lane between the houses, but we found nothing, and no sign that anyone had passed.

CHAPTER 17

❦

THE next day I set plans in motion. If I were to marry Lydia Westin, and I had fixed upon this course, I had many things to do.

Long ago, when I had first married, I had swept my bride away in haste without thought to jointure and settlements. This time, I would go more carefully. Lydia was a widow, a very wealthy one. I had nothing. When Lydia married, unless wills and settlements said otherwise, I would gain control of her money.

I did not wish to be perceived as what both Allandale and Lady Breckenridge intimated, a fortune hunter. I would need to ensure that barriers would be set in place against me so she'd have use of the money for her lifetime, and leave it to whom she wished.

Then there was the matter of my first marriage. My wife had abandoned me fourteen years ago. I had no idea now where she was, or even if she still lived. When she'd first left me, I had been ready to drag her back in shame. Louisa had argued with me day and night against it. For abandon-

ing me, my wife could be tried for adultery, sentenced to
the stocks, or much worse. I'd come to realize that I
wanted her back only to assuage my pride, not to assure
her safety. The frail girl would never have survived the
censure and the ruin of her character, let alone trial and ig-
nominy. I'd finally convinced myself to let her go.

Later, I'd attempted to find her and so discover what
had become of my daughter, but the trail had gone cold. I'd
attempted a search several times, wasting money with no
result. I'd not found her to this day.

I could not have done much, in any case. Divorces were
costly and difficult to obtain—only those in the upper
classes managed to divorce and even then they could be
ostracized by their family and friends. An annulment could
be granted only under certain circumstance, such as my
wife and I being too closely related or one of us already
married to another party—or me being afflicted with
Colonel Westin's malady. So I had simply let her go. I was
a poor man with no prospects; likely she and my daughter
were better off without me.

I could, of course, simply declare her missing and
marry again without taking the trouble to search for her.
Others did so when wives or husbands traveled to far lands
and never came back. After seven years without word, one
could presume they had died and marry again without censure.

But I wanted to know.

Of course, my wife could very well no longer be living.
Her French lover might have abandoned her long ago, or
she might have married another. She might have died in
France. My first step was to find her, and decide what to
do after that.

I swallowed my pride and approached Grenville for advice.

First, he professed astonishment, because I had not yet
told him I had once been married. Once he'd recovered his
surprise, he admitted he knew a man of business in Paris
who could help me.

As he wrote the letter, he quizzed me. "You are certain you want to pursue this?" He sat at his ornate writing table in the center of a private sitting room, a chamber decorated with mementos from his travels. A scarlet tent hung from one wall, and fascinating gold miniature cats from Egypt occupied a shelf beside whimsically carved ivory animals from the Orient.

"Quite certain," I said.

"I do not mean your marrying Lydia Westin. For that, I can only applaud your taste. I mean delving into the past. I know from experience that sometimes the past is best left buried."

I paced across his silken carpet from Syria, my hands behind my back. "I cannot marry Mrs. Westin under false colors."

"I know that. But it was so very long ago. Who knows what person your wife has become? Or what her life is now? Is it worth raking up what was, for either of you?"

I stopped. "You mean she might have married under false colors herself? I have thought of that. I have also realized that she might no longer be living. But I cannot marry Lydia if I am anything but honest with her. Not discovering the truth might only haunt us later."

Grenville gave me a cynical smile. "Such as the previous Mrs. Lacey turning up on your doorstep threatening suit? Yes, I can understand why you would want to prevent that."

He did not understand in the least. I could not let Lydia marry a lie. Even if my first wife never turned up, I would know the lie, and it would fester. Also, I wanted to finish what had been between myself and my wife, now that I could finally put my hurt behind me.

In addition, I could learn what had become of my daughter. I probed that thought as delicately as I would an abscessed tooth. So long I had debated whether or not to search for my daughter and bring her home. By law, she belonged to me, not her mother. But always I feared the knowledge that investigation would bring. If I learned

Gabriella had died, I would know oceans of pain. If she lived, she would not know me.

"You do know," Grenville was saying. He toyed with the end of his pen and did not look at me. "There is a man in London who could find your wife quickly, and what is better, discreetly. With little disturbance to her, I imagine, if you so chose. I would even offer to put up the fee."

I eyed him coldly. "You mean James Denis. Know this, Grenville. I do not want Denis anywhere near my wife or anyone close to me. Imagine what he could do with such knowledge once he had it."

Grenville shrugged, but his mouth tightened. "A thought only. I will write to my man in Paris. But it may take time."

"I understand," I said.

He wrote his letter, and my quest was set in motion.

ANOTHER task I assigned myself was to keep an eye on the Spencer brothers. I visited Pomeroy again and told him of my interview with the Spencers, and asked him also to watch them. If John Spencer were carrying out his revenge, then he would strike again, probably soon. Breckenridge and Westin were dead. Eggleston and Connaught would be next.

Two days later, when I returned to my rooms from a meager dinner at the Gull in Southampton Street, I found young Leland Derwent waiting for me at the bake shop.

I shook his hand with pleasure. I had enjoyed myself at his sumptuous supper, where his family had made me feel welcome and wanted. He had brought with him another young man of his own age, whom he introduced as Gareth Travers. Travers was a clean-looking young man with light brown hair and small brown eyes. This gentleman, however, lacked the unworldly look of the more innocent Leland.

Because they were the same age, I concluded they were

school friends. Travers referred to Leland as "Eely," which I assumed was a somewhat dubious play on "Leland."

I hoped we could visit in the bake shop, with Mrs. Beltan's bread and coffee, but Leland said he had some important news to relate and wished to speak privately. He looked about as though he expected conspirators to lurk in the corners of Mrs. Beltan's cheerful and clean-scrubbed shop.

I led the way upstairs. The stairwell was dim and cool, with light filtering through the dirty skylight high above. I heard nothing from Marianne's rooms, which relieved me. I shuddered to imagine Leland encountering her.

I let Leland and his friend into my rooms and opened the windows against the stuffy heat. Leland looked about in awe, his gaze roving from the flaking plaster ceiling to the threadbare carpet. "Did you live in tents in the army, Captain?" he asked.

I limped back to the pair. "Not always. I lived in barracks or inns whenever we stayed put. Usually near the stables."

"So that you could ride out at a moment's notice?"

"So that we could better care for the horses. A cavalryman needs a decent horse beneath him, or he should simply stay in bed."

"With a pretty woman?" Travers said slyly.

"That is preferable," I answered with a straight face.

Leland did not laugh. He nodded, as though he were taking particulars for exams.

"You said you had news?" I asked, trying to steer them back to the reason for their visit. "Are we to move the appointment to meet Sir Edward Connaught?"

Leland jerked his attention back to me. "That is just the trouble, Captain. We will not be meeting with Major Connaught at all. He is dead."

I stopped. "Dead?"

Leland nodded unhappily. "He died in his sleep at his house in Sussex. Quite peacefully, his valet said."

I sat down on the chair behind me. So the killer had already struck again. I had asked Pomeroy to tell me if John Spencer made a move, and I'd heard nothing. I fumed in frustration and regret. "You spoke to the valet?"

Leland shook his head. "That is what the valet said at the inquest. Father had it from the magistrate."

"The inquest was already held? When?"

"Last week. By the time father found out what happened, Major Connaught had already been buried. Father knows the magistrate in that part of Sussex. The magistrate says the valet says Major Connaught was not feeling well one night. He went to bed, and sometime in the night, he died."

Travers looked at me. "The verdict was not murder, if that worries you."

Surprised me, rather. But then Breckenridge's death had been put down to an accident. Connaught *might* have died naturally, but I was unprepared to believe it. Of the four officers who'd known the truth about the death of Captain Spencer, only one remained alive.

One other man had known, too—Colonel Spinnet—and he had been killed along with Captain Spencer at Badajoz. I rested my head in my hands. If only the dead could speak.

I jumped to my feet before that thought fully formed. The dead *could* speak. The murderer had forgotten that.

Leland and his friend were staring at me in concern. I snatched up my hat and walking stick. "Come with me," I said.

They followed me in curiosity. Leland's coach waited nearby in Russel Street, and I commandeered it. Leland did not seem to mind. I directed his coachman to Mount Street and the home of Lord Richard Eggleston.

"Why are we going there?" Leland asked as we rattled toward Mayfair. "Do you think Eggleston will be murdered, like Lord Breckenridge?"

"Anything is possible," I answered, then I kept silent for the rest of the journey.

Lord Richard Eggleston's front hall was narrow and shadowy. Little thought had been given to decoration, and the walnut paneling and heavy-legged furniture of the last century darkened it still further. The butler who answered my knock looked like a shadow himself, thin and drawn and gray-faced.

"I regret to say that his lordship is not at home," he said. "He has gone to the country."

"His doorknocker is here," I said, motioning to the shiny doorknocker on the black painted door. Only when a family left town did the staff remove the doorknocker to show that the inhabitants were not in residence.

"Her ladyship is still here, sir. But I regret that she is not at home, as well."

Doubtless she was upstairs and still in bed. Not that I wanted to speak to the spoiled child.

"Is Lord Richard in Sussex, by chance?"

The butler's eyebrows climbed. *Sussex,* they said, as though horrified at such a gaffe. "His lordship's country house is in Oxfordshire."

In the opposite direction. But my elusive murderer had managed with ease to go to Sussex and visit with Major Connaught. He might manage Oxfordshire as easily.

"Excellent," I said. "I will write him there. If he returns, please have him look me up." I thrust a card at the butler, which he took with another disdainful rise of brows.

We retreated, and he closed the door on us. Far above, a curtain moved. Another servant looked out, perhaps, or else Lady Richard peered down to see who had knocked. We apparently were not fascinating, because the curtain dropped almost at once.

"May I take charge of your conveyance one more time, Mr. Derwent?" I asked in the act of scrambling aboard.

"Of course." Leland climbed happily in after me. Travers followed, curious but much more contained than the pup-like Leland.

We did not go far, only around the corner to South Audley Street and the house of the late Lord Breckenridge.

This hall was much less shadowy—in fact, anything from the past had been ripped away and the house redone in the utmost modernity. The butler who answered our knock was much younger and looked a bit harried.

He began his "I regret—" speech, but I pushed a card into his hand.

"If Lady Breckenridge truly is at home, please let her know that Captain Lacey requests a moment of her time."

The butler looked doubtful, but left us in a small, cold, square reception room and reported to his lady. Ten minutes later, we followed the butler upstairs to a sitting room, where Lady Breckenridge awaited us.

She wore mourning, as did Lydia Westin, but her gown showed off her plump bosom and arms, and its long skirt, falling in a graceful line to the floor, clung to her long legs. Otherwise, she looked much the same as she had in Kent— cool blue eyes filled with slight disdain, hair curled and pinned under a lace cap. The only thing missing was the cigarillo.

"Good evening, Captain," she said. "Did you call to convey your further condolences?"

Her gaze flicked to Leland and Mr. Travers. I had worried a bit about bringing the innocent Leland into this woman's presence, but Leland had insisted on not being left behind. He regarded Lady Breckenridge with polite indifference.

I introduced the two young men. Lady Breckenridge looked them over, frowned slightly, and returned her full attention to me.

"I called to inquire about your husband's papers," I said. "Do you still have them?"

"How flattering you are, Captain. My health is quite well, thank you."

I inclined my head. "I beg your pardon, my lady. I am anxious to review his letters or journals, or anything you will let me see. They might help me unravel who murdered him."

Her brows arched. "His horse murdered him."

I knew differently. I had suspected; now I *knew*. "If his

papers no longer exist, then I apologize for my intrusion. But if they do, may I persuade you to let me see them?"

She made a show of considering. Lady Breckenridge owed me nothing, and in Kent, I had insulted her greatly. I probably had not hidden my disgust well when I'd walked in and found her in my bed. Also I had not yet paid her the five guineas she'd claimed she'd won at billiards. I'd written her a vowel for it, and no doubt she'd call in the note soon.

"Very well, Captain," she said at length. "If my husband's private papers are still in the house, they will be in his study. I will have Barnstable escort you."

I nodded my thanks. I doubted she'd gone through his papers herself. She'd seemed singularly uninterested in anything involving the late Lord Breckenridge.

A small smile hovered around her mouth. "While you read them, perhaps Mr.—Derwent, was it?—can remain here and speak with me."

I glanced at her sharply. Her smile was all innocence, but her eyes said, *Ha, that's got you, Captain.*

I turned to Leland. He managed to look polite, but I sensed the acute disappointment that he would not accompany me. Solving a murder with me far outweighed the young man's desire to speak to widows ten years his senior.

I made my decision and hoped his father would forgive me. "Of course. Mr. Derwent would be happy to keep you company."

Leland bowed and responded politely that yes, he would. A more blatant lie I had not heard in a long while.

Lady Breckenridge rang the bell and the harried butler returned. At her instruction, the man led me and Travers down a flight of stairs and opened the door of a small study that overlooked a minuscule patch of garden.

The butler unlocked the desk. "His lordship kept his papers in here, sir. His man of business has not yet sorted through them."

"We will remove nothing, I promise," I said. My fingers twitched, itching to begin. "Thank you."

I seated myself when he departed, opened the drawers, and began to pull out their contents. I found stacks of letters and documents that had to do with properties and investments, instructions to Breckenridge's staff and stewards, and correspondence with friends and colleagues.

Travers looked at the piles in dismay. "Good lord, are you going to read all that?"

"I hope I do not have to," I said, beginning to sort things.

Travers dragged a chair to the desk, lifted a bound bundle of letters, and untied the ribbon. "What are we looking for?"

I gave him a grateful glance. "Anything that mentions the names 'Eggleston,' 'Connaught,' 'Spinnet,' or 'Westin,'" I said. "Or 'Spencer,' for that matter." I doubted we'd find anything about the last, but it was worth a try. Travers silently mouthed the names, and bent over the letters.

Lord Breckenridge seemed to have been quite orderly, or at least his secretary had been. Documents were neatly organized into categories, as were his private and business correspondences.

I skimmed through papers, opened letters, read through notes to his man of business or secretary. I'd hoped to find a journal that readily fell open to the entry reading, "This evening, we murdered Captain Spencer," but nothing came that easily.

In the end, Travers and I created a dismally small stack of papers that in any way concerned the gentlemen I'd named.

One was a letter from Eggleston, dated late in 1811. "I have oiled the levers as much as I dare," it said. "If Spinnet will not have you as major, Westin will not be brought to bear, I wager. They are close as thieves in the night. I do not believe the toad-eater Westin breathes when Spinnet tells him not to. But I have a few ideas on this, my friend."

He did not elaborate in this or any other letter. Whatever his ideas had been, he'd either kept them to himself or told them to Breckenridge in person.

Another letter documented a large sum of money paid out to Colonel Roehampton Westin of the 43rd Light Dragoons and a smaller payment to Colonel Spinnet. This had been dated January 1812.

I found a letter from Major Connaught written in June 1812 on the back of a letter from Breckenridge to him. I read this eagerly. Breckenridge had written: "Badajoz went well, confound you. I should be major. Have you taken a leaf from Spinnet's book? What must I do?"

Connaught's reply had been terse. "Do nothing. The wheels turn. Doing things will be the death of you."

Interesting, if cryptic. "Doing" had been underlined three times.

"Here's something," Travers murmured. He handed me the letter announcing Breckenridge's promotion from captain to major in November 1812.

I contemplated this for some time. It had always struck me as odd that Breckenridge had never risen further in rank than major. Lydia had mentioned that Breckenridge had pestered her husband to be made a colonel, but Westin had resisted. I myself had been a lieutenant for years, then made captain during the Peninsular campaign for some of my actions at Talavera. For a man of my wealth and standing—which was to say, none—that I had risen as far as I had was commendable. Breckenridge, wealthy, connected, and a lord, ought to have been at least a colonel. Wellesley—the Duke of Wellington now—had risen through the ranks from ensign to general by the time he was thirty-three. And yet, from all evidence, Breckenridge, no older than I, had struggled to make even major.

The letter of promotion had been signed by Westin, the regimental colonel. Breckenridge had won his rank of major—after Colonel Spinnet had died.

I sat back, my thoughts spinning. John Spencer viewed the rioting at Badajoz as culminating in the death of his fa-

ther. But what if we viewed it not as the murder of Captain
Spencer, who had come across the melee by chance, but as
the murder of *Colonel Spinnet,* an annoying cog in the
wheel who had prevented Breckenridge from advancing in
rank?

Eggleston had claimed he'd had ideas. Had one of those
ideas been to corner Colonel Spinnet, under cover of battle or the revelry following, and murder him? Had Eggleston seen in the rioting at Badajoz a golden chance to rid
his friend of the bothersome Spinnet?

I remembered the confusion at Badajoz, the drunken violence, the fear and horror, the futile attempts to stop it.
Who could have said whether a man had been killed by a
stray bullet or deliberately murdered by his fellow officers?

It was true that one of the four men killed Captain
Spencer. Which of them had pulled the trigger was still un-
clear, but from out of the chaos, facts emerged, and crystallized.

I sat back, drumming my fingers on the desk. Good
lord. No wonder they worried about what Westin would
say on the dock. He might very well blurt the whole tale.

"What is it?" Travers asked.

I came out of my reverie and forced myself to calm.
Discovering the murder of Spinnet did not mean I'd discovered who'd murdered any of the others, or even if the
same person had done so.

"I do not know," I said. "Maybe something, maybe
not."

Travers looked puzzled. He'd read everything over my
shoulder, and he seemed an intelligent enough lad. But he
had not been at Badajoz, could not know how justice had
gone up in the smoke of the siege fires and the aftermath.
Breckenridge and his friends had escaped that justice. At
least then. It was catching up to them now.

I swallowed the lump in my throat. "We should finish,"
I said, "and rescue poor Leland."

Travers gave me the ghost of a grin. "Do not worry about Leland. He is most resilient."

He must have been correct, because Lady Breckenridge gave me a look of angry annoyance when Travers and I arrived upstairs to fetch Leland. I had not played fair once again, her expression said. Leland took his leave politely, seemingly untarnished by his encounter with her.

She was right, I had not played fair. But I had needed truth, and had been ready to take it in any way possible. I bowed as I took my leave. Doubtless she would have spit on me if we had but been alone.

LELAND obligingly instructed his coachman to take me to Grenville's. I wanted to tell him of my findings and ask what he made of them. Grenville had a way of examining facts without emotion, turning them over to see if they were what I'd believed them to be. I thought sometimes that he ought to have been a barrister.

When I arrived at his home in Grosvenor Street, however, Bartholomew announced that Grenville had gone out and was doubtless at White's. I started to turn away, but the blond giant stopped me. "Wait, sir. I had an urgent message from Mrs. Westin's footman, William, a few hours ago. He asked that if you turned up here, would I send you down the road to the Westin house? Mrs. Westin is gravely ill, he said."

CHAPTER 18

❧

THE sweltering afternoon suddenly chilled. The day's
heat still radiated from the brick houses around me and
the stones beneath my feet, but I no longer felt it.

A strawberry seller approached the carriage, smiled at
the two young gentlemen. "Strawberries?" she queried.
"Ripe and sweet."

"Ill?" I repeated.

"Yes, sir," Bartholomew said. "The lad was fair agitated."

I thought of Louisa and her recent "illness." I thought of
Major Connaught dying in his sleep in Sussex.

I swung away and began striding down Grosvenor
Street in the direction of Lydia Westin's home.

"Captain?" Leland's voice floated after me.

It would make more sense to press my way down the
street in his carriage. But I could not stop. My feet moved,
my body automatically avoiding passersby, vendors,
horses, carriages.

I reached the Westin house. The doorknocker was still
gone. I pounded on the door with my gloved fist.

After a long time, and more pounding, I heard male voices inside, and then William pulled open the door.

He had been weeping. His eyes were red, and mucus puddled on his upper lip. "Sir!" he cried in obvious relief. "You'd better come in."

He reached for me, then stopped, as though just in time he remembered he was a footman and I was a gentleman. I heard Leland's carriage halt behind me, but I could not turn around, could not explain. I strode inside and left William to face them.

The other voice I'd heard belonged to Mr. Allandale. He hurried toward me as I sought the stairs.

"She is very ill, Captain." His handsome face looked strained. "I have sent word to her daughter. I believe the best thing we can do now is leave her alone."

I did not waste breath telling him what I thought of that idea. I plunged up the stairs. Pain nudged my bad leg, but I did not heed it.

I reached the second floor to see a maid rush from Lydia's room, a soiled basin in her hands. She hastened toward the back stairs and another maid scurried up past her with a clean one.

Below me, Allandale called, "Captain, there is nothing you can do."

I growled something and pushed my way into the bed-chamber.

Lydia lay among tangled sheets, her nightrail pasted to her limbs with dark sweat. The room was close and stinking, the window tightly shut. Lydia's face was dead white, her eyes red-rimmed. Her long hair hung in loose hanks, snarls of dark brown tangling her wrists and lying limply across her breasts.

As I entered, she put her head over the side of the bed and vomited into the clean basin that the worried maid had brought.

Spent, Lydia collapsed back into the pillows. Montague, the lady's maid, leaned down and wiped her mouth.

Lydia's dull eyes focused on me; her cracked lips parted. "Gabriel."

I came to the bed. I touched her forehead, her cheeks. She was warm, but not fever-hot, thank God. I brushed a lock of hair from her face.

A spasm wracked her, and she hastily sought the edge of the bed. When the episode ended, she lay back weakly, and Montague cleaned her mouth again.

I took her hand.

"Gabriel," she whispered. "I am so sorry."

This was not a miscarriage. This was something else. My fear did not abate.

"She needs a doctor," I snapped to the maid.

"She has had a doctor," Montague said at once. "He gave medicine. Shall I get more?"

"No!" Lydia jerked her hand from mine. "No, I cannot." Her eyes were bright, worried. "I will only bring it up again."

"Fetch her water," I said. "Lots of it. And brandy. At once."

Montague looked doubtful. "I tried to bring brandy before, sir. Monsieur Allandale said that she should not have spirits."

"Monsieur Allandale is a horse's ass," I said. "Fetch the brandy."

The maid with the basin whitened. Montague sent me an approving smile. "Yes, sir."

"Gabriel." Lydia tried to sound reproachful. Her lips trembled.

I laid my hand across her lower abdomen and gently pressed it. I met only softness like eiderdown. I looked quickly at her.

Her eyes were dark with hurt. "I am sorry, Gabriel," she repeated.

Fresh pain flowed through me. I had been wrong. She'd had a miscarriage. Just like Louisa.

At this moment, I finally understood the grief that had lived in Louisa Brandon's eyes for years. A child, a being, gone forever. A part of you, ripped away in an instant, and you helpless to prevent it. If John Spencer had done this, I would kill him myself.

My hand tightened on hers. Our gazes locked, hers filled with trepidation. Did she fear my anger? Some gentlemen, Brandon included, blamed their wives for miscarrying. An army surgeon had once told me that miscarrying was not necessarily the woman's fault. The child could be sick or dead, or there could be a disease of the womb.

I leaned down and kissed her forehead, having no words to reassure her.

Montague returned at the moment with a flagon of brandy and a pitcher of water. She set both on the night table, sloshing water onto the wood. I took up the glass she handed me, filled it with water, and added a liberal dollop of brandy.

I lifted Lydia's head and pushed the glass to her lips. "Drink."

She opened her mouth and let the liquid spill in. Almost instantly, spasms began, and she started to turn for the basin.

I held her fast, pressing my hand to her mouth. "No. Swallow it. Take a deep breath, and swallow."

She obeyed. Her body spasmed and trembled, but the water stayed down. For now.

I fed her more, small sips at a time. She began to breathe more easily.

"Monsieur," Montague said. "William says there are two gentlemen downstairs. They are arguing with Monsieur Allandale."

Leland Derwent and Mr. Travers. "Good," I said, tipping more brandy water into Lydia's mouth. "Tell Mr. Derwent that I want him to drive to Greenwich. He is to find a boardinghouse called The Climbing Rose, and fetch Mrs. Brandon from it. Tell her I need her here most urgently, and on the moment. Can you remember that?"

"Of course, monsieur. I will go at once." She suited action to word.

"Do not," Lydia whispered. "I do not want—"

I hushed her. "Louisa will know how to help you. I will not let you die, love."

Tears leaked from her eyes, and she looked away.

I fed her that glass of water, and another, until at last her heaving stopped, and she lay quietly. I gently stripped the sodden nightrail from her body and bathed her limbs in cool water. I lifted her in my arms while Montague smoothed out the bed, then I laid her down again, covering her with new sheets.

She slept for a time, her body still. I stayed next to her in a chair the maid brought for me. When Lydia twitched awake, I was there to soothe her. She sought my hand with hers, and I held it until she slept again.

Darkness at last consumed the room. I ordered the window open. Softer air slid through the closeness, the coolness breaking the heat.

The clock struck two. I dozed, Lydia's hand still in mine, her breathing even. I dimly wondered what had become of Mr. Allandale. Had he left in a huff? Or did he still wait downstairs, genuinely worried about his fianceé's mother?

I wondered as well, pain still holding its fist around my heart, if Lydia, now that she had lost the child, would want to marry me. The thought wove around the dark hours and made them darker still.

And then Louisa was there. I started from my doze to find her bending over me, her golden hair a pale smudge in the darkness. Her hand on my cheek was cool, her whisper soothing.

In the glow of the candle she held, she looked well again, no longer pale and wan. Unhappiness still lingered in her eyes, but she had regained strength.

She told me softly that I should go home and sleep. I could not obey the directive to leave, but I did seek a bed. The nearest one was in the chamber of the late Colonel Westin. By the light of my lone candle I saw that the room had been rigidly cleaned and stripped of any personal me-

mentos Colonel Westin might have brought home from his
campaigning days. It was an anonymous room, reflecting
nothing of the man who'd lived there.

I laid myself on the bed Lydia's husband had been
found dead in, and pulled the coverlet over me. I fell asleep
upon the instant, but I kept my face turned toward the door.

IN the bright light of morning, William, whom I thought
should long be remembered as a saint, brought me coffee,
soft, buttery croissants, ham, and eggs. I consumed the
feast hungrily, washed it down with more coffee, and tried
to see Lydia.

The maid stationed outside the door told me that I was
on no account to enter. When I started to protest, she added
that the order came from Mrs. Brandon, and would I please
meet Mrs. Brandon in the downstairs sitting room?

"Mrs. Westin is all right?" I asked in some alarm.

To my relief, the maid nodded. "Yes, sir. She is sleeping. Mrs. Brandon says all is well."

My knees went weak with relief. I turned on my heel so
the maid would not see my wet eyes and marched down
the stairs.

I waited not many minutes for Louisa in the sunny back
sitting room. She looked tired, but otherwise her eyes were
bright and alert, and her waxen hue had gone.

I held out my hands. She took them, rose on tiptoe to
kiss my cheek, and released me.

"You were supposed to go home," she said.

"Did you really suppose I would?" I looked at her. "It
was good of you to come."

"How could I not? Your Mr. Derwent came tearing in
begging me to return with him as though the whole town
were on fire. I feared . . ." Her smiled dimmed, and she
stopped. "We were halfway to London before he could tell
a coherent story."

I wondered what she had feared. That I, or Brandon,
had done something foolish?

"How is Lydia?" I asked.

"Weak. Quite weak. And tired. But she will mend. She ate some bread and kept that down. I believe the danger has passed."

"Good," I said fervently. "Thank you."

She gave me an unreadable look. Her golden curls were mussed, tangled strands of hair glinting in the sunlight. "You knew she was carrying a child?"

"Yes."

"And that the child is gone?"

My hand sought the curved back of the nearest chair. "Yes."

She looked at me for a long time. Emotions chased themselves across her face, but those that lingered were pity, and strangely, anger. After a long time, she said, "She did it herself, Gabriel."

For a moment, I could not comprehend her words. Then they sank into me, one after the other. My hand tightened. "I do not understand."

"She went to a quack, and she asked him to remove it. He did. What made her ill was the medicine he gave her after. To rid her of any lingering bad humors, he'd said."

I was so cold. My hands were numb, my blood moved like treacle. "But . . . why should she?"

Louisa gave a little shrug. Anger burned deep in her eyes, a palpable fury that her calm stance belied. "I do not know. She would not tell me. I was a bit sharp with her, I am afraid." She hesitated. "But she does feel great remorse. That is certain."

I was silent. My mind, my entire body, believed at that moment that if I did not speak of it, it would not have happened. She had not wanted the child. Fury like a howling demon rolled through me, and a voice from far away cried, *Why?*

"The child was mine," I said.

Louisa gave me an odd look. "She was ten weeks gone, Gabriel."

I stilled, staring at her, staring at the lips that had pronounced the words. The entire world dropped from beneath my feet. *"What?"*

"Her lady's maid said so, and Mrs. Westin did not correct her."

The enormity of it sent shock through me the like of which I had not felt in years. Lydia and I had been conducting our affair for five weeks. She had known. They all had known, she and Montague and William and Millar. I remembered the change in William when I had come to the house for the second time, his suspicion gone, his greetings welcoming. He'd known what they all had known, that I'd been brought in to become the father of Lydia's child.

Rage and grief and burning coldness swam through me. Louisa watched, powerless to help, Louisa who had stood by me throughout every hardship in my life.

"I wanted . . ." My throat hurt. "I was going to ask Lydia to marry me. I had taken steps to look for . . ." I took a shaking breath. "To make certain I could marry."

Louisa only looked at me. I wanted to storm and swear, I wanted to swarm upstairs and shake Lydia until she told me why she had done it, I wanted to break down and weep until I was sick.

I opened and closed my fists. "I do not . . ." I stopped. "Dammit."

She placed cool hands over my agitated ones. "Go home, Gabriel." She squeezed my fingers when I started to protest. "You cannot see her yet. She needs time to heal. As do you."

I drew a breath. "I do not want to see her." If I saw her now, I might hurt her. Anger was overtaking grief, and I did not want to let it have full rein.

"Then go home," Louisa repeated. "I will stay with her. I promise." She smiled faintly. "It is either that or face my husband, and I am certainly not ready to do that yet."

I put my hands on her shoulders, held her hard. I wanted to say things, but words lodged in my throat. But she knew. She knew everything I wanted to say, and everything I felt.

She could read me like no other. It had ever been so, even to the day that Aloysius Brandon had introduced me to her when she had been twenty-two years old and I had been twenty.

I left her. I went home, but I did not sleep.

I lay awake long into the afternoon. The events of the previous day jumbled themselves in my head—verbally fencing with Lady Breckenridge, the tedious chore of sorting through Breckenridge's papers, my excitement at what I had found, then Lydia's illness.

Questions beat at me like the wings of a terrified bird. She had lied to me, lied from the very start. She had gone to the bridge that night because, as the vulgar women there had put it, she'd been belly-full. I'd saved her life that night. She had looked at me and seen what I'd told her she'd seen—a fool who would fall on his knees and be her willing servant.

I had known even then I was being a bloody fool, and I had taken great pains to prove myself right.

What had Lady Breckenridge said? *Gentlemen have dashed themselves to pieces on those rocks before.* She had smiled at me with her world-wise eyes, knowing my fate better than I had.

I squeezed my eyes shut. Lydia's husband had only once been capable of copulation with her, no matter how many times he'd visited his doctor, no matter how many aphrodisiacs he'd tried. The chance that Colonel Westin had been the father of this child was remote. I remembered her declaring that she had gone to her husband's chamber the morning she discovered him dead, because, she'd said, *I wanted to tell him everything, the entire truth.*

I did not want to examine the truth.

The truth was that Breckenridge or Eggleston had murdered Colonel Spinnet that night at Badajoz. Westin had known the truth as well. And he'd died. They'd both died.

Another truth was that John Spencer had made an appointment with Westin the day of his death.

Kenneth Spencer did not like his brother trying to uncover the truth.

I did not blame him. Truth was a terrible thing.

I sensed the viscid fingers of my melancholia reaching through the hot, bright room to me. I had not been encased in my malady in months, and had even begun to believe myself free of it. Now it beckoned to me, dark and seductive.

Lie still, it said. If you do not rise, do not move, nothing can hurt you. Simply do nothing, say nothing, be nowhere.

I began to close my eyes to embrace it.

No. I slammed my eyes open. I would not. I forced myself from my bed, though it was like moving my limbs through heavy mud. Through great effort, I bathed, shaved, and dressed myself, then limped my way to Bow Street and the magistrate's house.

I found Pomeroy explaining to his patrollers that they were to go to Islington and wait for him. He looked up, annoyed, when I entered and asked to have a few words with him.

He dismissed his men with a sergeant-like bellow, and took me into the corridor. "What is it, Captain? Thought you'd have dragged in Lord Breckenridge's murderer under your arm by now. What is keeping you?"

"The last link in the chain," I replied tersely. "What have the Spencers been up to these last few days?"

Pomeroy shook his head. "Not much, sir. Living very quiet-like. Excepting Mr. Kenneth Spencer left London a few days ago."

I came alert, and the melancholia slid away. "Did he? Good lord, why did you not tell me at once? Did he go to Sussex?"

Pomeroy's brows climbed. "Sussex? No—"

"Oxfordshire then?"

"No, sir."

My heart pumped. "Where then?"

"I would tell you if you'll give me half a minute, Captain. He went to Hertfordshire."

I stopped. "Hertfordshire? Why?"

"Now I don't know, Captain. I'm only watching him to find out where he goes. Not why. That's your lookout."

"Well, what is he doing there?"

"I don't know." Pomeroy frowned. "I pulled my men off him, soon as he went somewhere harmless. None of your lordships live in Hertfordshire. And I need my men in Islington. Someone's gent killed his wife—at least so his wife's sister says, but no one's found the wife's body. Not the first time the gent's murdered his wife, so this sister says. Not the same wife twice, you understand, but wife one and wife two. Either he is very clever, or the sister's for Bedlam."

I could get nothing more helpful from him. I left Bow Street and returned to my rooms.

The cure for melancholia, or at least a method of staving it off awhile, was action. I acted. I wrote to John Spencer, asking to meet with him. I wrote to Eggleston in Oxfordshire, also requesting a meeting.

I then wrote Grenville to apprise him of what I had discovered. I had not spoken to him in some days, and he had not sent for me in his imperious way. I wondered what the devil he was doing, and at the same time was a bit relieved that I had not seen him and would not have to explain my current agitation.

I heard nothing from Louisa, and I sent no inquiry to her. If Lydia had wanted to see me, or if she had grown worse, Louisa would have informed me. Likewise I heard nothing from Brandon, from which I concluded Louisa had not yet returned to him or even sent word.

John Spencer replied by the next post that he'd see me. We met the next day in the same tavern we had before. He confirmed that his brother had gone to Hertfordshire to visit an old school friend, then I discussed Colonel Spinnet and my speculations with him.

He admitted that when he'd read Colonel Spinnet's diaries, he'd found references to Breckenridge wanting promotion, but he'd drawn no conclusion but that Breckenridge had been incompetent and annoying.

I asked Spencer if he would show me what he had found, and after regarding me sourly for a time, he took me to the rooms in Piccadilly he shared with his brother and fished out Spinnet's diaries.

I flipped through them eagerly. *Breckenridge,* Spinnet had written early in 1812, *that ass, yearns to be a major. He is the sort who likes to strut about in braid and lace, and knows nothing of commanding or warfare. Old Nappy will not go away because Breckenridge waves his balls about. I have told Westin to not, for God's sake—for all our sakes—give him major. Such a thing would make a mockery of all other majors in the Army.*

No doubt Breckenridge had not been pleased to hear this news.

It all fit now. Breckenridge and Eggleston had contrived between them to murder Spinnet and remove him from Breckenridge's road to promotion. Lydia's husband had known, and they had somehow persuaded him to take the blame when the deed came to light.

I thanked John Spencer and took a hackney back to Covent Garden market. As I emerged onto Russel Street, two large men closed on either side of me. Startled from my thoughts, I quickened my pace, but they kept with me. They steered me toward a finely appointed carriage, and when I turned, a third man had closed behind me.

I raged, but they had me penned in. I could not flee without a fight. James Denis had gotten wiser. I wondered if he would call in his favor today.

I would know soon enough. The three bullies more or less loaded me into the carriage, and there I found Denis waiting.

CHAPTER 19

HIS gloved hands rested on his elegant cane and he looked me over with cold eyes.

"Well," I said. "I am here. What do you want?"

"As blunt as ever. To answer you just as bluntly, nothing. Not yet."

The footmen closed the door, shutting me in the elegant, satin-lined box with the man I fervently despised. He was not very old—barely thirty if that—but he had already acquired more power than most dukes knew or understood.

"I have come to do you another good turn," Denis went on.

"Can I stop you?"

Sometimes, he smiled at my sallies, but today, his face remained mirthless.

He dipped his kid-gloved fingers inside his coat and pulled out two papers, each folded and sealed.

"I have information here that could be of great help to you, Captain. I offer to share it."

I eyed the crisp, folded sheets tucked between his

gloved fingers. "Why should you believe I will be interested?"

His expression did not change. "I know."

I shifted uneasily. "For what price? I already agreed to what you asked for Mrs. Brandon."

"The same price. You aid me when I need it."

"You are keeping tally of favors?" I asked dryly. "Favors in the debit column versus favors in the credit?"

His brow lifted the slightest bit. "Exactly, Captain. You are perceptive. I told you before that I wanted to tame you, but that is not quite true. What I want is to own you utterly."

I regarded him in silence. Outside, the daily life of Russel Street went on, the wagoners moving through to Covent Garden market, vendors crying their wares, street girls teasing passing gentlemen.

For years, I had given my life to the King's army, and I had given myself and my loyalty to a man I had admired more than any other. That man had at the last spit upon me, and the King's army had not done much better.

My freedom from both had been bitter. A man who could not give himself to another was useless and alone. But I at least wanted to choose who received my loyalty. James Denis did not deserve it.

"You need have no interest in me," I tried. "I care nothing for your business and what you get up to."

His fingers twitched on his cane. "That is not what I perceive. You dislike me and what I do and I foresee a time when you will try to stand against me. I cannot afford that." He paused. "You should take my precautions as a compliment. You at present are my most formidable enemy."

I snorted. "I am a half-crippled man with no fortune. I can hardly be a threat to you."

"I disagree. But we digress." He held out the first paper. "This is the name of the house in which Lord Richard Eggleston has hidden himself."

I scowled at the stiff edge of the paper hovering before

me. "That is no secret. Eggleston went to his country house in Oxfordshire."

"He did not. You took the evasive word of his butler as fact. He is not in Oxfordshire. He has gone to visit a paramour. I have written here the name of the paramour and the house in which they now dwell in lovers' bliss."

Denis's eyes were ice cold. He was handing me an answer, an important one. I had but to take it and know—and be obligated further to this man I reviled.

I think I hated him more at that moment than I had ever before.

In a swift movement, I jerked the paper from his fingers and broke the seal.

I had once remarked that Grenville had wasted half a sheet of expensive paper on a short letter. Denis had wasted one on one line—it listed a name, the name of a house, and the name of the county in which the house resided. Hertfordshire.

I stared at the words, dumbfounded. "Dear God."

Kenneth Spencer had gone there. And Pomeroy had sent no one to follow him, believing him to be traveling nowhere important. John Spencer had said his brother had gone to visit a school friend.

My pulse quickened. I looked from the paper to Denis, who looked, very slightly, satisfied.

I did not ask whether the information was accurate. I knew it was. Denis could uncover things with far more efficiency than any Bow Street Runner or exploring officer during the war.

He was holding out the second sheet of paper. I barely saw it, my head was so filled with implications of this new knowledge. One thing was certain—I had to go to Hertfordshire. Now.

"This," Denis continued, "concerns another matter entirely. It contains the direction of a lady called Collette Auberge."

I stared at him blankly. The name meant nothing to me. He went on, "She used to call herself Carlotta Lacey."

I stilled. Thoughts of Eggleston slid away like water from my hand.

This was the real information he offered me. The whereabouts of the woman who had been my wife—might still be my wife. One fact crystallized, hardening into facets I could touch, could cut myself on.

She still lived.

All I had to do was take that paper, open it, and discover where she was.

"You fucking bastard," I whispered.

He said nothing.

My hand trembled. I clenched it. I looked up at him, met his cold eyes.

"You are misinformed," I said, forcing my voice to be light. "I no longer require that information."

His eyes flickered the tiniest bit. In surprise? I felt a small amount of satisfaction. Not what you expected, was it?

He wanted me to crawl, even with greatest reluctance, but I would not.

He sat still for a second longer. Then he gave a faint shrug and slid the unbroken paper back into his pocket. "I will keep it safe for you," he said. "When you require it, you have only to ask."

Of course. If nothing else, he had learned how important the information was to me. He had a card he could hold until needed.

A few months ago, I had formed a half-crazed plan, born of frustrated anger, to kill him. Even if I hanged for it. Later, I had realized how foolish I had been. Now, I wondered.

Perhaps he was right. I was dangerous. I was someone he did not control, might never control, and he did not like that.

He returned both hands to his cane. "Then good day to you, Captain," he said.

As though his minions had heard his cue, the door opened, and I was ushered out.

•   •   •

MY emotions churned and tumbled as I returned home, packed my few belongings, and sent a note to Grenville. *We must away at once. Lacey.*

I knew the cryptic lines would catch his attention more speedily than an explanatory letter. It was uncharitable of me, but I took pleasure in summoning him the way he often peremptorily summoned me.

As I packed my shaving gear, Marianne wandered in. "Leaving again, Lacey?"

I looked up, ready with an irritated quip, but I saw her smile. She was goading me. "Yes," I answered shortly.

She wandered to my writing table. "An interesting journey? With Mr. Grenville, perhaps?"

"Not far. And yes, with Grenville."

I supposed she'd come to filch paper or ink, but under my nose, she opened my writing box, extracted a letter, and began to read.

The letter was one of Grenville's. I recognized the seal, a stylized "G" in red wax. I contemplated snatching it from her, then decided there was no harm. Grenville and I did not discuss dark secrets after all. I continued to pack, doing my best tō ignore her.

"He is quite fond of you," she remarked after a time.

"Grenville? I would hardly say that."

"Perhaps he fancies you."

I looked up. I expected to find her smiling at me, teasing me with barbs to hurt, but she was still studying the letter. Her eyes were tight. "No," I said. "He does not." I had seen enough of the world to know when a man preferred the company of another man to ladies, and Grenville had showed no sign of it.

"I see." She folded the letter.

"Do not toy with him, Marianne," I said. "He does not deserve that."

She dropped the paper back into the box. "Do you know, Lacey, if you were not so proud, you could get much from him. From what I hear, he has vast wealth, houses all over England, business interests in France and America. He could at least set you up in a house with servants to wait on you."

I fastened the leathers on my kit and hoisted it to my shoulder. "Yes, but I am that proud. So I stay here." At the door, I looked back at her. "You may have my bread and coffee in the mornings. I have already paid Mrs. Beltan for them."

A ghost of her usual smile lit her face. "How kind you are," she said in a mocking tone. "But do not worry about me, Lacey. I can take care of myself."

With this lofty statement, she brushed past me and made her way back upstairs.

I ate a half-loaf in Mrs. Beltan's bake shop, then went to the end of Grimpen Lane to await Grenville, reasoning he'd either send his carriage or Bartholomew with a message.

I found Colonel Brandon there instead. He was striding toward me down Russel Street, his own carriage halted among the press of wagons and carts. As usual these days, he exuded anger. He emanated violence in his every step, as though he just stopped himself drawing a weapon on me.

"Where is she?" he began once he was within earshot. "I know you have her, devil take you." His ice blue eyes were bloodshot, his mouth white. "Where have you hidden my wife?"

His voice climbed. Passersby stopped to stare.

I kept my own voice low. "I have hidden her nowhere. She does as she pleases."

His hands balled to fists, stretching his expensive gloves. "A man called Allandale paid me a visit. He thought it would interest me that one Captain Lacey had summoned my wife from a boardinghouse in Greenwich like a servant." He glared at me in fury.

Damn Allandale. I remembered giving the order for Leland to find Louisa and bring her back. Allandale must still have been in the house then. I imagined him gleefully relating the tale to Brandon. "Louisa?" I asked, incredulous. "Do you believe she would scuttle to me just because I called?"

"What I believe is that you knew where my wife was all along and you fetched her back to London at your convenience."

I lost my temper. "I asked her to look after a friend who is ill."

"But you knew. You *knew*." He stepped close to me. "I will kill you for this."

"At least you are no longer pretending you want reconciliation," I snarled.

"That was for Louisa's sake. You have forfeited any reconciliation with me."

"Thank God for that."

His eyes blazed. "I will have you up before a magistrate. If you are not hanged for the abduction and rape of my wife, I will shoot you myself."

If I'd had a pistol in my possession, I would have already potted him with it. "You idiot, do you realize that any move you make against me will ruin her? If you disgrace her, I will certainly find a way to kill you."

"Do not use her reputation to hide behind. Adultery is a foul crime and I will sink you for it."

I laughed humorlessly. "Lower than you have already sunk me? Ruining my life was not already good enough for you?"

His face and neck went brick red. "You took her from me. You must pay for that."

"You drove her away, you stupid fool. How much did they pay you to testify against Westin? What did they promise in exchange?"

His breathed hoarsely. "Why the hell can you not attend to your own affairs?"

We had collected quite a gathering now. Street girls stopped, hands on hips, to watch us. Mrs. Beltan had left her bakery. Mrs. Carfax and her companion slid by at the edge of the crowd.

"Because you drag me into yours," I answered him. "She is furious with you over Colonel Westin. Why the devil were Breckenridge's lies more important to you than your wife's good opinion?"

"You understand nothing."

"No, I do not. Were she mine, I would move the sun and the moon to please her. You seem to think you can do any idiotic thing you like and she will simply understand. No matter how slow-witted you are."

"She is *my* wife. Mine!"

"And that gives you leave to hurt her?" I was nearly dancing in rage now myself. "Know this. Whatever you believe, I care greatly for her honor. I would do nothing, ever, to disgrace her, even if that means not kicking you as I'd like to. Her honor is more precious to me than anything else in the world. Do you understand me?"

"So," he said, his voice shaking. "You choose between her honor and mine."

"Exactly, sir. And hers will ever win."

"Then for God's sake, why not tell me where she is?"

I looked him in the eye. "Because she asked me not to."

He stared at me for a long moment, then his lips pulled back in a fearsome snarl. "Damn you—"

He got no further, because Grenville's carriage and its fine matched grays on that moment stopped beside us.

Bartholomew hopped down from his perch, opened the door, and extended the stairs. Grenville leaned forward, his eyes alight. "Well, I am here."

"Where are you going?" Brandon barked. He blocked my way to the carriage. "Are you going to her?"

I gave him an irritated look. "Did you hear anything I've just said to you? No. I am leaving London on other business."

But he had a mad light in his eyes. "But you will go to her sometime. I will not let you out of my sight until you do."

"Oh for God's sake, get out of my way. I am in a hurry."

Bartholomew straightened from unfastening the stairs.

At any moment he'd offer his cheerful assistance to remove Brandon from my path, just as he had with Denis's
thug.

I could not let that happen. I suddenly remembered
Louisa's words—*He was a great man, full of fire and able
to inspire that fire in others.*

And he had been. I still saw it in him. His heart had
been broken, partly by me, partly by Louisa, and he was
bewildered and hurt. In any event, I could not let him simply be moved aside on the street by the towering
Bartholomew.

"Get into the coach," I said.

Brandon blinked at me. "Pardon?"

"I said, get into the coach. If you must dog my footsteps, we may as well make room for you."

Grenville's well-bred brows rose, but he voiced no ob-
jection. He must have sensed that even touching the ten-
sion between Brandon and me might shatter the very air.

Brandon fixed his gaze on me for a long, furious moment, then he flung himself up and into the waiting carriage.

ALONG the road north through Hatfield, I told Grenville—
and Brandon—about Denis's information and Pomeroy's
report that Kenneth Spencer had headed to Hertfordshire,
the same place Eggleston had gone to ground with his
lover.

The road we traveled was, fortunately for us, rather dry
this day. July had segued to August, with its still warm
days but cooler nights. The heat wave, I hoped, had broken.

This road marked the route that eloping couples took to
Gretna Green, in Scotland, where they could quickly
marry. I had eloped with my young wife, but we had not
had to travel the long way to Scotland. The man now sitting next to me had managed to obtain a special license for
us. That license had allowed us to marry at once, without

calling the banns in the parish church, thus preventing my father from standing up and voicing his most strenuous and foul-worded objections. If he had not managed to find impediments to our marriage, he would have created them. As it was, I had been of age, my wife's family had not objected—their daughter had been, in fact, marrying up—and I'd had the license in hand. My father had raged and roared, but the deed had been done.

Colonel Brandon now glanced at the paper I'd handed Grenville, and read the words with great disgust. "Eggleston's lover is a man?"

"Yes," Grenville mused. "And a famous one at that. Surprising. I had thought he was Breckenridge's toady."

"I would not put much past the team of Eggleston and Breckenridge," I said.

"Well, we shall see when we arrive." Grenville returned the paper to me, then pulled out a lawn handkerchief and dabbed his lips. "Forgive me, gentlemen," he said. "I am afraid—"

The coachman was able to halt and Bartholomew able to lift his master out just in time. Poor Grenville rushed into the trees to heave out whatever had been in his stomach. Brandon watched the procedure in great puzzlement but, to my relief, said nothing.

We reached our destination, a house east of Welwyn, at seven o'clock. The waning sun silhouetted a rambling brick cottage covered with climbing roses. It was a quaint little house, one entirely out of keeping with Eggleston. But it was remote, well off the road and five miles from the nearest village.

Grenville descended shakily from the carriage and came to rest on a little stone bench beside the walkway to the front door. He breathed in the clean, warm air, and color slowly returned to his face.

Brandon and I proceeded to the door. No one answered my knock. Above in the brick walls, casement windows stood open, but I spied no movement, heard no noise from within.

I knocked again, letting the sound ring through the
house. Again, I received no answer. On impulse, I put my
hand on the door latch. The door swung easily open.

Brandon peered over my shoulder. We looked into a
tiny entranceway, not more than five feet square, with open
doors on either side. I stepped in and through the door to
the left.

The large square room beyond was part sitting room
and part staircase hall. A ponderous wooden stair wrapped
around the outer walls and led to a dark wooden gallery on
the first floor. An unlit iron wheel chandelier hung from
the ceiling at least twenty feet above us. Dust motes
danced in sunlight from windows high above.

"Eggleston!" I shouted.

My cry echoed from the beams and rang faintly in the
chandelier. No footsteps or voice responded. No servants,
no paramour, no Eggleston.

Brandon whispered behind me, "Breckenridge truly
murdered Spinnet to gain his promotion? Dear God, I was
ready to defend him and his honor."

"Breckenridge had no honor." I put my foot on the first
stair, holding my walking stick ready.

"Lacey!"

It was Grenville, shouting from outside. His voice held
a note of horror. Brandon and I turned as one and sped out
again to the brick path.

Grenville was no longer on the bench. He had followed
the path around the house to the garden. Roses climbed
everywhere, twining through trellises, rambling across a
wall, tangling in the grass. On the other side of the wall,
which was about five feet high, the earth had been over-
turned into rich, dark heaps. Brambles of roses sat in pots,
ready to be planted.

As we approached, Grenville moved his stick through
the soil and brought up a white hand in a mud-grimed
sleeve.

"Good God," Brandon whispered.

The hand and arm belonged to a body lying face down

and shallowly buried in the dirt. Grenville brushed earth from the man's back, studying him in somber curiosity. In the back of my mind, I marveled that a man who grew nauseous traveling ten miles in a carriage could observe a dead body without a twinge.

He leaned down and, without regard for his elegant gloves, turned the body over.

I drew a sharp breath. Brandon gave no hint of recognition. Grenville got to his feet. "It's Kenneth Spencer," he said.

CHAPTER 20

HE had been dead perhaps a day. His face was drawn and gray, his eyes open and staring at nothing.

"His neck is broken," Grenville said slowly. "Just like Breckenridge's."

Brandon stared at him. "But Breckenridge fell from his horse."

"Did you see him fall?" I asked him.

"No. I told you, I found him on the ground. I thought . . ." He stopped. Grenville and I both watched him. He reddened. "Very well. I followed you when you rode out that morning. But I lost you in the dark and there was a mist. Later I walked the same route I thought I had seen you take. And I found Breckenridge. I thought it was you, fallen from your horse." His brow furrowed. "Good God. So you were right after all? Someone killed him?"

"But who?" Grenville asked, studying Spencer. "Eggleston?"

"No, I do not—"

A sharp crack sounded in the summer air and shards of brick from the top of the wall suddenly stung my face.

"Good lord," Grenville said.

Brandon and I were already on the ground. I reached up, grabbed Grenville's coattails, and dragged him down to the mud.

Brandon sat up, his back flat to the wall. "Where did the shot come from?" he whispered. "The house or the woods?"

"Devil if I know," I hissed back. "Too quick."

"The house, I think," Grenville offered. We looked at him. "The direction of the gouge the bullet made in the wall," he explained.

Another crack, and another pistol ball winged off the wall and whizzed over our heads. "Definitely from the house," Brandon muttered.

"My coachman and Bartholomew are still in front," Grenville said. "They could sneak into the house while he's firing at us."

"And be shot for their pains," I said sharply. "Both of them are in there."

Laughter sounded over our heads, from the open casement windows that overlooked the garden.

"Do we lie here the rest of the day?" Grenville asked. His usually pristine cravat was caked with black mud. "Or try to get in there and disarm them?"

"If there are two of them," Brandon said, "both shooting, or one reloads while the other fires, we could be here a long time."

"At least until dark," I said. I leveraged myself up to sit next to him, keeping my head well below the lip of the wall. Kenneth Spencer's outstretched arm nearly touched my boot. "We can slip away then. They won't be able to see well enough to aim."

Grenville gave me a sour look. "They could always hit us by chance."

"Or . . ." Brandon looked at me. "Do you remember the ridge near Rolica?"

I knew what he was thinking. Eight years ago, at the beginning of the Peninsular campaign, he and I had been trapped together on a path we had been reconnoitering. Our horses had been frightened away and we were cut off from our troop by a gunman who kept us pinned in a small niche in the rocks. We had lain there together, tense and certain we would not live the day, while bullet after bullet struck the rocks inches from where we huddled. Shards of rock had stung my face; Brandon's cheeks had run with blood.

We had escaped by sheer daring and not a little foolhardiness. I knew what he had in mind. It would still be foolhardy.

Running footsteps sounded suddenly on the brick path. "Sir? Are you all right?"

I sat up in alarm. It was Bartholomew, running to see if his master needed assistance.

"Go back!" Grenville shouted.

We heard the explosion of the pistol, heard Bartholomew cry out, heard the sickening crash of his large body falling to the brick path.

"Damn it!" Grenville sprang from his hiding place, his face and suit black with mold. He took three steps toward his fallen footman before another shot sent him scrambling back to the safety of the wall.

I risked a look. Bartholomew lolled on the dusty bricks between us and the house. He held his shoulder with his large hand, his glove crimson with blood. Grenville cursed in fury.

Brandon glanced at me. "We will have to risk it," he said in a low voice. "If the lad is hit again—"

"It was a stupid idea the first time," I said. "And I cannot run as fast as I used to."

"Neither can I," he shot back.

"What idea?" Grenville panted.

"He can only shoot one of us," Brandon said. "If we go in three different directions at once, we may get away. He cannot watch all sides."

I was perfectly certain that he could. When Brandon and I had agreed, on that ridge, to split and run, so that one of us at least would have a chance, we had each been willing to sacrifice our life so that the other could live. The ruse had succeeded, and we'd both survived. But Brandon had missed being shot in the head by a fraction of an inch.

He was asking for that same kind of sacrifice now. I saw in his light blue eyes that he was willing to take the chance that the gunman would hit him. *It does not matter what happens to me,* his expression seemed to say, *as long as we get the bastard.*

I remembered, dimly, why I had once admired him.

"All right," Grenville said. "Better than lying here."

Brandon nodded once. "Best to wait until he fires again. He'll need a moment to take up the next weapon."

"Unless he's got a double-barreled pistol," Grenville said.

"He does not," Brandon replied. "The sound is wrong."

I nodded agreement.

We whispered our plan. Grenville hissed a protest, but Brandon replied, "I am stronger. I can carry your footman, you cannot."

Grenville looked back and forth between us, then nodded glumly. "How do we draw his fire? Stick our heads over the wall?"

Brandon gave him a brief smile. "That is one way."

As it turned out, we needed to do nothing. Laughter sounded once more, then a pistol shot, then Bartholomew cried out in renewed agony.

We stared at one another in stunned horror, then Brandon hissed, "Now!"

We dove from hiding. Brandon ran toward Bartholomew, I around to the right of the house, Grenville toward the woods.

The gunman decided to shoot at me. I slammed myself around the corner of the house, pressing myself against the climbing roses. Thorns pierced my coat and skin.

Breathing hard, I risked a look back. Brandon had

seized Bartholomew under the arms and was dragging him toward the front of the house. I hurried around the other side to help him.

My shoulder blades prickled as Brandon and I carried the footman between us past the front windows and through the gate. Bartholomew was still alive, though his face was white, his breathing shallow, and blood stained his scarlet livery still darker red.

The coach had moved a little way down the road. The coachman had halted there, holding the frightened horses, not daring to leave them. Grenville came panting up, reaching the carriage the same time we did.

I wrenched open the door of the coach, and we slid Bartholomew in. Grenville climbed in beside him. When Brandon and I hung back, he stared down at us incredulously. "Come along, gentlemen. We will go for the magistrate."

I shook my head. "They might run, and we might never find them again."

Brandon said nothing. Grenville looked at Bartholomew, who lay groaning and bleeding on the luxurious cushions, then at us, waiting on the ground.

With a grunt, he swung down again. "Three against two is better odds. But at least, let us go armed."

He opened a cabinet under the seat and pulled out two boxes that each held two pistols and bullets and powder horns. He took two pistols himself and handed the other two to me and Brandon. We loaded and primed them, and then filled our pockets with extra balls and powder.

Grenville sent the carriage off with a curt directive to his coachman to find a constable and a surgeon. He joined us, his anger palpable.

Brandon led the way back to the house. It felt natural to follow him as I had for many years, across India, Portugal and Spain, and into France. At one time, I would have followed him to hell itself. Too much had passed between us since then, but somehow, as I kept my gaze on his broad back while we moved stealthily against the blank wall of the house, I felt a glimmer of the old bond the two of us had so thoroughly pulled apart.

We abandoned the idea of entry through the front door. We could go only single-file through the tiny hall, and anyone on the gallery could pick us off one at a time. Brandon forced open one of the downstairs windows and entered that way. While he made plenty of noise doing so, Grenville and I crept in through the cellar door we found on the left side of the house, then up through a cool deserted kitchen and back stairs to the ground floor.

Silence met us. I peered into the staircase room and spied Brandon on the other side, waiting in the shadows. We had agreed to try to disarm the two upstairs or, barring that, to at least pin them down here until the constable arrived.

One of them stepped out onto the gallery, a pistol in either thick hand, an affable smile on his face, just as I remembered from the boxing match at Lady Mary's.

"Evening, Captain," Jack Sharp said cheerfully. He peered into the gathering shadows in the hall, then upended his pistols against his shoulders. "Thought I'd frightened you off."

I said nothing. When I'd read his name on the paper James Denis had handed me, many things had fallen into place. In Kent, I had reasoned that only a very strong man could have broken Breckenridge's neck. A very strong man had been on hand—the pugilist Jack Sharp. I had dismissed him at the time because he had been laid out by the farm lad, as Bartholomew had told us, but that entire scene had likely been a farce. Jack Sharp, probably instructed by Eggleston, had simply taken a fall, making certain to show a great deal of blood on the way down.

"I won't shoot you, sirs," Jack Sharp called down. "Not my manner, not at all."

We remained in place, and silent. I believed Sharp—he probably preferred hand-to-hand combat, a bout in which the strongest and most skilled would win. But Eggleston waited up there, and I imagined *he* would shoot anything that moved.

"Stalemate, then, gentlemen?" Jack said. He spoke no differently than he had in the garden at Astley Close, cheerful, friendly. He was a mate you would join at the local tavern. "Well, well, if you will not come up, I will come down."

"No!" Eggleston's voice rang out.

Jack kept grinning at us. "Now, now. I'll leave my shooters here." He leaned down and dropped both pistols to the floor. They clanked heavily against the boards. "They are honorable gentlemen. We'll just have us a chat, me dears, won't we?"

He was spoiling for a fight. He wanted to fight the three of us at once, to see what he could do. It was a challenge to him, a game. I saw no remorse in him for Kenneth Spencer's death, nor for Breckenridge's.

He was wrong if he thought I would not shoot an unarmed man. I would shoot him even if Grenville and Brandon were too punctilious to; I'd shoot to bring him down until the constable came to put him in chains.

Eggleston stepped into the light. His face was white, his blue child's eyes protruding. "Lacey, you interfering bastard, go away!"

Jack grinned. He turned and pattered along the gallery to his lover and kissed him on the mouth. Then, his manner still oozing friendliness, he turned back and started down the stairs.

"Go away, all of you!" Eggleston shouted desperately.

Jack kept plodding toward us. Brandon came forward to meet him, pistol ready, despite my signaling for him to stay back. If he got in my way, I could not fire at Sharp.

Behind me Grenville quivered with rage. "If we rush the bastard—"

"Eggleston will shoot us," I said. "And Sharp probably has a knife up his sleeve."

Brandon reached him. "I am arresting you, sir," he said to Sharp in stentorian tones. "For the deaths of Colonel

Roehampton Westin, Lord Breckenridge, and Mr. Kenneth Spencer."

Brandon carried power in his voice. So he had sounded in the days when he'd commanded an unruly band of cavalry troops and kept them all alive. For a moment Jack Sharp gazed at him in astonished apprehension, the face of a clever pickpocket who'd at last been nicked. Then he moved.

Everything happened very fast. Ringing footsteps sounded without, and a man burst through the door. It was John Spencer. Before I could be startled at his sudden appearance, or wonder that he'd followed us here, he ran at Jack Sharp, howling murder, his face a mask of rage and grief.

A blade flashed in Sharp's hand. Brandon grabbed Spencer, stopping him just before he reached Sharp. Eggleston aimed his pistol at the both of them.

I saw this in a split second before I was racing up the stairs to Eggleston. Sharp pain flashed through my leg, then it went numb. I hurled myself at Eggleston, even as he fired.

The shot went wide. The ball struck the chain of the heavy iron chandelier, shattering the links. Below, Brandon hurled Spencer out of the way, just as the iron wheel of the chandelier crashed down.

Eggleston screamed. Grenville, swearing hard, ran forward. John Spencer, panting, turned back in horror.

Brandon lay face down beneath the chandelier, the wheel of iron pinning him. The legs of Jack Sharp protruded from the other side of the massive thing, and he lay still beneath it, his face a mass of blood.

Eggleston screamed again. He came at me, fists waving. I ducked a blow and punched him full in the face. He went down, crying and cursing. I hit him again, and he collapsed to his hands and knees to the smooth floorboards.

I wrested the pistol from him, searched his pockets for any other weapon, then seized him by the collar and marched him down the stairs. The numbness in my leg wore off on a sudden, and the pain returned with head-spinning fervor.

"Lacey," Grenville said. He was crouching by the fallen chandelier, his hand on Brandon's shoulder.

I dropped Eggleston to the floor. He folded up into a ball and wept.

"Sharp is dead," Grenville told me.

"Brandon," I said hoarsely.

"Still alive. But this damn thing is heavy. I fear that . . ."

He did not finish the thought, and I did not want him to. The iron wheel lay across Brandon's lower back. The chandelier could have crushed his legs, or the organs in his body. I might be facing Louisa tonight, explaining why I had killed her husband.

John Spencer, still breathing hard, took hold of one side of the chandelier. I, too, locked my grip around the cold iron wheel, my hands shaking. Brandon lay utterly still.

Spencer and I strained to lift the thing. While we held the chandelier raised, faces reddening, Grenville grabbed Brandon under the arms and dragged him from beneath.

We rolled the chandelier away, exposing Jack Sharp's crushed and dead body. Eggleston cried out and crawled to him.

Grenville had turned Brandon over onto his back. I sat down on the floor and gently lifted Brandon's head to my lap.

His breathing was ragged and shallow. I gently slapped his face, his beard stubble scraping my fingers. "Brandon, old man," I said. "Wake up, damn you."

He did not move. His face was pasty white, and gray lined his mouth.

"Do not dare to die on me. Louisa will never forgive me." I patted his face again. "You know what she will say. 'Could you not take care of my husband any better than that, Gabriel?' And then she will *look* at me. You know how she does."

I kept babbling. Stupid, stupid—It had been just like him, to try to save Spencer at the expense of himself.

Never risk yourself unnecessarily, he had once told me. *But when it is necessary, by God, go out fighting, and make every blow count. Make your sacrifice mean something.*

He had brought down a killer and saved Spencer's life and mine and Grenville's.

Grenville's muddy buff boots, buckles coated with grime, stopped next to me. His leg bent, and his knee in fine lawn breeches touched the board floor. He held a pewter cup of strong-smelling spirits. "Help me make him drink."

I raised Brandon's limp head. His hair was graying more than I'd noticed before, white strands mixing with the black. He'd be completely gray in another few years.

Grenville guided the goblet to Brandon's lips and poured a few drops of liquid inside. For a moment, Brandon lay unmoving, then his body spasmed weakly, and he coughed. Ruthlessly, Grenville poured more brandy into his mouth. Brandon coughed again, harder, then his eyelids moved and he groaned.

His light blue eyes remained blank for a moment, then his gaze fixed on me, and his pupils widened.

"Oh hell," he said. His voice was little more than a croak. "It's you."

CHAPTER 21

I feared John Spencer would kill Eggleston before the constable arrived. The young man was beside himself with grief. I guessed correctly that he had followed Grenville's carriage here to Hertfordshire, as he confirmed. When I had left him earlier that day, excited about Spinnet's letter and my conclusions, he had grown suspicious of me and followed.

Upon arriving at this house, he had heard the noises inside, walked around the house to see if he could discover another way in, and had found his brother lying dead in the garden.

"You killed him, you dung-eating son of a bitch," he said now.

Eggleston shook his head hard. "No! I killed no one. I swear to you. Jack did it. He said Mr. Spencer was spying upon us. And he was."

We had removed Jack's bloody body to a shed outside, and laid Kenneth Spencer more reverently on the grass.

Brandon lay on his back on the hearth rug in the sitting

room. One of his legs had broken. My own leg ached and throbbed, but I had not broken it, as I'd feared. I'd simply wrenched and strained the muscles. I often forgot I could no longer run about with impunity. I sat now in a chair near Brandon, resting my foot on a stool. It did not help.

We had bound Eggleston's hands with rope found in the shed and sat him on a chair. Grenville held a loaded pistol loosely in his hands. He, too, was angry enough to use it.

"I for one will be happy to see you hang," Grenville said. "For my footman, if nothing else."

Eggleston's round eyes went rounder still. "I did not shoot him! I swear to you. It was Jack."

"You'll hang for Westin's murder," I said. "Or Spinnet's. Or Captain Spencer's. Which would you like?"

Grenville shot me a puzzled look. "Westin?"

My feelings of loyalty to Lydia had dimmed, and I decided it was time for truth. "He was murdered. Stabbed in the neck. His wife pretended he'd died accidentally, because she feared the savagery of the newspapers."

Grenville's eyes widened. "Good lord. You do know how to keep secrets, Lacey."

"He is ever the champion of the ladies," Brandon said dryly from the floor.

"I do not understand this," John Spencer barked. "He murdered Colonel Westin?"

"Yes," I said. I eased my leg to a slightly less painful position, gritting my teeth as I did so. "He learned that Colonel Westin had made an appointment with you and your brother, and feared that Westin would tell you the entire truth—how he and Breckenridge had conspired to murder Colonel Spinnet back in 1812 and make it look as though he had died in the rioting at Badajoz." I looked at Eggleston. "Captain Spencer saw you shoot Spinnet deliberately, did he not? He was so horrified, he ran to try to stop you. So he died as well."

Eggleston stared. "How do you know this? Westin did not tell anyone! He swore to us."

"He kept his word," I said. "Of course, you and Breck-

enridge made certain of that to the last. You and he together went to see Westin the day he died, early in the
morning, probably, say, when you would be returning from
a gaming hell and Breckenridge would be up for his early
ride. You either made an appointment with Westin, or he
saw you approach, but he must have let you in himself, in
his dressing gown, and taken you quietly upstairs."

I gave him an inquiring look. Eggleston only stared.

"You must have argued with him long," I continued.
"Perhaps he agreed to keep silent, perhaps he did not. You
must have known some secret Westin desperately did not
want revealed, but perhaps Westin had decided he would
rather humiliate himself then let you get away with murder. I imagine Breckenridge was not satisfied, in any event.
I think it was he who actually murdered Colonel Westin.
Just as he murdered Spinnet at Badajoz, and shot Captain
Spencer."

Eggleston nodded readily. "He did. He killed Spinnet
because he knew Spinnet would forever block his way to
promotion."

I gave him a hard look. "The plan was yours. It smacks
of the kind of sneaking subterfuge you would dream of.
You advised him not to challenge Spinnet directly, oh no.
Instead, take away a good man's life and hide it in the
chaos of the destruction around you. What was one more
death in the Peninsula campaign, after all?"

Eggleston put his hands to his face. "It was not like that.
We saw an opportunity. That is all."

"Which you urged Breckenridge to take. Did you urge
him on to kill Westin?"

"No, no. Breckenridge decided that himself. Westin refused to listen to us. He vowed he would reveal all. When
he turned away, Breckenridge took out a stiletto and
pressed it right into Westin's neck. He died at once. Went
down in a heap."

"So," I continued. "You tucked him up in bed, rejoicing
that so little blood had been shed to give things away, and
let yourself out of the house."

Eggleston's throat worked. "Yes. That was it."

I wanted to rise from the chair and kick him, but I was too tired. My melancholia danced just beyond my vision.

"The death of Westin must have upset you greatly," I said. "Soldiers dying at Badajoz was one thing, but I think you realized after Westin's death that Breckenridge was a cold-blooded killer. You were a witness; who knew when he might turn on you? So you sought the comfort of your lover. Jack probably advised you to leave everything to him." I paused. "He killed Breckenridge, did he not?"

"He did," Eggleston whispered. "To protect me."

The knowledge that I had been right all along comforted me little. "Sharp must have killed Breckenridge somewhere in the garden. Perhaps you had not known he would do it right then. You decided it best to make his death seem an accident, a riding accident—Breckenridge was so fond of rides at ungodly hours of the morning. I doubt you were prepared to handle the body, so Sharp did it all, am I right? He must have, because you would not have made the mistakes he did. He saddled Breckenridge's horse, using the saddle I'd left, not realizing that a cavalryman who took the trouble to travel with his own saddle would certainly use it. He put my coat on Breckenridge's body . . ." I paused. "I confess, I do not know why he should, or why Breckenridge was in shirtsleeves at all."

Eggleston flinched. "They were boxing. In the garden. Sharp offered to show Breckenridge exactly how he'd been felled by that farmer's lad. Breckenridge took off his coat." He swallowed. "I could not find it in the dark."

Grenville sucked in a breath. "Good lord. So Sharp must have found Lacey's coat and put it on him. He reasoned one gentleman's coat was as good as another."

"I thought it so amusing," Eggleston said. "Breckenridge was so careful about his clothes. And to be caught dead in a shabby coat several years out of date . . ." He wheezed a little and tears leaked from his eyes. "I laughed so."

I did not find it in the least amusing. The sniveling little twit deserved to have John Spencer lay him out.

Grenville still looked puzzled. "But Major Connaught,"
he said. "He died peacefully. Or seemed to."

Eggleston shook his head fervently. "We had nothing to
do with that. He really did die in his sleep. That was a bit
of luck." He eyed us with the smugness of one who was at
least innocent of *something*.

"No," I corrected softly. "Your luck changed when he
died. His death renewed my interest in deciphering the
truth. And I found it. Colonel Spinnet was the key."

John Spencer cleared his throat. His eyes were red with
grief, his hair tangled where he'd raked it. "What about my
brother? Why did you kill him?"

Eggleston met his gaze with something like defiance.
"He was spying on us," he repeated.

"He must have worked out the truth," I said. "And came
here to confront you. He was just as grieved as his brother,
even if he kept it quiet. You are not blameless in his death."

"But I killed no one," Eggleston protested. "Jack and
Breckenridge did it all."

From the fireside carpet, Brandon opened his eyes.
"You were an accomplice to five murders. You will definitely hang for that, my friend."

His brisk, matter-of-fact voice seemed to penetrate
Eggleston's haze of denials. His eyes widened. Then the
gentleman who had sneered at my clothes and dismissed
me as less than nothing wet himself, then fainted.

LORD Richard Eggleston's trial was held a few weeks later.
His brother, the Marquis of Hungerford, protested on the
strongest terms, but there had been no denying that Eggleston had, at the very least, shot at me, Brandon, and
Grenville, and had been party to Kenneth Spencer's murder. Grenville's word on this counted for much. The marquis, however, pointed out that we could produce no
concrete evidence that Eggleston had been present at the

deaths of Breckenridge or Westin. In the end, the Lord Chief Justice and the marquis made an agreement that if Eggleston wrote out a confession, explaining all, he could commute his sentence to transportation.

So Eggleston's argument that he had not actually murdered any of these gentlemen won out. He wrote the confession and signed it, and was taken to Newgate to await passage on a ship to New South Wales. I had no doubt that his wealthy brother had ensured he'd have a fine room in the jail with servants and wine and food. Such were the wheels of justice for the privileged.

Lady Richard, his child wife, I learned later through Louisa, had gone to the north of England to live with the marquis and his wife.

After the sensational trial, the journalists turned to other fodder. Pomeroy had discovered the bodies of two women in a cellar in Islington and arrested the gentleman who had married, then murdered, them. He was quite pleased with himself, and the journalists, Billings included, lauded him.

Louisa Brandon returned home after I dragged her husband back from Hertfordshire with his leg in splints. She had nearly flown from the carriage that had deposited her at her front door and rushed to her husband's bed with rage and fear in her eyes. I walked away from their reunion and closed the door on their rising voices. I did not see or hear from either of them for a long time after that.

Bartholomew recovered from his gunshot wounds, though for a long time he limped from the bullet that had pierced his leg. Grenville had spared no expense on surgeons and doctors, and the lad had lived like a prince while he convalesced. He was young and strong and brave-hearted, and he recovered quickly.

August slipped into September. The days at last cooled, and the evenings became crisp. Grenville talked of going to the country to go hunting. He invited me along, but I'd had enough of country houses. The vice of the city at least wore a face I could recognize.

In mid-September, long after I'd believed Lydia Westin must have quit Town herself, she sent for me.

WILLIAM greeted me with subdued wariness. He led me in silence to the upstairs room with the pianoforte and Lydia's portrait. He ushered me in, then took the double doors one in each hand and backed out, closing us in, leaving us alone.

Lydia sat on a damask chair, her hands in her lap. She avoided my gaze as I entered. She had given up mourning black and wore a gray high-necked and long-sleeved gown trimmed with lighter gray. The costume did not become her; her face was too pale for it, though it made her midnight blue eyes bluer still.

If only she would look at me with them.

I moved slowly forward, resting my weight on my walking stick. When I reached the halfway point between door and chair, I stopped.

Silence hung in the air, broken only by the ticking of the clock and the faint crackle of the fire. The September day had turned cool.

"I had not thought you would come," she said.

"As ever," I answered, trying to keep my voice light, "I fly to your side when you call."

Still she would not look at me. She transferred her gaze to a corner of the carpet. "You cannot imagine how long it took me to work up the courage to face you. Even now I falter."

"You have no need to."

My anger at her had long since ground itself to dust. After the arrest of Eggleston, my melancholia had taken over, as I had known it would.

The last time I had discovered the identity of a murderer, the sheer cruelty of it all had sent black waves of melancholia crashing over me. I had been expecting it this time; nonetheless, the malady had laid me in bed for nearly a fortnight, and had not yet completely subsided. I currently could only view the world through a fog, as though I watched everything through a thick, waved glass. Although I walked and spoke, I often could not say whether what I did was real or the vestiges of a dream.

She smiled faintly. "Before you remonstrate with me, or scold me, allow me to thank you for clearing my husband's name. Lord Richard's confession absolved him of all crimes in the Peninsula. The *Times* even praised Roe for his bravery."

I looked straight ahead. "Yes, I read the story."

"Well." Her voice was soft, whispery. "I wanted to thank you. To see you when I did it. Writing seemed—an inappropriate method."

"I would have treasured such a letter."

At last, she looked at my face. Our gazes met, stilled. "Please do not say such things when you do not mean them," she said. "I know that you long to tell me what you think of me."

I slowly closed the distance between us. I reached down and lifted her hand, the one with the heavy gold and sapphire ring. I stroked my thumb gently across her fingers, the same smooth fingers that had caressed me while we lay together in her bed.

"I did not come here to scold you." I lifted her hand and pressed it to my lips. "But to learn whether you were well."

She watched me kiss her fingers, then she withdrew her hand and crumpled it on her lap. "Please, Gabriel, do not be kind to me."

"If you prefer that I rail at you like a drunken waterman, I am afraid I cannot oblige."

"It might be easier for me." She lifted her gaze and looked at me fully. I saw in her eyes everything that had been between us, and great pain, and loneliness. She was lonely because of the grief she faced, a grief she could not share.

"You are a good man, Gabriel. You did not deserve what I did to you—tried to do to you. In the end, I simply could not." She tore her gaze away. "Oh, please, sit down. I cannot bear you standing there looking so patient."

I was not patient. Anger was stirring beneath my fog, and the mists had cleared a little. I obliged her and seated myself on the divan.

She studied the carpet again, seeming to gather strength from the gold and black oriental pattern. "Do you know why I made my way alone that night to the bridge?"

I remembered her sliding through the rain, her dark cloak blending with the night, the fire of diamonds in her hair, her lovely, distressed face beckoning me to follow, follow.

"You wanted to end your life," I said. "Because you carried a child that you dared not bring into the world."

She looked at me, startled. Then she shook her head. "No, Gabriel, I had not intended to kill myself. I would never have left my daughter alone, no matter how wretched I was, believe that." She paused. "It was not to end my life, much as oblivion would have been sweet to me at the moment. I went to meet someone."

"The beggar who tried to cut you."

"He was not a beggar." She drew a breath. "I had been told to meet him there, by a—a woman to whom I spoke about my predicament. She assured me that this man would tell me where to go to rid myself of—my so unfortunate burden."

I remained still. Likely she had managed to consult a high-flying courtesan or an actress who would know all about removing unwanted children.

She went on, her face pale. "When I met the man, I did not like him. He was wretched and stank and leered at me so. He wanted to lead me to this doctor himself. I suddenly did not want to follow."

I nodded. "You were no doubt wise. He and your high-flyer might have been conspirators, and he leading you off to rob you."

"I thought of that. I realized how utterly alone I was. I

tried to run away. He took out his knife. And then you were there."

I ran my finger over the engraved brass head of my walking stick. "I am pleased that I at least saved you from danger."

"I was so grateful to you." She smiled a little. "Do you know, that was the first time in my life that someone had taken care of *me*. It has always been me, you see. I looked after Roe, and Chloe. Neither of them was ever very strong. I was the one who held my head up and faced it all, no matter how terrible, and kept them safe. But that night, I at last learned what it was to lay my head on someone else's shoulder. I so craved that comfort, and you offered it for nothing."

I remembered how she'd twined her arms about my neck, pressed her lips to mine, how she'd whispered, "Why not?"

"I am pleased I was able to help," I said.

She gave me a rueful smile. "Always so polite. By rights, you should hate me."

I looked away and let out my breath. "I cannot hate you, Lydia. I admit that I tried to when Louisa made it clear that the child was not mine." I paused. "I gather from your actions that the child was not your husband's either."

"It was not. Roe and I . . ." She stopped, grief filling her eyes. "No, it was not his."

"I know about your husband's—difficulties," I said.

She glared at me, suddenly indignant. "You know? How the devil could you? Did Richard Eggleston—"

I held up my hand. "You asked me to discover the truth and so clear your husband's name. I am afraid that when one searches for truth, one uncovers it all, not simply the parts that are not ugly. I am sorry."

She sank back. "Oh, it does not matter anymore. I resigned myself long ago that I would never have a natural marriage. After a while, I no longer cared. I could still be a partner to him, if nothing else."

"But he gave you Chloe."

She nodded, a faraway look in her eyes. "Yes, on a moonlit night in Italy. I was so happy. I thought everything would be all right after that. But it was not. It never was."

I felt sweet relief. If she told the truth, then Grenville had been wrong. She had not taken a lover to give herself Chloe. She was innocent of that at least.

We sat in silence for a time, listening to the crack of the flames and the wind in the trees outside the window.

I still did not have one piece of information. "I could have wished that you had told me from the start what Eggleston's hold over your husband was."

She glanced at me uneasily. "Hold?"

"The reason your husband promised to go to the gallows for what Eggleston and Breckenridge had done."

Color filled her cheeks. "I did tell you. For honor."

"That is true, in part. Colonel Westin, from all I have learned, held honor in high regard. But what was the other side of it? A gentleman might die for another when the cause is just, and worthy. Even Brandon is willing to chance death to save his fellows from harm, but I doubt he'd have crossed the street for Eggleston. What was your husband's reason?"

She gave me an anguished look. "Gabriel, must you?"

"Damn it, Lydia, might we at least have perfect clarity between us? If we can have nothing else?"

She hesitated a long time, then she sighed. "You are right, Gabriel. I can at least give you the courtesy of my trust. There was something. It happened ten years ago, but Eggleston could not leave it lie." She looked at me limply. "Roe had an affair with a young subaltern. Eggleston, the toad, brought it about, helped them meet in secret, and kept it quiet for them both."

CHAPTER 22

I stared at her. "An affair? But I thought—"

She toyed with a button on her cuff. "I believe it surprised Roe most of all. Eggleston instigated it, of course. He suggested that where Roe could not succeed with a woman, he might with a man. I suppose Roe was desperate. So he let Eggleston lead him, and discovered that, indeed . . ." She faltered.

"Good God."

Lydia nodded. "Roe was so ashamed. And yet, for a long time, he could not stop."

But he had at the last. He had returned to the good Dr. Barton, trying desperately to learn how to go to his wife.

"How did you discover the truth?" I asked.

She lifted her head. Rage sparkled in her fine eyes. "Eggleston told me. He sat down with me one evening and told me all, giggling in that horrible way of his. He hoped, you see, that I would destroy my marriage with Roe, that I would shame him, perhaps go so far as to have him arrested. Eggleston kept suggesting ways I might go about proving a case of sodomy against my husband, which would have taken Roe to the gallows. I do not know why Eggleston wished that; he might have been jealous, or he might have been angry that Roe would not put through a promotion for his dear friend Lord Breckenridge." She fixed me with a steely gaze. "But Lord Richard Eggleston read me wrong. Perhaps I could not have a real marriage with my husband, and perhaps I had not loved him for a long time, but I was still his friend."

I could imagine her rising before the astonished Eggleston, rage and scorn radiating from her. I hoped she'd made Eggleston crawl away on his belly.

"Colonel Westin was lucky to have you," I said.

"Roe was a good man. I wish you could have known him. He did not deserve to be in thrall to someone like Richard Eggleston." Her expression softened. "I also recognize that you are a good man. And you did not deserve what I did."

"I did it to myself," I said, knowing the truth. "You beckoned to me, and I was willing to oblige. I would have done anything for you, even lived a lie."

She held up her hand. "Do not, please, Gabriel, I do not think I can endure gallantry just now."

"I did fall in love with you," I admitted. "But do not worry, the madness has passed."

She pressed her shaking fingers together. "I am so sorry. I had realized that day—the day you found me ill—that I could not go on deceiving you. But you had made me feel . . ." She broke off, smiling faintly. "I had never had a lover before. I had not known I could feel what you made me feel." She made a helpless gesture. "I so did not want to give that up."

"Few people do."

"But I realized how unfair it was to you. I was ready to lay my burden upon you, to let you ruin yourself to take it up. When I lay ill, Mrs. Brandon explained to me about your first marriage. You ought to have told me you were al-

ready married, Gabriel. I certainly would never have tried
to trap you."

"My life was already in ruins. Taking up your burden
could only have improved it."

She flushed and did not answer. We sat in silence again.

"You are lying about one thing," I said after a time.

She looked startled. "Am I?"

My anger, nearly forgotten, began to simmer again.
"You have just told me you'd never had a lover before.
That is a lie. Someone fathered the child you destroyed.
Who was he?"

Her face whitened, and she looked swiftly away.

Behind my stillness, the anger reached out and clawed
the last of the fog away. "I believe I have guessed it," I
said. "But name him."

She shook her head. "Please do not make me. He is
gone. I have sent him away."

Outside, a sparrow began singing a belated summer
song in the flowerless lilac tree. A soft September breeze
whistled in the chimney.

I said, "I thought he was to marry your daughter."

Her eyes glittered. "I would never have let that happen.
I persuaded her to cry off. Do you think I wanted him married to her?"

"Why did you go to him?" I asked in a hard voice.

When she looked up at me, her eyes held the imperious
defiance I remembered from our first meeting. The great
lady had returned. "Know this, Gabriel. I never went to
him, never. He looked upon me, and he wanted me." She
shook her head. "Other gentlemen have done so in the past.
I do not know why they should—when I look into a mirror, I see only Lydia the silly schoolgirl who has grown
into a woman with wrinkles about her eyes."

If she did, she saw so little. Those eyes held a dark fire,
a passion burning beneath her cool and aristocratic gaze.
The elegant way she carried herself only made a gentleman wish to smooth that delicate skin, to feel her blood
pulsing beneath his fingertips.

"But he wanted me," she went on woodenly. "He wanted my daughter as well, but he knew he must hold himself from her. Mr. Allandale always obeys the rules! He must keep pure the young maiden he was to marry, because to do otherwise would be wrong. Scandal must never touch their pristine marriage. But a married woman, she may take a lover if she is discreet."

Even if that lover was his fiancée's mother. The fury within me danced and snarled.

"And so he proposed it. I was shocked and showed him the door. The next day he had the audacity to return and ask if I'd changed my mind. Of course I had not. I threatened to tell my husband. And then . . . Oh, Gabriel it was horrible. He changed. He had always been polite and soft-spoken to all of us, so friendly, such a help. And then all that vanished in an instant. His face . . . he was like a beast. He terrified me. He said he would hurt Chloe if I did not oblige him. He said he had ways of hurting my husband. Still I defied him—I thought that I could go to my husband and we could defeat Mr. Allandale between us. And so . . ." She closed her eyes. "He took it from me. I tried so hard to stop him. I tried and tried, but he was too strong. I have never before not been strong enough to stop anything . . ."

She trailed off. The room went silent.

Within me I was anything but silent. She had described a beast in Allandale's eyes, which I, too, had seen, but one also lurked inside of me, its red-hot rage holding me in its grip.

I did not think she lied. Her anguish was real. When she spoke his name, her voice filled with loathing. During the wars I'd served in, I'd known women who had been raped, by enemy soldiers, by our own soldiers. They had all shown what Lydia did now—fear, anger, remembered terror, the shrinking inside themselves when something startled them. Their trust had been ripped away, their comfortableness with themselves gone.

I forced my lips open. "You did not send for a magistrate?"

"To prosecute him for rape? Who would believe it? I am a married woman, older than he; I should know better. And there are those who knew that Roe could give me nothing. They would say that doubtless my own behavior must have provoked him. What a depraved thing I must be to cause Mr. Allandale to lose his respect for me . . ." She trailed off again.

She was right, she likely would be blamed, I thought bitterly. And Allandale, with his soft-spoken politeness, his gentle smile, would have been viewed as the victim, perhaps even pitied.

I rose to my feet. She looked up in consternation. "I swear to you, Gabriel, I never meant to hurt you. I am ashamed. I have lived with so much shame. What I have done—"

"Is done," I said.

I leaned down and gently kissed the tear that trickled down her cheek. She touched my face with trembling fingers. I straightened, and her hand slid away.

"Go to your daughter," I said. "She will need you."

Lydia nodded. Tears beaded on her lashes. "I am taking her away. Abroad." She smiled a little with a mother's fondness. "She wants to go to Italy and paint. She is romantic."

My lips should have curved into a returning smile, but they would not move. "Give her my compliments," I said. "Good-bye."

I turned and walked to the door, neither swiftly nor slowly.

She must have seen something in my face, because I heard her draw a sharp breath. "Gabriel?"

I did not answer. I reached the double doors, opened one. William, stationed down the hall, came alert.

Lydia's silk skirts rustled as she rose. "Gabriel?" Her slippers swished on the carpet behind me.

I pulled the key from the door's lock, shut the door be-

fore she could reach it, inserted the key, and turned it. She
rattled the door handle. "Gabriel, what are you doing?"
The imperious tones returned, though her voice was still
weak with tears. "William!"

I passed the open-mouthed William on my way to the
stairs. He started for me, but I gave him a hard look, and
he stepped hastily back.

I pocketed the key and started down the stairs. "Let her
out in an hour," I said. And I departed.

FATE allowed Mr. Allandale to be out when I called. I knew
he was truly out, and not simply "not at home," because I
backed his valet to a wall and demanded he tell me where
Allandale was. The man stammered that his master had
gone out to his club. Which club, the valet could not say,
though he looked quite unhappy that he could not.

I took pity on him and went away.

I expected to find Grenville ensconced at his own club
at this time of day, but he was in fact at home in his dining
room.

Bartholomew's brother Matthias, who opened the door,
looked neither surprised nor dismayed when I appeared
without invitation, but led me through the quiet stateliness
of the hall to the main dining room.

Grenville was sitting at one end of his dining table, with
Anton hovering at his left elbow. A maid, hands ready to
snatch dishes away as soon as they were dirtied, lingered
nearby. As I entered, Anton reached down and, with a
flourish, removed a silver cover from a tray. Beneath it lay
a small, perfect oval of pudding.

"This is it, is it?" Grenville looked the pudding over,
turning the silver tray all the way around. "The grand mas-
terpiece?"

Anton nodded, clearly beyond speech. At his signal, the
maid produced a ladle and decanter of brandy. Anton
poured brandy into the ladle, then set fire to it by holding
it over one of the candles. He poured this burning liquid

straight over the pudding, and the whole thing flamed merrily.

I tramped into the room. The members of the tableau started, looked up.

"Lacey," Grenville said. "You are just in time. Anton has just perfected his summer pudding. Berries and custard and cream, he tells me. Flamed without, cold within."

The little fire burned itself out. Anton lifted a silver cream boat, and carefully poured yellow-white thick cream around the base of the pudding. He pressed two raspberries into the pudding, in its precise center. He stood back and let out a sigh of satisfaction.

"I need to find Mr. Allandale," I said abruptly.

Grenville's famous eyebrows elevated. "On the moment?"

"Yes." At any other time, I would have eagerly seated myself and rubbed my hands in anticipation of another of Anton's concoctions, but rage and darkness churned within me, leaving no room for elegant puddings.

"I must find him," I repeated.

"Now?" Grenville said, his voice cooling considerably. "Yes."

"Lacey," he said with forced patience, "Anton has spent three days creating this."

I dragged out a chair and dropped into it. "Enjoy it, then."

Grenville stared at me for a long time, then gave Anton a curt nod to proceed.

Any other time, I might have found the whole thing amusing. Anton handed Grenville a spoon. With exaggerated care, Grenville scooped up a minute portion of custard and inserted it into his mouth. He closed his eyes. Anton held his breath. Grenville chewed, very slowly. He swallowed. He remained motionless for a long moment, then he opened his eyes, and sighed.

"Exquisite," he said. "You have outdone yourself."

The maid relaxed. Anton beamed. All was well in Grenville's world.

"Certain you will not have some, Lacey?"

I shook my head. It would have been dust in my mouth. "Just tell me where to find Allandale. I will go alone if I must."

"No, you will not." Grenville gave his chef a placating nod. "Set this aside for me. I will have it with my supper."

No one in that room was terribly happy with Gabriel Lacey.

Once we were settled in Grenville's carriage, he said to me, "I know you rarely do anything without purpose, usually good purpose. So why are you so eagerly pursuing the very dull Mr. Allandale?"

I told him. I told him the entire story, not even suppressing the bits that wounded my pride. When I was finished, he stared at me in astonished horror. "Dear God, Lacey, if that is true, I apologize to you for my coolness. I ought to have known you would not ask favors lightly." He paused. "Are you certain he has done this?"

"Yes," I said. "I do not think she was lying. But, of course, I will ask him."

He cast me a wary glance, but subsided.

CHAPTER 23

WE found Allandale at Brooks's. He was playing billiards with a few desultory members who looked bored in the extreme. They brightened when Grenville appeared.

Allandale looked a query. "Gentlemen?" he asked in his smooth, polite voice.

I wanted to smash my fist into his face right then and there. "A word with you in private." My teeth were so tightly clenched I could barely speak.

His brows flickered. "Of course." He laid down his cue and excused himself from the other gentlemen. They did not look in the least displeased to see him go.

Allandale led the way down a short hall to another room. I came behind him, my fists clenching. Before we'd gone halfway, Grenville stopped me. "Lacey," he said. "Let me just hold your walking stick."

He eyed me steadily, his hand out. I frowned, but slapped the walking stick into his open palm.

Allandale had already entered the little room. I quickened my pace and gained the threshold several steps ahead of Grenville. I turned, abruptly closed the door in his face, and locked it.

"Lacey!" Grenville's alarmed cry came through the panels. Like Lydia had, he rattled the handle.

Allandale faced me, puzzled. The room we stood in was quite small, containing only a table and chair, a small bookcase, and a window. Here a club member could pen a letter or read away from the noise and bustle of the billiards and card rooms.

"I have some advice for you," I began. "Leave England. Today."

Allandale's politeness wavered. "I beg your pardon?"

"I said, leave England and do not return."

He studied me uneasily. "And if I choose not to?"

"Then I will certainly kill you."

He stared for one more bewildered moment, then his oily smile slipped into place. "Please tell me what you are talking about, Captain Lacey."

He ought to have been afraid. I had locked us in here, and no one was here to aid him against me. "You raping Lydia Westin." I took a step toward him.

He gave a sharp laugh. "Is that what she told you? She is a termagant, have you not discovered this? She turned her daughter against me and bade her break the betrothal. I plan to bring suit against them for breach of promise."

I lifted him by his coat and slammed him against the wall. I held him there, my face inches from his. "You touched her, you little worm. You deserve to die for that."

His too-pretty face flushed. "She is a whore. You ought to know. She whored for you."

The man was a fool. I banged his comely blond locks against the moiré wallpaper. "You do not dare speak of her. Do not even speak her name. Pack your things and get out of England. And if ever I find that you have gone near her, or in any way made yourself known to her, I will kill you. You have my word on that."

His polite mask vanished. The eyes that looked out at

me were filled with disdain and scorn and a darkness even beyond what I had imagined. "You know nothing about Lydia Westin. She is a cold bitch who seduces gentlemen then turns them away. You poor fool, she did the same to you."

I put my hand on his throat. "I believe I told you not to speak her name."

"You are nothing, Captain. Even your association with the great Mr. Grenville does not make you important. If you try to fight me in court, you will lose, and then all will know what kind of woman Lydia Westin truly is."

I kept my voice deadly quiet. "I have no intention of fighting you in court or anywhere else. And you have spoken her name twice since I told you not to."

He sneered, unafraid. I saw now in his eyes a man who viewed all of humanity as fools to either use or step around. His politeness kept us at bay, but beneath that politeness, he looked upon us all with loathing. He took what he wanted, and his practiced courtesy and smooth handsomeness deluded others into thinking him kind.

"You had better open the door for your Mr. Grenville," he said now. "He sounds quite anxious. Then we can finish this foolishness."

"Yes," I said, not releasing him. "We will finish."

Grenville had taken away my walking stick and its concealed sword, knowing what I might do. But I had not told him about the knife in the pocket of my coat. I removed it now. It was a small thing, a souvenir from Madrid, with which I cut open books and broke seals on letters and frightened away footpads. It fitted nicely into my palm, the thin, pointed blade only as long as my index finger.

I touched it to Allandale's cheek. He focused nervously on the tip. "What are you doing, Lacey? Are we going to fight like drunkards in a rookery?"

"No, we will not fight. I have no intention of letting you fight. I am going to reveal to everyone your true face, so that when they look upon you forever after, they will know you for what you are, and loathe you."

He stared, his mouth a round "O," uncomprehending.

I pressed the blade into his skin and cut him. He screamed.

Grenville's voice rose on the other side of the door. "Lacey! Bloody hell!"

My knife worked. I sliced stroke after stroke across his alabaster cheeks, shallow cuts that would heal and close and leave a criss-cross of scars all over his face. Scars that would remind him, every time he looked in the mirror, of me. They would tell him that he could not merely smile in soft politeness and have what he wanted. He would never, ever be able to trick anyone with his handsome face again.

Such coherent thoughts would come much later when I reasoned out why I had done what I'd done. At the moment, I only shook with rage and hatred and deep hurt.

This man had broken my beautiful Lydia, wounding her so deeply that she had gone deliberately into despair and shame. The Lydia Westin who had so resolutely stood by her wronged and innocent husband, in the face of all who opposed him, would never have dreamed of lowering herself to a courtesan's tricks, or to using a man who had showed her the slightest kindness. Allandale's actions had turned her into someone she herself had hated in the end.

He had taken her from me before I'd even met her. I would never know that other Lydia, the one true and steadfast and honorable and beautiful. He had shamed her and hurt her, and I doubted she would ever recover from that.

And so I cut him. My knife moved across his lips, his eyelids, his brows. All the while he screamed and wept and pleaded. He tried futilely to claw himself free, but a too-soft life had made him weak. I pinned him firmly and sliced again and again into his ever so handsome face.

Behind me, the door burst open. Strong hands seized me and hauled me away from Allandale.

I went without fight, because I'd finished. Allandale's face streamed blood, cuts covering his face in a bizarre pattern. Tears mixed with the blood, smearing it, dripping to his cravat.

"Good God, Lacey, are you mad?"

Grenville was glaring at me. He seemed to have brought other gentlemen with him, but I could not see them through the haze of my rage.

"Yes," I said. My hands were shaking as I slid the knife back into my pocket. I looked at Allandale. "The wilds of Canada will not be too far. Be gone by tomorrow."

Grenville still held me. I jerked from his grasp and strode past him and the gibbering Allandale and out of the room. Outside, club members had gathered to peer into the room and discover the source of the fuss.

I heard Grenville come behind me. He gained my side as we reached the foyer and plunged out into Saint James's Street and the sweet September air.

Grenville's efficient coachman had the carriage waiting for us. Matthias bundled the both of us in. The door slammed and I fell into the seat. I was shaking and sick, and my hands were sticky with Allandale's blood.

"Are you insane?" Grenville asked incredulously. "He will bring you up before a magistrate."

"Good. Then I can spread far and wide what kind of man he is. No one will ever trust him again. Even if I go to the gibbet for it."

I leaned against the cushions and passed a hand over my brow. My fingers were shaking so hard, I stopped and gazed at them in amazement.

"Are you all right?" Grenville asked sharply.

"Yes," I said. Then I found myself on my hands and knees on the floor of his opulent carriage, gasping for breath and vomiting all over his elegant carpet.

ALLANDALE did try to prosecute. He began a suit against me the next day, which Pomeroy called round to warn me about. But before the constables could make their way to Grimpen Lane to arrest me, Allandale and his suit suddenly vanished.

I assumed that Grenville had influenced someone in

high places, but Grenville wrote that he'd not had the chance to make any plans before Allandale had suddenly left London.

The mystery was solved when I received a letter on thick, cream-colored paper, sealed with a blank wax seal. In it, a fine, slanting hand I did not recognize informed me that my recent trouble had been taken care of. The letter was not signed. I knew, however, in my heart, that James Denis had just made another entry in my debit column.

Somehow, the story put round was that I had taken Allandale aside and bruised him for trying to cheat me at cards. Such a motive was understandable, and I am sorry to say it won me a bit more respect in Grenville's circle. The knife was never mentioned, not by the gossipers, not by me, and not by Grenville.

Lydia Westin had also quietly departed London. When I passed along Grosvenor Street not a week after our final interview, I saw that her house had indeed been shut up, William gone, and the shutters closed. She had not said good-bye.

The only other final note in the business was that I at last gave in to Grenville's insistence and let his tailor make me a coat to replace the one I'd lost in Kent. The new coat was black and made of finest wool, so light I barely was aware of wearing it but warm enough to keep out the London damp. The thing fitted, glovelike, over my somewhat wide shoulders, a change from the secondhand, pinching garments I usually wore.

Grenville persuaded me into the coat because he'd said I'd earned it. I had sacrificed the old coat in my quest to clear Lydia's husband, and cleared him I had. Bow Street Runners earned their rewards; I must earn mine.

I also believe he regarded me in a new light after the incident with Allandale. I'd catch him looking at me sidelong for weeks after, and his conversation with me was more guarded, less impatient.

Louisa Brandon was the only person that autumn who did not avoid me. I confessed to her what I had done, and why, and she understood. I read anger in her eyes, not at me, but at Allandale, and at Lydia Westin.

I told her all as we walked together in Hyde Park on a day late in September. I'd spent intervening time staving off melancholia and not very successfully. The day was chilly, but I had needed to see her. She'd replied that she'd meet me, no doubt welcoming the chance to escape from her convalescing and somewhat irritable husband.

"I was a bit sharp with Mrs. Westin," Louisa said now. She strolled at my side, her hand on my arm. She had admired the coat and told me it made me look fine, but even that had not warmed my heart. "I know it was not her fault," she continued, "but even so, I was most annoyed at her actions."

"She could have done nothing else," I answered. "I would have given myself to her, you know, Louisa. Completely."

"I know."

We walked in silence for a time. I wondered if Brandon had raged at his wife when she'd confessed to him why she'd gone, or if he had wept. Both most likely.

Louisa had not written to me since she'd returned home, nor come to my rooms to see me, though she must have known I'd been ill with the melancholia. But I did not admonish her. I simply enjoyed her presence, savoring this walk and the warm pressure of her hand on my arm.

As we turned along the path toward the Serpentine, she spoke again. "Have you given up looking for Carlotta?"

I thought a moment about James Denis and the paper he had held out to me.

"Yes," I said. "I have given it up."

We stopped to gaze at the gray surface of the water. A breeze rippled it.

"I am sorry," she said softly.

I faced her, studying the rust-colored bow beneath her chin. In the shadow of the bonnet, her gray eyes held sadness.

I said, "I thought I had found something that I'd always

wanted. Instead . . ." I paused and drew a burning breath. "I found something I can never have."

Louisa touched her fingers briefly to my chest, then lifted her hand away. "Your heart will heal in time, Gabriel."

I looked at her, at the ringlets of gold that touched her face. "No," I said. "I think it never will."

Meet Captain Gabriel Lacey in

The
Hanover Square
Affair

by
Ashley Gardner

IN WAR OR AT PEACE,
CAPTAIN LACEY KNOWS HIS DUTY.

His military career may have ended with an
injustice, but former cavalry officer Gabriel Lacey
refuses to allow others to share his fate.
The disappearance of a beautiful young woman
sets Lacey on the trail of an enigmatic
crime lord—and into a murder investigation.

0-425-19330-6

**Available wherever books are sold or
to order call: 1-800-788-6262**